8 LANES

What do you do when your problems run faster than you?

Denisha Raychelle Hardeman

Dedication

To my family, I love you guys so much. I couldn't have done any of this without you guys. You all mean the world to me and I thank you for being there for me every step of this journey. I do this all for you. Mom, Dad, De'Angelique, Junior, Tristan, Bridgette, Aunt Bridget, Uncle Geral, Grandma, Papa, Tabitha, Tamay, Kenneth thank you for everything. I love you. To my friends that inspired the events in this book, Verlensia, April, Ebony, Lanissa, Kayci, Micki and JG…I love you guys so much! Uncle Keke thank you for protecting me from heaven. And to my family and friends thank you so much for everything! Couldn't have done this without your support!

Also, very special thanks to my little sister for designing the book cover and the "8 Lanes" logo. You're the greatest Lil Big Dede. I love you.

Denisha Raychelle Hardeman

Table of Contents

Introduction

This could be it. This could be the day he actually kills me. So why do I stay?

I'm scared.

I'm embarrassed.

I'm prideful.

I'm alone.

Why can't I just pack my bags and walk out of the front door. The door is right there. It's not that hard! I should just call my mom and tell her to come get me. Or I can walk down the hallway to my cousin's dorm and put an end to this right now! He took me away from my family. My friends think I'm ignoring them so they don't want to have anything to do with me. I'm not on the track team anymore and I'm hanging on by a thread in school. What am I doing? Why am I still here? Is it the sex? Is it the money? I don't know what it is but I'm becoming those women I used to laugh at. My only escape is the track. The only place I can run away from all of this foolishness I've put myself into! I have to go! But my legs won't move. My brain is telling me to get up, just run away. Right now! But my body won't move. I'm stuck here. My mind is gone. I've run out of tears. I can't continue to let this go on.

I have to get out of here. I'm going to leave and never look back. I'm going to fight my way out of this.

Tonight, I choose to live. I can hear his footsteps coming down the apartment hallway - his heavy feet hitting the pavement walking towards me. I can hear him stop outside the door as he sighs. The sound of the keys going inside the first lock made my legs tremble. It unlocks. I could hear myself stop breathing. My heart is beating 100 times a minute. I let out a loud cry. It becomes silent outside the door. Shit! He heard me. Silence. Then the keys go into the second lock. He's not going to just let me leave but God knows I have to go. I'm praying to God asking him to protect me. The warm tears run down my face and drop to my wrists. I looked at the cuts on my arms. I take my hand and rub my head. I feel the knot he gave me two days ago. My tears continue to fall on the blood stained carpet. The blood that dripped from my lip after he slapped me. I close my eyes as the door handle twists and swings open. I listen as he walked inside and dropped his backpack on the floor. The door slamming shut made me jump. Then the room grows silent. I could hear my heart beating inside of my chest. My head started pounding. I felt nauseous. I open my eyes slowly. My vision is blurred from the tears. I wipe my face with my right hand and I look up at him. His eyes catch mine. He knows something is up. I can't hide anymore. It's all over my face that something is wrong.

"I'm leaving you." I couldn't believe I said it. My hands were shaking but I said it.

He smirks at me. That creepy, evil smirk. "We'll see about that."

This is it. Bring it on.

1

The Starting Line

It was a sunny afternoon in Houston, Texas. Eleven-year-old Niyah Coleman and her friends were racing up and down the street. With her long hair in a ponytail falling down her back, Niyah raced a group of neighborhood boys and won. Eleven-year-old Mark was the fastest of the boys and wide receiver for the little league team. Tall and lanky with long legs, he was still no match for Niyah. Anthony, one of the cutest with his brown skin and gray eyes came in third place after Niyah and Mark. Steven was overweight and came lagging in last place breathing heavily. He pulled his asthma pump from his pocket and took three long puffs. Sweat falling down her face, Niyah panted to catch her breath, as she walked back over to the boys.

"I don't think any of you can beat me," she taunted.

Steven looked up at her after he finished taking his last puff from his asthma pump.

"You cheated!" Steven yelled at her, playfully trying his hardest not to smile.

"Now you know that's a lie," Niyah retorted. She stared at one particular tall and lanky boy, Caleb. Caleb was twelve-years-old and almost reached 5 feet 8 inches. He towered over all the girls and boys of the neighborhood. With his light brown eyes and curly hair, he caught the eye of all the girls, including Niyah. She smiled at him as he stepped forward, wiping the perspiration from his forehead with his blue Batman shirt.

"Y'all let a girl beat you! I bet she can't beat me," he said.

Niyah stepped even closer to him, her head only reaching the bottom of his chest. She was not intimidated by his tall stature and long legs. With her big brown eyes she looked at Caleb and said, "I could beat Jesus if I wanted to." The group of kids laughed.

"Well, let's race then!" yelled Caleb as he eyed her from head to toe.

Niyah glared at him, smirking. "Do you need a head start, Caaaaaaleb?" she replied mockingly. She walked over to her friends. They cheered and laughed as they gave each other high fives.

Caleb lowered his head a little angry Niyah was embarrassing him in front of their friends.

"Okay, since you think you're so good, let's make a bet!"

Niyah turned to him and smiled.

"What kind of bet?" she asked.

"If I win, you have to give me a kiss on the lips for five seconds."

All the girls screamed "Ewww," as the boys laughed and made kissing sounds with their lips.

Niyah laughed at Caleb's confidence.

"And when I win? What do I get?" she asked.

"Whatever you want because you're not going to win, Niyah!"

"Fine, Caleb, when I win you have to kiss my feet and tell me I'm the greatest runner ever!"

The girls clapped and cheered as Caleb turned to his friends, grimacing at the thought of kissing her clammy feet after they had been running all day in the heat.

"Fine, I'll kiss your little nasty feet if you win. Let's race!"

Niyah smiled and walked towards the light pole which was marked as the starting line. Caleb and his friends followed as Caleb said, "It's not like Niyah is Jo Flo or something."

Brooke, Niyah's best friend, overheard Caleb's remarks.

"It's Flo Jo, genius!" Brooke yelled.

"Thank you, Brooke," Niyah replied.

Caleb rolled his eyes as they reached the light pole. They stood next to each other, ready to take off. Brooke took her place in front of them to start the race.

Caleb's best friend Mark shouted, "Since you talking about us you better not let a girl beat you!"

Caleb turned to Mark and the rest of his friends.

"I got this. Let me show you how you're supposed to run," Caleb replied.

Brooke stood in the street facing Niyah and Caleb. She raised her hands high above her head as if she was trying to reach the clouds. She had her palms opened and anxiously looked at best friend. Niyah winked at her signaling that she was ready to run. Brooke nodded her head and smiled big.

"On your mark," Brooke yelled.

Caleb bent his knees slightly with his arms dangling by his sides, ready to run. Niyah started her routine for the starting blocks as if she was about to race in a track meet. She jumped high up in the air three times while bringing her knees to her chest then planted her left knee on the scorching concrete. She placed her hands by her sides with only her fingertips touching the blazing ground. She lifted her right knee up to her chest. As the sun beamed down, warm beads of sweat slid down Niyah's face unto the ground. She lowered her head and closed her eyes as she took a deep breath.

"Set!" Brooke yelled as she stretched her arms up higher.

Caleb looked straight ahead. Niyah lifted her butt and knees. Her legs were powerful and ready as she erected her head. She opened her eyes and looked down the street to the finish line. Caleb took one more glance towards her then focused his attention back down the street. Brooke dropped her hands shouting, "Go!"

Niyah and Caleb flew down the street with their hands driving up and down as they raced towards the finish line. Niyah was breathing in her nose and out of her mouth as she drove her knees, and her legs propelled her body as fast as they could. Niyah and Caleb were neck and neck.

"Let's go, Niyah!" her friends shouted as they watched Caleb struggle to keep up with her. As they came closer to the finish line, she started to pull away from Caleb. Sweat flew from his face as he panted heavily. He got nervous as he watched Niyah inch closer and closer in front of him. Niyah reached the finish line leaning her head and shoulders in for the win. Caleb reached the finish line a split second behind her. Caleb dropped to the hot concrete as he gasped for air. Niyah bent over, breathing heavily but smiling. The group of kids ran over to them cheering Niyah on. Mark looked at his best friend on the ground in disgrace.

"I can't believe you got beat by a girl!" he said.

Barely able to speak, Caleb replied, "You try racing her then. Oh wait, you did and you lost too!"

Brooke gloated, "he doesn't want to get beat again either and have to kiss feet."

Niyah finally caught her breath and walked over to Caleb. She extended her hand out to him and helped him up. He stood in front of her and smiled.

"I guess you are the next Flo Jo, huh?"

She smiled and said, "I guess I am. Good race."

Caleb grinned happy that she wasn't throwing the win in his face.

"But you still got beat by a girl," Niyah told him, and everyone burst out laughing. She stood in the middle of her friends who cheered, proud of her victory. She took off her shoe and sock and her foot was aloft.

"Someone has some kissing to do," she teased as she wiggled her red painted toenails.

Arriving home, Niyah burst through the front door. Her older brothers, Junior and Tristan, were playing video games with a few boys from their football team.

"Somebody didn't make it before the lights came on!" said Tristan laughing.

Niyah flipped the middle finger at him.

"Hush. I made it!" she said and ran past her brothers into the kitchen as they continued to play their game. "Mom, I made it home!" she screamed.

Tammi Coleman was short and gorgeous with long hair and big brown eyes. She looked younger than she was. Her father, David Coleman, was preparing a big pot of spaghetti. He was still dressed in his football coaching clothes, whistle around his neck and a jumpsuit on. Niyah looked exactly like her father with his caramel complexion, light brown eyes and a beauty mole on his right cheek. Tammi and David had been married for eleven years. Niyah's nine-year-old little sister, Rochelle, was sitting at the table with their mother. She was the spitting image of Niyah and they were often mistaken as twins.

"Those street lights are on, Miss Niyah," Tammi said as she stared at Niyah.

Niyah tried to crack a smile. "I was outside beating the boys, Mom."

"Yes, but I want you in before the street lights come on."

Niyah ran over and kissed her mother.

"I know, Mom! I know! It won't happen again," she said and ran over to kiss her dad. "Hey, Daddy!"

Her dad smiled and kissed her on the cheek.

"Outside beating the boys, huh?" David asked as he continued cutting the onions.

She smiled big and said, "I sure was!"

"She still needs to be in before it gets dark." Tammi said.

David stopped stirring the pot of spaghetti.

"What did I say wrong?" he asked.

Tammi rolled her eyes as Niyah sat at the table silently. Niyah's smile disappeared. She knew there was about to be an argument between her parents.

"Tammi, relax she's right outside."

"I don't care where she is. I told her to be in this house. I don't want her outside this late with all these crazy people outside."

"She's here."

"And what would you do if she got kidnapped or something? Because she wants to be outside racing the neighborhood. If she's that fast, she can be home on time."

"Tammi, relax. Besides, she would be faster than the kidnappers anyway."

David glanced over at Niyah, and they both snickered.

"That's not funny!" Tammi yelled.

Niyah stopped laughing. Lately, her parents had been arguing more and more frequently. Niyah and her siblings didn't know Tammi and David had discussed separation. They didn't know that they'd been having conversations about seeing other people. Tammi looked at Niyah and sighed. Niyah looked up at her mother with tears in her eyes.

"I'm sorry, Mom. I won't be late again," Niyah said.

"It's not you, baby. I'm not mad at you. I promise. Go wash up for dinner and tell them it's time to eat."

As darkness filled the sky, Niyah's house was quiet and still. Niyah and her sister were asleep in the room they shared on the second floor of the four bedroom home. The pink walls glinted in the starlight which came through their window. Tristan and Junior were sleeping in the next room in their bunk beds. A loud thud from the downstairs bedroom and louder yelling awoke Niyah. She sat in her bed listening to her parents argue. She could hear glass breaking and shouting.

Rochelle jumped out of her sleep and ran over to Niyah's bed.

"Are they fighting again?" she asked.

Niyah held her little sister close.

"Yeah, but it's going to be okay," she said, grabbing Rochelle's hand as they tiptoed to their door. They opened it slowly, hearing their parents still arguing downstairs. They lightly walked to their brothers' room and opened the door slowly. Their brothers were still sleeping. As the shouting from downstairs got louder, Junior woke up surprised to see Niyah and Rochelle standing there.

"What the heck are y'all doing? What's all that noise?"

Niyah pulled back the covers and put Rochelle in the bed with Junior.

"Mom and Dad are fighting again. Rochelle was scared. I'll be back," Niyah said.

"And where are you going?" Junior asked.

"I'll be back, okay?" Niyah said, pulling the covers up to Rochelle's face. Junior closed his eyes again as Niyah kissed Rochelle on the forehead repeating, "I'll be back."

Rochelle looked at her with tears but finally closed her eyes, attempting to go back to sleep. Niyah walked slowly from the room back to her own where she put on some socks and her running shoes. She threw on her summer track sweatshirt. She went to her mirror and put her long, black hair in a quick ponytail. Still slowly, she crept from her room down the stairs to her parents' door. It was slightly opened, so she could see her parents were still in the middle of their fight. Niyah watched as warm tears rolled down her cheeks. She wiped her face and walked to the kitchen where she opened the window, pushed the screen back and crawled out. She shut the kitchen window, quietly letting the cool breeze from the night hit her face. She shivered as she began to sprint down the street.

Niyah pumped her arms and legs, running as fast as she could. Tears continued to fall down her face as she ran to the school behind her house. She slowed down as she got to the gate to the track. Out of breath, she opened the gate and went in. She sprinted up and down the lanes angrily. Eventually, she stopped to sit. She put her head between her legs, breathing in and out then she fell on her back, still trying to catch her breath. Looking up into the sky, she stared at the stars winking at her from above, the only light on the track. Tears once again formed in Niyah's eyes. This time she couldn't control herself. She cried so hard she started to cough.

"God, please! Please make it better! I don't want them to fight anymore. I don't want them to fight no more," she said looking up at the sky. She buried her head in her knees, continuing to pray as the night breeze swept across the track, whistling through the trees.

2

Friendly Sibling Rivalry

In the scorching heat of spring in Houston, Texas, teams from all over the state were ready to race for medals and bragging rights. In the Rice Stadium, Niyah, now seventeen-years-old, was preparing for her 400-meter dash. She was standing off the track with her seven female competitors, watching the guys four by two-meter relay finish. The winners celebrated as they walked off the track. Niyah's breathing became heavier, knowing it was time for her to race. She looked at the competitors then shifted her gaze to the roaring crowd. Her coach came up behind her, causing Niyah to jump as she touched her shoulder.

"Woah, Relax! You got this!" Coach Dana, a dark-skinned, fit woman reassured her. Her afro glistened in the sunlight as she smiled big at her star athlete. Coach Dana gently grabbed Niyah by the shoulders and asked, "You ready?"

Niyah nodded her head yes.

"All right remember, Nini, push out of the blocks. Hit the first twenty meters with everything you got. Relax on the back stretch, but not too much. When you get to that 200-meter point, I need you to pick it up. When you get to the 300-meter mark, bring it home."

"I got it," Niyah said.

"I know," said Coach Dana smiling.

Just as they finished talking, Niyah's little sister Rochelle walked up. Now a tenth grader, she was dressed in her Wadson Eagles track uniform in red, white and blue. Rochelle and Niyah now attended two different high schools. With the overcrowding of the main high school, their town decided to build a new high school, Wadson, for the upcoming juniors, sophomores and freshmen. The two schools were zoned by neighborhoods. Since Niyah was already a senior, she stayed at her school making her and her sister competitors. Niyah and Rochelle were about to run the 400-meter dash together. The crowd had been anticipating the race between the two sisters all year long. Rochelle walked over and hugged Niyah.

"You ready, big sis?" Rochelle asked.

"You know I have to beat you today, right? But, I still love you!" Niyah said, hugging Rochelle tightly.

"Every track meet y'all act like y'all didn't see each other this morning at breakfast," Coach Dana chuckled.

They all laughed as the official came and stood in front of the competitors.

"All right, ladies 400, let's get on the track," he said, pointing to the lanes.

Niyah took off her sweatshirt and tights, her running spikes tied tight. Coach Dana gave her one last push. Niyah grabbed her starting blocks and walked to lane four. Rochelle grabbed her blocks and walked to lane five. They placed the blocks behind the 400-meter starting line. Niyah could hear the crowd roaring with excitement, waiting for the race to begin. She looked up into the bleachers and spotted her family and friends. "Let's go, Niyah! Let's go, Rochelle!" they shouted at the Coleman sisters. Niyah looked back down the track. She knelt down and began to pray. "Dear God, thank you for this day. Please guide my feet and my legs around this track as fast and safely as I can. Please let me not only prove to my teammates and family that I can do this, but let me prove it to myself, Lord. Amen."

Rochelle ran over and gave Niyah one last kiss.

"I love you," she said. "Good luck."

"I love you too. And you better run your ass off. Do not just let me beat you. Earn it," Niyah said.

Rochelle laughed as she ran back to her spot. The official blew his whistle, notifying the girls it was time to run. Niyah stood up, looked to the sky and then down the track.

"Quiet at the start," the announcer's voice boomed from the intercom.

The crowd became dead silent allowing the runners to hear the official. The starting official walked up to the edge of the field.

"Runners, behind your blocks!" the shooter yelled.

Niyah and her competitors stood behind their blocks. She could hear herself breathing. She stared at the four girls in front of her, including her sister. They were bigger and taller than her, but Niyah was not intimidated. She relaxed her breathing and stood quietly waiting for the race to begin. The shooter stood on the podium.

"On your mark!"

Niyah stepped in front of her blocks. She jumped into the air three times bringing her knees to her chest. She breathed in her nose and out of her mouth. Placing her hands on the track in a downward dog position, she walked backwards into her starting blocks. Under her knees she felt the sting of the hot rubber surface of the track. The sun gleamed down her back as she placed her feet in position. She looked up at the track, and then bowed her head. She began to imagine herself as a little girl racing the boys down the street.

"Set!" the official said, raising his starting gun into the air.

Niyah raised her knees, legs, and butt. Her breathing continued to increase as her heart beat faster. She was anxious, ready to hear the gun. She remained still. Pow! The official shot the starting gun, and the ladies took off.

Niyah raced around the track, leaning her body forward to hang on to the curve. Her hands were pumping, and her legs were throbbing. Her knees came to her chest as she ran towards the finish line.

"Let's go, Niyah! Relax! Relax!" Coach Dana yelled, running with Niyah, coaching her from the sideline. Niyah began to slow down just a little to conserve energy for the end. She could hear footsteps close behind her. She had caught up to the four ladies in front of her. She had a slight gap on the rest of the competition. She reached the 200 meter mark, knowing she was halfway done. She began to pull away from everyone with Rochelle on her heels.

"Let's go, Niyah! Let's go, Rochelle!"

As she flew by her teammates and family in the stands, she could hear them going crazy. Niyah knew Coach Dana was looking at her stopwatch. She tuned out the crowd as she listened for Coach Dana's voice.

"Let's go, Niyah, you at a twenty five. Pick it up now!"

She heard her coach and began to pick up the pace as she rounded the last curve of the race. She reached the 300-meter mark. She was on the home stretch now, pumping her legs faster and faster. She moved her arms harder. Exhaustion was all over her face. Her legs wanted to give out, but she kept pushing. The sweat from the 100 degree Texas heat rolled down from her forehead into her eyes. Her competitors were trying to catch up now. Rochelle was a half a second behind her sprinting to the best of her ability. The crowd stood to their feet.

"Home stretch! Go! Go! Go!"

Niyah ran as fast as she could, eyes set on the finish line. Finally, she crossed it, leaning in with her shoulders. She looked up at the scoreboard seeing she won the race.

She grinned from ear-to-ear. Her competitors finished the race shortly after her. They all walked up to her and hugged her, so they could tell each other, "Good race."

Her sister ran up and jumped on her. They both sat on the track giggling as the reporters snapped pictures.

"I almost had you!" Rochelle said.

"You thought you almost had me! You're the little sister for a reason!"

Niyah and Rochelle got off the track as Coach Dana ran and hugged her.

"I told you that you had it!" Coach Dana said.

She walked over to Rochelle and hugged her as well.

"You did great too, lil' bit," Coach Dana said.

She turned back to Niyah and smiled at her proudly. In the distance, Niyah could see her family and friends going crazy with excitement. She waved to them as she gloated in glory. As she stepped off the track, she was swarmed by a reporter from the local news who covered high school athletics and his camera crew.

"Niyah, great race! Congrats on the win. How do you feel?" the reporter asked.

"Ummm…tired," Niyah replied as everyone laughed. She then looked into the camera and said, "I feel great. This is my last year, and I definitely have my eyes on the state track meet."

"Speaking of your last year, have you chosen a college yet?"

Niyah looked at him and laughed. "No, I'm still undecided. When I know, you will know," she said.

The reporter smiled, satisfied with that answer. "How was it running with your sister? Did you think she was going to beat you? Were you nervous?"

Niyah smiled and said, "Well, I couldn't let her beat me. I'm the big sister. I think secretly everyone wanted her to beat me. But that's my baby. I want her to be better than me in everything. I told her before the race not to let me beat her. But, if she would have won I wouldn't have heard the end of it. I love her, and she's going to be a force to reckon with when I'm gone."

The reporter smiled and replied, "That is so sweet. We all love the relationship you guys have. No sibling rivalry, just pure love for the sport and each other. Thank you for your time, Niyah, and good luck with the rest of the year."

"Thank you." She shook the reporter's hand, waved at the camera and ran over to the podium to receive her first place medal.

The reporter turned to the camera saying, "That was Niyah Coleman who has just breezed her way to another win in the 400- meter dash with the time of 55.8 seconds. We will see her later in the four by four relay."

After receiving her medal, Niyah and some of her teammates ran into the bleachers up to her mom. "Mom, I have a cramp," Niyah said.

Tammi, now forty-four, still looked younger than her years and physically fit, was sitting in the bleachers watching the meet. She dug through her cooler filled with fruits, sandwiches, water and Gatorade. She pulled out a sandwich bag filled with pickles. Niyah took the bag from her mom and began eating. Tammi watched her daughter eat the pickles and laughed. "That's because you don't drink water. I need fifty-two seconds honey. When I was in high school I ran a-"

Niyah cut her mother off. "Yes Mom we knoooow!"

Everyone laughed. Tammi smiled at her daughter. "Where is your sister? We were cheering for her! We wanted her to win," she teased.

"That's messed up. Y'all wanted me to lose?" Niyah laughed.

"I was cheering for both of you. Since you're fast like your daddy, you don't have to worry about nothing," David said.

Niyah laughed at her dad's statement. Tammi smacked her lips. "Now you know she don't get her speed from you."

"You just mad!" said David.

"As long as her butt gets to state!" Tami retorted.

"Don't worry, y'all. Niyah is going to state!" Brooke said, jumping into the conversation to have Niyah's back.

"Thank you, Brooke. *Somebody* knows!" Niyah gave Brooke the thumbs up.

"She better! Talkin' all that shit!" Tammi said, rolling her eyes playfully.

"I believe in you. You have to watch out for these girls coming after you. You're going to have to get out faster," David said.

"Okaaaay, Dad," Niyah said, playfully rolling her eyes.

Everyone laughed. Niyah handed Tammi the bag of remaining pickles. Tammi nudged her back towards the track.

3

The Great Coin Robbery

Niyah was in her bathroom taking a shower. She got out and wrapped herself in a towel. She had moved into her brothers' old room after they'd gone to college. Trophies and medals filled the room everywhere along with newspaper clippings of her on the walls. Her cell phone began to ring. She ran over to the bed and grabbed it to see who was calling. She smiled when she saw who it was and answered. "What do you want, slut?" she said.

On the other end of the phone was seventeen-year-old Destiny, one of Niyah's classmates and closest friends. Standing at 5'2", Destiny was known for her hazel eyes, long, sleek hair and her fit body.

"Where were you yesterday, trick?" Destiny asked.

"Language, ma'am! Our track meet was canceled so I went to work out then slept. How was Cam's party?"

Destiny hesitated before answering.

"It was ummm… it was cool. Anyway, what you doing today? Come get me. I'm bored!"

"You have gas money?"

"Yes! Come get me and stop playing."

"All right, I'm on my way." Niyah laughed as she hung up the phone and got dressed.

Niyah pulled up to Destiny's house and blew the car horn raucously. Destiny came running out carrying her purse and a jar of coins.

Niyah laughed as Destiny got in the car.

"Don't blow the horn at me like I'm one of your side chicks," Destiny said.

Niyah laughed, looking at the jar of coins.

"Why you got coins like an old lady?" she asked.

"This yo' gas money. Take me to the ACU Bank up the street."

Niyah rolled her eyes, laughing as Destiny shut the door. She drove off toward the ACU Bank, noticing Destiny playing with the coins in the jar.

"So where are we going after this, Grandma?" Niyah asked.

Destiny looked at her and smirked.

"Mike wants us to come to his dorm," she said.

"No, Mike wants you to come to his dorm. Not me," Niyah said, smacking her lips at Destiny.

"Leslie is going to be there."

"So, what's your point?"

"You know you like her. I don't know why you be fronting," Destiny said, giving Niyah a pointed look.

"For one, I don't like girls."

Destiny stared at her. "Who are you trying to fool, Nini?"

Niyah hit Destiny and laughed.

"And for two, I have a boyfriend, Caleb. Remember him?" Niyah said as she flashed a charm bracelet she was wearing. She beamed at the bracelet. "I've never taken this thing off since he bought it for me like five years ago. Reminds me of him when I'm not with him. So no, I don't like girls crazy. I love Caleb." Niyah smiled and looked over at Destiny.

Destiny looked at her as if she wanted to say something.

"Why you looking like that?" Niyah asked as her smile faded.

Destiny hesitated then replied, "Nothing. It's nothing."

The girls pulled in the ACU Bank lot and parked the car in the back of the parking lot. Niyah grabbed her letterman jacket from the backseat and threw it on. On the back of her letterman was her last name in huge letters with the phrase "I Show No Mercy" underneath. Destiny looked at the jacket and giggled.

"I always laugh when I see your letterman. But why do you have that on? It's hot as hell!"

"I mean, I really don't show no mercy. Not even to you. And this ain't any kind of leather. You can wear it in any weather," said Niyah, looking her jacket over.

"Oh so you got bars?" Destiny said.

They laughed as Destiny grabbed her purse and the jar of coins. The girls closed the car doors and walked towards the ACU Bank entrance.

"Hey, don't they take like five dollars from your total when you use the coin machine?" Niyah asked.

"Not when you have an account like me!" Destiny smiled and tapped the jar of coins.

The girls walked inside of the first entrance of the bank. They spotted the coin machine and walked over to it. Destiny began to drop her nickels, quarters and dimes from the jar inside the machine. The coins clinked as they hit the machine and fell inside. Niyah watched as the money counter went up. Destiny continued dropping her coins into the machine when she suddenly stopped. She realized she was about to throw two Chuck E. Cheese tokens inside the machine.

Niyah looked at the Chuck E. Cheese coins and shook her head. "Why do you have those?" she asked.

"Those damn kids I be babysitting be dropping them everywhere," said Destiny, attempting to toss the tokens in the machine.

Niyah stopped her.

"If you throw those in the machine it's going to spit them out," she said.

"Spitters are quitters."

Niyah laughed uncontrollably. "You're disgusting! Throw them in then. Break the damn machine."

Destiny shrugged and tossed the two Chuck E. Cheese tokens in the machine. The machine froze for a moment and then the money counter went up two dollars.

"Hold up. Did you see that?" Niyah asked, noticing the money counter.

Destiny looked confused as Niyah started thinking.

"What are you talking about, Nini? You smoking and I don't know about it?"

"No! No! You got some more tokens? I'll show you."

Destiny rummaged through her purse and found three more Chuck E. Cheese tokens.

"Throw them in, Des."

She threw them in the machine and the money counter went up again.

"Didn't you see that?" Niyah asked.

Destiny shook her head no.

"I'll explain to you in the car. Just go cash out," Niyah said.

Destiny grabbed the receipt and walked into the building as Niyah followed. Destiny handed the bank teller the receipt.

The bank teller looked at Destiny and smiled. "Do you have an account with us?"

"Yes, I do." Destiny went into her purse, pulled out her wallet and handed her license to the bank teller.

"Okay, Miss Mitchell. We only take two dollars since you have an account with us. That leaves you with fifty dollars and sixty three cents. How would you like your cash?"

"Ummm… twenties and tens."

The bank teller walked away to get the cash.

Destiny turned to Niyah and whispered, "Nini, what the hell are you thinking about?"

Niyah put her finger to her lips. "Ssshhh! I'll tell you when we leave."

The bank teller came back with the money. She counted it aloud and handed it to Destiny.

"Thank you," Destiny said as she took the cash and began to walk out. Niyah followed as she walked to the parking lot. She was still in deep thought as Destiny grabbed her shoulder and stopped her.

"Okay, so what happened, Sherlock? What has you all hype?" Destiny said.

"Get in the car first."

Niyah unlocked the car door, and they both hopped in anxiously.

"Well, are you going to tell me or not?" Destiny asked as she anxiously closed the car door.

"Did you see the machine? When you threw in those coins it went up two dollars."

"Yeah… So?"

"So this means that either the machine has a glitch, or it prices by weight. When you threw in the tokens, the machine went up a dollar for each. Those tokens are the same weight as say… gold dollars. So for every dollar at Chuck E. Cheese, you get four tokens right?"

Destiny continued thinking about it as she replied, "Yeah…"

"If we go to Chuck E. Cheese and spend one dollar, bring them back here and put them in the machine, we would get four dollars. So if we took that fifty dollars to a Chuck E. Cheese, we would get two hundred tokens. If we bring them back here and put them in the machine, we would get…"

It finally dawned on Destiny.

"Two hundred dollars! Oh shit!" she screamed in joy at the thought of the fast cash.

Niyah continued, "And if we do the same thing again from that two hundred, cash those in for coins, come back…You get what I'm saying now?"

"Hell yeah I get what you're saying! We going to Chuck E. Cheese!"

They both laughed as Niyah started the car and drove off.

Niyah and Destiny walked into the Chuck E. Cheese. The employee at the front greeted them.

"Hi, are you here for a party?"

"No we just want to play," Destiny said as the employee stamped their hands to get inside.

"Okay come on in."

Niyah and Destiny ran straight to the token machine. Destiny pulled out the fifty dollars.

"Oh my gosh! I bet we look crazy just in here with no kids or nothing. Like some pedophiles," she said.

"Shut up. No we don't. Put the money in there, crazy. I'll go get a cup to hold the tokens," Niyah laughed.

Destiny put the first twenty dollar bill inside the machine, and it spat out eighty coins. Niyah returned with a big Chuck E. Cheese cup to put the tokens in. Destiny continued with the remaining money. The girls watched excitedly as the tokens came out of the machine and put them in the cup.

"We got two hundred dollars sitting here," Destiny said.

Niyah hit Destiny on her shoulder. "Girl, don't say it where the entire world can hear us. Let's go."

Clutching the cup of tokens, the girls ran out of the Chuck E. Cheese. The employees watched confused as the girls left the building not sure why they only came in for tokens. They hopped in Niyah's car and sped away.

Thirty minutes later, the girls pulled back up to the ACU. They looked at each other and smiled. The unusually cool afternoon gust of air brushed their faces. Niyah buttoned up her letterman jacket as they walked towards the bank. She stopped Destiny before they walked inside.

"Do you have any more pennies or nickels or something? I don't want it to be exact. Might look funny."

"No, I think I used all of them the first time," Destiny said.

Niyah rumbled through her pants pockets and letterman jacket. She found some quarters and nickels.

"I'll throw these in too," Niyah said.

The girls walked over to the coin machine. Destiny opened the jar, looked at Niyah and smiled.

Niyah smiled back at her and said, "Go ahead, girl!"

Destiny dropped the coins in the machine. At first the machine did nothing. "Damn, please don't tell me we spent all our money…"

Suddenly, the money counter went up. It showed ten dollars. The girls cheered in excitement. They continued to throw the coins in the machine. Once they finished, the money counter read two hundred dollars and forty five cents.

"Okay, Des, you go in and I'll stay out here. Just go to a different teller and don't use your account. Okay?"

Destiny acknowledged that she understood and walked inside the bank. Niyah watched from outside the glass doors as Destiny walked up to a teller. The teller looked at Destiny then back at the receipt.

Niyah whispered to herself, "Come on, lady. Just give her the money. Come on."

The bank teller walked to the back of the bank. Destiny turned around and looked at Niyah then back towards the teller. Niyah's breathing got deeper. The bank teller walked back to Destiny with a stack of cash, and Niyah let out a sigh of relief. Destiny grabbed the money and rushed towards Niyah. They smiled as they hurried out of the bank. They swiftly ran to the car, got inside and counted the money.

"Two hundred dollars in less than an hour. Niyah, you are a genius!" Destiny said.

Niyah popped her collar. "I just noticed the machine glitch! You had the coins. Thank God. So what do you want to do now?"

Destiny stared at Niyah and flashed the money in her face.

"What you think I want to do? Go back to Chuck E. Cheese! Let's see if we take this two hundred back we can get..."

"Eight hundred! And I have another hundred with me we can use," Niyah said.

"You have a hundred dollars, Niyah, and you had me scraping up coins for gas money?"

Niyah started laughing hard. "That's some money my grandma gave me for a rainy day. You the one that wanted to go an hour away. Besides, it worked out didn't it?"

"Yeah, you right! Let's go!"

"Let's go to a different Chuck E. Cheese, so they won't be looking at us crazy!"

"Let's do it!"

Niyah cranked the car up, and they drove away.

Forty-five minutes later, the girls pulled back up to the ACU Bank. This time, they had a water jug with the coins in them.

"These water jugs will make it seem like we just had a lot of coins for a long time," Niyah told Destiny. She looked over at Destiny who had put on some sunglasses. "Can you take those glasses off? You look stupid."

"We're robbing a bank, these are a must," Destiny said.

Niyah snatched the glasses off of her face and laughed.

"No, silly we are not robbing a bank. It's the machine's fault. Let's go. God, I hope it's a different teller in there. We keep coming in here. I don't want to look too suspicious," she said.

The girls got out of the car and walked into the bank. At the coin machine stood a father and son. The father looked back at the girls and smiled as the son poured the coins in the machine. Niyah and Destiny gave him a nervous smile. Destiny turned around so the father couldn't see they had Chuck E. Cheese coins in the jar.

"See, now he's seen our face. I should have worn my glasses," she said.

Niyah nudged her in the stomach. The father and son finished at the machine and walked inside the bank. Niyah pulled out some more quarters and dimes and tossed them in the machine with the tokens.

Destiny took the receipt and looked at Niyah. "Can you come in with me this time? Please? I'm nervous. This is a lot of money."

"Hell no!"

Destiny looked at Niyah with a shocked look on her face. "Are you serious?"

Niyah began to giggle as she hugged Destiny.

"Yes I'm going in with you! I wouldn't let you go in alone this time. What kind of friend do you think I am?"

They smiled and walked into the bank. The two tellers from earlier were nowhere to be found.

"Good. Those other ladies aren't here, Des," Niyah whispered.

They walked over to the teller next to the father and son they saw at the coin machine. The teller greeted them as Destiny handed the teller the receipt. She looked at it and then looked back up at them suspiciously.

"Wow, this is a lot of money," the woman said.

Destiny stood there smiling nervously, so Niyah spoke up. "It's our graduation. Our grandmother has been saving these coins for a long time! Hence the big water jugs we have in our hands," she said, holding up her jug.

The teller looked at the jugs and back at them. She smiled and said, "Will you excuse me for a second?" She walked to the back of the bank and spoke to an older lady. She handed the receipt to the lady. They stared at the girls and continued to talk.

"Oh my God! We are so busted!" Destiny said. Her legs and arms began to shake.

"Stop it, Des! There is nothing wrong. Chill out! You making *me* nervous!" Niyah said.

"*You're* nervous? *I'm* the one with the account here! They know me!"

"Des, chill!"

The father looked over at them and smiled. The girls smiled back at him anxiously. "You ladies must have had a lot of coins. How much did you get?" he asked.

Destiny blurted out, "Twelve hundred dollars!"

The father and the teller in front of him looked at them shocked.

Niyah stared at Destiny. Destiny mouthed, "I'm sorry."

"Wow! We only have fifty dollars," the father said and patted his son on his shoulder. "We should have come with you guys!"

"Yeah, our grandma saved a lot of coins over the years. Graduation present!" Niyah smiled at him hoping that he believed her.

"I wish my grandma was that nice," he said chuckling. Niyah and Destiny nervously laughed with him. Then he took his money and walked away with his son.

Just then, the older woman and the bank teller came back to Destiny and Niyah. The older woman said, "Hi, Ladies, my name is Veronica. I am the manager today. This is quite a lot of money to get from that machine, so that's why it's taking a while."

The two girls stared at her as she eyed at the receipt.

"And you *did* get this out of our machine. There was no funny business, was it?"

Veronica looked at the girls.

Destiny replied, "No! No funny business."

Veronica smiled.

"Well good! Heard it was a graduation present. Must have taken forever to get this many coins," she said. They all laughed. "Okay, do either of you have an account with us?"

Destiny shook her head and started to say, "Yes," but Niyah quickly chimed in and said, "No!"

Niyah looked at Destiny then back to Veronica.

"No, ma'am, we do not have an account."

Veronica continued to type on the computer. "Okay, ladies, well the bank will be taking fifteen dollars from your total leaving you with one thousand, one hundred and eighty five dollars and forty cents. How would you like your bills?" she asked.

Both Destiny and Niyah shouted at the same time, "hundreds!"

The sun was beginning to set for the evening as Niyah and Destiny hopped into Niyah's car. The lasting sunlight shined through the windshield onto the girls.

Destiny held up the money. They both looked at it and screamed.

"It worked! It actually freakin' worked! Oh my God!" Niyah shouted. Destiny was in shock as Niyah smiled brightly.

"Who's a genius? No, really, who's a genius?" Niyah laughed as Destiny kissed her on the cheek. Niyah grabbed some of the money and began counting it. "We just got twelve hundred dollars in less than an hour. It's not a million dollars but like seriously this is kind of crazy."

Destiny smiled at her as she continued counting her half.

"So, where to now, Thelma? Still want to go to Mike's?"

Niyah looked at her and smirked.

"I was thinking more like the mall, Louise!"

Destiny gave her a high-five and said, "I'm down with that!"

Niyah pulled out her phone and grabbed some of the money and Chuck

E. Cheese cups. "Let's remember this day! Robbed a bank with Chuck E. Cheese coins. Say Cheese!" They both smiled as Niyah snapped a picture.

It was seven in the evening. The sun had finally set and the moon was shedding light on Niyah's home as she pulled her car into her driveway. She walked inside her house carrying numerous shopping bags. Rochelle was sitting on the couch watching television. She noticed Niyah and the bags. Rochelle hopped off the couch and started rummaging through the bags.

"What did you get me?" she asked.

"What happened to hey, greatest big sister in the world? I love you? How was your day? I don't get none of that?" Niyah joked.

Rochelle smiled and replied, "again, what did you get me?"

Niyah laughed as she set the bags down and sat on the couch. "I ain't get you nothin', sucka!" She looked around the house and over her shoulders. "Is Mama or Daddy here?"

Rochelle shook her head no as she sat on the floor to continue to go through the bags.

"No, not yet. Mama is still at football practice, I think. Daddy should be on his way. Where did you get all this stuff from?" she asked.

"Man, the craziest thing happened today!" Niyah said, as she embarked on telling Rochelle the whole story.

"Wait, what? How in the hell did you do that?" Rochelle questioned, open mouthed.

"We went to the Chuck E. Cheese, got some tokens, put them in the coin machine at the bank, and got some money! That's basically what happened!" Niyah exclaimed.

Rochelle's eyes brightened up with excitement. "What you going to tell mom?" she asked.

Just as Niyah was about to answer, Tammi walked in sifting through mail. She was wearing her football practice uniform. Tammi had joined the Houston Women's Professional Football League as a wide receiver in Houston.

Both girls yelled out, "Hey, Mama!"

Niyah laughed at the tired expression on her mom's face. "How was practice?" she asked.

"Hey, babies. I'm tired as hell, but we have to get right for this game on Saturday." Tammi walked over to the couch without lifting her head from the mail. "Here, Niyah, you got some more college letters from that school in California. I don't know if I want you going all the—" Tammi looked up from the mail and spotted the shopping bags. She put her hands on her hips and asked, "What's all this?"

Rochelle looked at Niyah. Niyah replied, "It's mine. Caleb took me shopping with some money his dad gave him."

"That boy using his child support money on you?" Tammi said.

Niyah laughed at her mother. "It's not child support, Mom," she said, going through her bags then pulling out a woman's suit. "I got you guys some stuff too."

"It's cute!" Tammi said. "Maybe that boy is good for something. Did you get your sister something?"

Niyah pulled out some new track running shoes. "So she can be as fast as me!" she said.

Rochelle grabbed the shoes and hugged her sister. "Thank you! Love them! But I'm already faster than you!"

Niyah laughed as she continued going through the bags. "And I just got some clothes and stuff," she said.

Tammi smiled, about to say something as David walked in. The girls ran and hugged him. He kissed them both on the cheek then turned to Tammi. "Well, good evening," he said.

Tammi smiled and said, "Good evening. You being nice today?"

"I'm nice every day."

"Yeah, whatever."

They all laughed as David gave Tammi a kiss. "How was practice?" he asked.

"It was good, I guess. You need to come out there and coach us," Tammi said.

"My coaching days are over. I would probably make y'all tired and sore from all that running y'all would be doing," he said. They laughed as David looked at all of Niyah's bags. "What's all this?"

Tammi looked at him and said, "Caleb took her shopping. Boy's in love with her."

"Mom, we've been together since we were like twelve," Niyah said.

David looked at her. "Excuse me?"

Niyah smiled, grabbed the bags. "Just kidding!" she said, running up the stairs.

"Go put all that stuff away," Tammi yelled after her daughter.

Rochelle grabbed her stuff and ran upstairs too.

David yelled after the girls, "So I didn't get nothing? Man I work hard all day and don't even get a shirt!"

Niyah laughed from the top of the stairs.

"I got you something, Dad. I'll bring it down later!"

David laughed. Tammi stared at him, smiled and walked into the bedroom. David went into the kitchen to begin dinner.

4

Red-Handed

Later that night, Niyah was laying in her bed asleep when her phone rang waking her. She steadily opened her eyes. "Hello," she answered slowly.

"Baby, wake up!" Caleb was on the other end of the phone snickering.

"Baby, what time is it?" she asked smiling.

"It's midnight, but I need to see you. I'm outside."

Niyah sat up in the bed.

"Where are you?" she asked.

"Look out your window."

Niyah looked out the window and spotted Caleb's car in the street in front of her house. He poked his head out of the window and waved at her. She laughed and waved back.

"You're such a creeper!" she said.

"A creeper for you. Now bring that ass!"

"All right, I'm coming! Give me a minute," she said, laughing as she hung up the phone. She ran to her mirror and unwrapped her hair. She threw on some sweatpants, a sweatshirt, and tennis shoes. She put on her charm bracelet and grabbed her phone. She also grabbed a bag with a box of shoes in it and put it in her backpack. She crept slowly out of her room and tip-toed towards the kitchen, carefully placing each of her feet gently on the stairs. Everyone in her house was sound asleep. The house was pitch black dark aside from the moonlight coming through the windows. Niyah grabbed on to the wall as she walked down the stairs while her eyes adjusted to the dark. One of the stairs made a creaking sound. She closed her eyes and paused. She didn't hear anyone stir, so she continued downstairs and finally made it to the kitchen. She quietly lifted the window and pushed back the screen, placing the backpack she had on the ground as she steadily climbed out of the window. She closed the window behind her, grabbed the bag and ran to Caleb's car.

She got in and Caleb immediately grabbed her face. He kissed her lustfully. "I missed you, sexy," he said.

"I missed you too. How was your weekend?" she asked, blushing.

"It was cool."

"Were you being good at that party, Caleb?"

Caleb smiled at Niyah and grabbed her face. "You know me. I'm always good," he said.

"Yeah, right," she said, rolling her eyes. "You better be."

"Why you bring your backpack? You spending the night with me?" he asked playfully.

Niyah smiled as she opened her backpack. She pulled out the bag and gave it to Caleb. He opened it and saw a new pair of basketball shoes.

"Baby, did you get these with that Chuck E. Cheese money?" he asked.

Niyah laughed and nodded her head yes.

"My little bank robber thinking about me. I love them," he said.

"Good, I knew you would."

Caleb kissed Niyah on the cheek. "Thank you so much, baby."

"You're welcome."

Caleb grabbed Niyah's arm and started to play with her charm bracelet. "Always wearing the charm bracelet I bought you," he said.

"It's my favorite thing in the world. I love it," Niyah replied, smiling at him. "So what did you call me out here for?"

"I just wanted to see you. It seems like I barely get to see you nowadays," he said. "And I need to talk to you."

"Talk to me about what?" Niyah nervously asked.

He put his hand on Niyah's thigh. "So I got a call from Louisiana today!"

"Baby, that's great!" She kissed Caleb on the lips. "I knew you were going to get that call!"

"Yeah, I know. But it had me thinking, what are we going to do when we both go to college?" he said.

"Why do we keep talking about this?" she sighed.

"Because it's coming up soon, and I just want us both to be on the same page."

"I don't know, baby. I love you, and I want to be with you," she said. "I just want to be able to trust you."

He grabbed her hand. "You can trust me," he said. "I would never hurt you, and you know that. I love you, but…"

"But what?" she said, breaking her gaze with him to look at the floorboard.

"I mean, it is college. We're going to meet thousands of other people."

"Are you fucking kidding me right now, Caleb? Is this what you called me outside to talk about?"

"I'm just saying, let's be real about the situation."

She opened the door and tried to get out of the car.

"You're unbelievable," she said. "Fuck you."

Caleb grabbed Niyah's arm and pulled her back in the car.

"Hey, close the door. Let's talk like adults. Chill out," he said.

Niyah sat back in her seat and closed the door. She folded her arms as tears welled up in her eyes.

"Nini, I'm not saying it's not going to work," he said. "I'm not saying it is. But I'm a basketball player. You're a track star. We both are going to be extremely busy. Hell, we're both busy right now. And neither of us have picked a school yet but most likely we're going to be far from each other. But I'm not saying I don't want to try. Okay?"

Tears stung Niyah's eyes as they streamed down her cheeks. She reluctantly nodded her head in agreement. Caleb wiped her tears.

"Come on, stop that. You know I love you. Don't do that," he said kissing her lips softly.

Niyah gave in to Caleb's soft kisses and grabbed his neck as she kissed him back, full of lust. Caleb grabbed the inside of her thigh. Niyah moaned and smiled as Caleb found himself sucking on her neck. She snickered as she pushed him off playfully.

"Don't give me a hickey, crazy."

"Let's go somewhere," he said as he licked his lips staring into Niyah's eyes.

"Where are we going to go?" Niyah asked, looking back toward the house.

"To the park or something."

"You're such a freak," Niyah laughed.

"Only for you."

"Let's go then."

Caleb cranked the car up and drove off.

Caleb and Niyah pulled up to a park around the corner and got out of the car. The stars twinkled beautifully in the night sky as they got out of the car. Caleb grabbed a blanket from the trunk and took Niyah's hand. They found a discreet spot behind the playground, out of sight from the street. He laid the blanket on the ground as Niyah took off her shoes and sweatshirt, lying down on the blanket. Caleb took off his jacket and shoes and lay next to her. They both looked up at the stars.

"The stars are beautiful," Niyah said.

Caleb looked and Niyah and said, "You're beautiful."

Niyah laughed as she continued to look up at the sky. "You're so corny, baby."

"I'm serious. I really love you, Niyah," he said. "I want this to work out. I do."

Niyah leaned in and kissed Caleb's lips, then his neck. Caleb rolled her on her back, taking off her shirt and then his own. Caleb then moved down and took off her sweatpants and underwear. He licked her from her neck down to her stomach. Niyah began to moan as he went down on her. He took off his pants as he stood there erect.

Niyah stopped him before he unbuckled his pants. "Wait! Do you have a condom?" she asked.

"We don't need one."

"Yeah but you know what happened last-" Caleb placed his finger on Niyah's lips to quiet her.

"Shhhh… It's not going to happen again. Trust me." He said climbing on top of her and rubbing her face. "Do you trust me?"

She looked up at him worried, then slightly smiled. "I trust you," she said.

"Do you want me?"

"I want you."

Caleb finished unbuckling his pants and lay on top of Niyah. She let out a loud moan as he went in. He began thrusting as she gripped the blanket tightly. Her toes curled, and she scratched Caleb's back as he continued to stroke. Her legs wrapped around Caleb tight as he gently grabbed her neck. Suddenly, they were interrupted as Caleb and Niyah saw a flashlight coming towards them.

"Who's over there?" a man's voice called out.

Caleb briskly hopped off Niyah as they both rushed to throw on their clothes. They got dressed as quickly as possible as the police officer approached. They both sat on the ground panting heavily.

"What's going on over here?" the cop asked.

Caleb put his arm around Niyah's shoulders. "Nothing, we're just talking," he said.

The officer looked at Caleb and pointed the flashlight in his face. "Talking, huh? It's past curfew, and you're trespassing."

Niyah's legs shook nervously as she sat there. The officer turned his attention to her. "So were you guys smoking or something?" the officer asked.

Caleb jolted up. "Naw, we wasn't smoking! We were just…"

"Hey! Sit your ass back down! I wasn't talking to you. I was talking to her. You don't speak unless you're spoken to you, understand?" said the cop as he stepped up to Caleb and pushed him down. Caleb peered into the officer's eyes. Niyah grabbed his hand praying he didn't get back up.

The officer looked back at Niyah. "Young lady, I asked you a question."

"No, sir. We weren't smoking. We were just talking," she said.

"Just because you were talking don't mean you weren't smoking."

"No, sir. I run track. I don't smoke."

"Really now? Where do you live?"

"Around the corner," she said, pointing in the direction of her street.

"Well, let's go," he said.

Niyah and Caleb got up slowly. They walked to the car where another officer was looking inside with his flashlight. The bright lights from the two cops' cars flashed in their faces.

The first officer looked at them and asked, "Okay, whose car is this?"

Caleb stepped forward. "It's mine."

"You need to call someone to come pick it up for you. Officer Daniels will stay here with you, and I will take her home."

Niyah looked at Caleb, not wanting to leave him. They didn't move. Officer Daniels, the officer looking inside the car, became impatient.

"Hey! Did y'all not hear the officer? He said let's go!"

Caleb glared at the officers before he kissed Niyah on the forehead. "I'm sorry, baby. I'm so sorry."

"It's okay," Niyah said. She climbed into the police car, terrified.

"I'll call you when I get home, Nini!" Caleb said.

The officer got in the driver's seat and drove away.

"What happened?" Tammi asked, staring at her daughter standing on the porch with the officer.

"Hello, ma'am. My name is Officer Fredericks. I was doing my rounds in the neighborhood, and we found your daughter at the park with a male companion," he said.

"Niyah, what the hell-" Tammi began.

"Don't worry, ma'am," the officer interrupted. He looked at Niyah. "They were just sitting down talking." Niyah lowered her head as the officer turned back to Tammi. "I just wanted to make sure she got home safely. I've seen your daughter run, so I know who she is. They were just trespassing in the park, and it is past curfew for anyone under eighteen years of age. She has one more month before she can be out at this time."

"Thank you, officer. This will never ever happen again," Tammi said as she glared at Niyah.

Officer Fredericks smiled and replied, "You're welcome, ma'am. Have a good rest of your night. See you on the track, Ms. Niyah."

Officer Fredericks walked off as Niyah went in the house, trying to stay as far away from her mother as possible. Niyah stood there shaking, trying to calm herself as her mother slammed the door. Tammi turned to Niyah and folded her arms. She walked up to Niyah and snatched her by her shirt.

"I should kill you right now! What the hell were you doing?" Tammi said.

"I just wanted to talk to Caleb," Niyah replied with fear in her voice.

"Talk?" Tammi said. She let go of Niyah's shirt angrily. "That's what your damn phone is for! You should be asleep any damn way. You lucky your daddy didn't wake up! What the hell is going on with you? Stop making stupid ass decisions, Niyah, or you're going to end up in the same situations over and over just like before! Caleb doesn't care about you, and I will not go through that shit you went through again! You're too smart and too beautiful to be throwing your life away and getting in trouble over some guy that you're probably not going to see after this year! So stop doing crazy shit, finish school, run and keep your head on straight! Do you understand me?"

Niyah stayed silent. Tammi walked up to her and grabbed her arm. She tightened her grip.

"Do you understand me?"

"Yes, ma'am."

"And don't think you're going nowhere. That car of yours is not moving until I say so," Tammi said. "Only to practice. And since you don't like to talk on the phone, you can hand that over too."

Niyah gave her mom her cellphone.

"Now go to your room before I punch you for doing this dumb shit. You lucky I'm too sleepy to see straight."

Niyah ran to her room, happy that she got off easy and closed the door. Tammi sighed and walked back to her room to go back to bed.

5
Caught Up

The early Monday morning school traffic of kids was busy throughout the hallways as kids were walking around, getting ready for their next class. Niyah was at her locker putting some books away as Destiny rushed up to her in a panic. "Niyah!" she yelled.

"Well good morning, Destiny," she said. "What's up?"

Destiny pulled her close and whispered, "The bank called me this morning."

Niyah's face went blank as she took a big gulp. Her palms became sweaty with nervousness. "What they say?" she asked.

"They were saying that they were moving their money. Inside their coin machine they found a lot of fake coins and were short some money in their vault. So they were calling everyone who used their account in the last two weeks. I just told them I knew nothing about that."

"Oh shit! I'm glad you only used your account the first time we went like I told you," Niyah said.

"I know. Thank God. I tried to call you this morning. Why you didn't answer? I was freaking out!"

"Man. Crazy thing last night. My mom got my phone! Caleb and I almost got caught making love in the park by some cops!"

"What the hell? Cops? And did you really just say making love? Stop it."

Niyah smirked. "I'll tell you about it at lunch. But I can't believe the bank called you! What the hell, man?"

"I know!"

Niyah calmed herself down and grabbed Destiny's face. "Listen, we are going to be fine. If they knew it was us, they would have been in here already. Other people were at the bank too. Just continue to say you don't know if they call again, okay? We got that money from our grandmother. They don't know it was us! We're good okay?"

Destiny nodded her head up and down and said, "Okay." She looked over Niyah's shoulders and rolled her eyes.

"What?" Niyah asked.

Caleb walked up behind Niyah and hugged her. She turned and kissed him on the lips. Destiny averted her eyes, disgusted.

Caleb took Niyah by her waist. "You okay, baby?" he asked.

"Yeah, my mom just took my phone and told me I can only drive my car to school, practice and that's it. I thought she was going to slap the shit out of me, seriously. I'm glad the officer reassured her that we were just talking, or I would have been dead! What happened to you?" she asked.

"Nothing. My mom and dad came to get the car. They started yelling. You know how that goes. I just wanted to make sure you were okay though."

Niyah smiled and kissed him. "I'm fine, baby."

Caleb looked at Destiny and smiled. "Hey, little bank robber," he said.

Destiny shot Niyah an angry look. Niyah shrugged her shoulders. "What? I had to tell him in case my mom asked," she said.

Destiny rolled her eyes and sighed. "And this is how we're going to end up in a women's prison with a broom stick stuck up our asses, eating shit for dinner every night!" she yelled.

"Well that was graphic," Niyah said laughing.

Caleb grabbed Destiny's arm. "Des, stop trippin'. I ain't gonna tell no one."

Destiny snatched her arm away from him. "Yeah, whatever you say," she said.

Caleb turned his attention back to Niyah. "Anyway, baby, you going to be at the game tonight, right? I need my good luck charm," he said, grabbing her wrist with the charm bracelet on it.

She blushed and replied, "Yeah, I'll be there with your jersey on right after practice. I'll just tell my mom something because she will be mad if my butt is not home. Oh well. Like they say. If you're out and you're already in trouble, might as well stay out... Or I'll just run from her."

"How many times I have to tell you? You slow," Caleb said.

"But if I recall I beat you when we were like ten."

"That was like seven years ago. I am bigger and faster now, so you can get it."

"I need to stop trying to get it. That's how we almost got in trouble last night. That's seriously how we keep getting into trouble."

"Man, that was crazy! Like where did they come from? I've never gotten soft so fast in my life!"

"You're so gross!"

Niyah and Caleb laughed as Destiny stared at them with a repulsed look on her face. Brooke suddenly came running down the hallway and grabbed Niyah.

"Niyah, come on, we're going to be late. I need you to help me study for this test real quick!" Brooke said.

"Well hey to you too, Brooke. You don't see nobody but Niyah standing here or what?" Caleb said.

Brooke glared at Destiny and Caleb. "Hi, Caleb," she said, rolling her eyes.

Niyah looked at Brooke then to Caleb confused but brushed the situation off. "All right, I gotta go. Des, we will meet you at the game tonight because I know it starts like right after school. I'll call you when I'm on my way," Niyah said.

"Okay, Nini," Destiny said, hugging Niyah.

Niyah kissed Caleb, and ran off with Brooke. Brooke looked back and rolled her eyes at Caleb and Destiny as the two of them stared at each other awkwardly without saying a word. Caleb finally walked off. Destiny stared at him and walked the opposite way as the bell rang.

School was over for the day. Everyone was leaving the campus as the track girls prepared for their workout. The boys football team was taking over the field for spring practice, so the girls stretched on the side of the track.

"Niyah, lead the warm up," Coach Dana shouted. "Let's go!"

Niyah ran over to the girls and began leading the warm up with her friends Stephanie, Brooke and Carmen.

At the end of their warm up and stretching, Stephanie looked at the track and sighed as the sun radiated down making it extremely hot and humid.

"I hope we don't have 300's today," Stephanie said.

Niyah looked at her and said, "How much you want to bet we definitely have 300's today?"

Brooke looked up into the sky. "I should have just stayed being a cheerleader. At least we practiced in the air conditioning."

Stephanie laughed as she looked at Brooke.

"Weren't you going to be captain? You were like the best cheerleader here. What happened?"

Niyah laughed hysterically as she answered for Brooke.

"Her ass got into a fight that's what happened!"

"Oh yeah I forgot about that!" Stephanie said as she laughed.

Brooke laughed as she rolled her eyes.

"That trick threw a drink at me. It's Niyah's fault. I been hanging around her too damn long. I still got it though!"

Brooke got up and did a series of backhand springs. Her friends cheered her on as she sat back down. Niyah smiled proud of her best friend.

"You always gonna have it. Just don't break your ankle before regionals! So how was the party? It seemed like I was the only one not there."

All the girls stopped laughing and grew silent. Brooke replied, "We need to talk to you."

Niyah looked at them baffled. "About what?" she asked.

"It's about Caleb. He-"

Coach Dana blew her whistle, interrupting Brooke. All the girls walked over to Coach Dana and sat down on the side of the field. Her assistant coaches, Coach Bailey and Coach Talba were standing behind her. Coach

Dana pulled out her clipboard. "All right, ladies, today we have 300's," she said.

Niyah, Brooke and Carmen snickered under their breath as Niyah leaned over to Stephanie and said, "Told ya!"

Stephanie looked down in disappointment. Coach Dana shot the girls a look. "Ladies…" The girls stopped laughing and continued to listen. "Like I was saying, today we have 300's. Long distance girls, you are going with Coach Talba. You have ten 400's. Coach Talba has your times. You know who you are. Let's go!"

The long distance girls got up and followed Coach Talba to the start of the 400-meter dash for practice. Coach Dana continued talking to the remaining girls.

"District and regionals are around the corner, so we have to get with it," Coach Dana said. "We are going to be running in five groups. You are in the same groups as you were last week. So group one will be Stephanie, Niyah, Brooke, Carmen, Melissa G., Lexus, Jada, and Toni."

Coach Dana continued to read off the groups from her clipboard. "Okay, y'all know how this goes. You will start over there." Coach Dana pointed to an orange cone across the field. "And across the field, Coach Bailey will be standing there reading off your times. Now, if anyone in any groups does not make their specific times, everyone will have to run another one! Everyone! No matter what group you're in."

All the girls sighed.

"Hey, if you all make your times you won't have to run. Pace yourselves. You have one minute to rest in between. So that means when you're done with one you jog back over here. Do not walk! You have eight of them. First group, your time is thirty two to thirty four seconds. Second group, thirty five to thirty seven seconds. Third group, thirty eight-forty seconds. Fourth group, forty one to forty four seconds. And group five, forty five to forty nine seconds. But before we go over there, what is the quote of the day?" Coach Dana said, looking around at all the girls. "Come on. It was on the wall in the locker room. If you don't get it, everyone has to do twenty push-ups." All the girls sighed as Coach Dana looked at Niyah. "Nini, what's the quote of the day?" she asked.

Niyah whispered, "Damn it, I knew she was going to pick me."

"Do you know it? Did you even look at it?" asked Brooke.

"I mean I think…"

Coach Dana clapped her hands saying, "Come on, Nini, and stand up. What is the quote of the day? This is very relevant in everyone's life right now."

Niyah stood up and looked at the girls. "We are not… We are not made wise by the recollection of our past, but by the…" Niyah paused trying to remember the quote while everyone stared at her. "But by the responsibility for our future, by George Bernard Shaw."

Coach Dana looked at her and smiled saying, "Take that quote and use it. Don't worry about the past. That's over. We are looking ahead at our futures. All right, get to the cone. Let's practice. Let's go!"

Niyah smiled, happy she got the quote right. All the girls got up and began walking to the cone. Coach Dana yelled at them, "I didn't say walk! What did I just say about walking?! Let's go!"

All the girls began to jog to the cone, and Coach Dana followed.

"All right, first group step on the track," Coach Dana said. The girls in the first group stepped on the track taking up all eight lanes. Niyah stepped in lane one.

Lexus noticed this and quickly got upset. "Are you kidding me?" she said.

Everyone looked at her. Coach Dana asked, "What's the problem?"

"Why she always have to be in lane one?" Lexus asked.

Everyone looked at Niyah. Niyah frowned. "Are you serious right now, Lexus? It does not matter!" she said.

"It does matter, you're running less than everyone else," Lexus said.

Brooke said, "Well then cut over, genius."

Everyone began to laugh except Lexus. "Naw, hell naw, she runs less. She always gets in lane one," she said.

Niyah walked over to Lexus. "It doesn't matter what lane you in as long as you make the time. Seriously, what's the problem? Either lane I'm in, I'm still gone beat you," Niyah said.

All the girls laughed as Lexus replied angrily, "Fine, then get lane eight."

Niyah smirked. "That's fine with me, slowpoke," she said. "I was just joking with you. Come on then. Let's go! It's too hot to argue with you." Niyah stepped in lane eight as Lexus stepped into lane one.

"Are y'all done with this mess? Y'all will alternate lanes. Let's go," Coach Dana said waving to Coach Bailey letting him know they were ready to start. She turned back to the girls and pulled out her stopwatch. "On your mark," she said. The girls all bent their knees ready to run. "Set." The girls were anxious and ready when Carmen yelled, "Wait, so we can cut over or no?"

Everyone sighed. Coach Dana rubbed her forehead in frustration. "Yes, cut over at the curve. Y'all are killing me. Keep talking, and I'm going to drop yawl's time to twenty four," she said.

"Coach, that's impossible!" Carmen hollered.

"Yeah, we could never make that!" Brooke yelled. The girls laughed as Coach Dana stood there glaring at them.

"Okay, y'all, let's go," Brooke murmured, not wanting their time to be dropped.

"On your mark," Coach Dana yelled, lifting her stopwatch as Lexus looked over at Niyah. Niyah stared down the track not paying any attention to Lexus. "Set." The girls dropped their knees even lower. Coach Dana put her whistle in her mouth. She blew it and the girls took off.

Niyah's stomach glistened with sweat in the sunlight as she ran ahead of the girls. The football team and boys track team stared at the girls in admiration. Niyah and the girls reached the curve. They all proceeded to cut over, trying to get to lane one or two. Lexus was in the lead with Niyah right behind her.

Coach Bailey began screaming out their times. "Twenty five...twenty six....Let's go!"

Lexus tried her best to reach Coach Bailey first, but she was no match for Niyah. Niyah smiled as she ran past Lexus. Brooke then inched her way past Lexus as she started to wind down. Niyah ran right past Coach Bailey, followed by Brooke and then Lexus. "Thirty... good job, Niyah! Good job, ladies!" All the girls were happy they made their times. They got off the track as the other groups ran. The first group walked back across the field to Coach Dana.

Niyah walked up to Lexus and said, "Next time keep your mouth shut, and I won't have to embarrass you like that, slowpoke."

"Forget you!" Lexus replied barely able to breathe. Niyah and her friends laughed as they reached Coach Dana.

Coach Dana smiled at Niyah and said, "Stop showing out."

Niyah smiled and she stepped back on the track. "Let's go!"

The girls were on the last 300-meter dash for the day. They were exhausted and hot. They all gulped down water as Coach Dana called for the first group. "All right, group one this is the last one. Step on the track."

Niyah and the girls stepped on the track ready to get the last one over with.

Niyah clapped her hands. "Come on, everybody! Last one. Let's make it."

Coach Dana stepped up next to them with her stopwatch in her hand. "Y'all were cutting it close on that last one. Megan and Lexus y'all better pick it up or everyone will have another one. Let's go!"

Brooke looked at the two ladies. "Come on, ladies. You can do it," she said.

"Yeah, because I am not trying to do another one. Let's go. We can do it!" Niyah said, looking down at them and then back down at the track.

Coach Dana held up her stopwatch saying, "All right. On your mark, set!" Coach Dana blew her whistle. The girls took off once again. This time Lexus was in the back as Niyah, Brooke, and Carmen rounded the curve in the lead. Melissa, Jada and Toni were close behind with Lexus still lagged in the back. Once again, Niyah crossed the line ahead of the other girls. "Thirty one! Good job, Niyah," Coach said. The rest of the girls crossed just in time except Lexus.

Coach Bailey yelled out, "Come on, Lexus, you're at a thirty six."

Niyah looked at Lexus then her friends. "Are you freaking kidding me?" she said irritably.

All the girls were mad knowing that Lexus didn't make the time and that they would have to run another 300-meter dash. When Lexus finally crossed the line, Coach Bailey called out, "thirty-eight" as he shook his head. Lexus ran to a water bottle and swallowed it down fast. She lay on the field out of breath. Coach Bailey said, "That cost you guys another one. Everybody! Run back over to Coach Dana."

All the girls sighed and began walking back as the other groups finished. While they were walking across the field, Brooke turned around to Niyah and said, "How in the hell you on varsity running a damn thirty nine? I'm too tired for this shit."

The girls started laughing. Lexus looked at Niyah. "You got something to say, Nini?" she said.

Niyah stopped walking and turned around. The rest of the girls stopped walking as well to watch. "First of all, that wasn't even me. But, since you asked, yeah I got something to say. You always talking shit but can't back it up. I would have been fine with running another one if you wasn't complaining about petty shit earlier. If you were more worried about making your time instead of what lane I was in, I could be on my way to see my baby play right now. But your slowpoke ass-"

Lexus interrupted her. "You know what, Niyah. Forget you! You think you're the shit. Well you're not! You ain't the fastest person walking."

"I never said I was," Niyah said. "I'm far from it. Never said I was the shit either. But I work my ass off in practice, and I don't miss times either. Just stop talking shit and run. That's it. Just run! Damn! Ain't nobody got no beef with you. You're my teammate. Like seriously. Hop off that pedestal *you're* on!"

"*You're* the one that has yourself high up on a pedestal. Your life ain't as perfect as you think!" Lexus blared.

"What are you even talking about?" Niyah said. "Yeah, it ain't perfect, but you wish you were me, bitch! Let that be known! You know what, don't talk to me for the rest of the season. Or there will be a problem." Niyah walked towards her friends.

Lexus screamed out, "No wonder Caleb cheated on you!"

Niyah stopped walking, abruptly. Her friends turned around and glared at Lexus. Niyah walked over to Lexus saying, "I'm sorry. What did you say?"

"I said, no wonder Caleb cheated on you."

Niyah began to laugh saying, "Caleb has never cheated on me. And our relationship has nothing to do with your slow ass."

"You think you run shit, but you don't. And yes he did. Ask your 'friends'."

Brooke yelled, "Lexus, shut the hell up!"

Lexus grinned at Niyah. "See they know," she said.

Niyah did not take her eyes off of Lexus. She stood there quiet. Her face turned red, and her legs started shaking.

Carmen screamed, "Lexus, don't!"

"At the party… with Destiny," Lexus continued.

Niyah's mouth dropped. Lexus smiled even harder. "I guess your life ain't so perfect. Is it, Niyah?"

Niyah slowly took a hair tie from her wrist. She put her drenched hair in a ponytail. Brooke's eyes widened.

"Uh-oh!" Brooke said.

Suddenly, Niyah ran and tackled Lexus. Lexus fell to the ground, hitting the back of her head on the field. Niyah got on top of her and punched her in the face. Lexus punched Niyah back and grabbed her hair. Niyah slapped Lexus hard across her cheek.

"I hate you, you stupid whore!" Lexus yelled then kicked Niyah in the face with her tennis shoes.

"I hate you too!" Niyah yelled.

Lexus yanked Niyah's hair as Niyah yelled out, "Ouch! I'm going to kill you!" Niyah punched Lexus in the stomach.

They continued to fight, hair pulling, punching and scratching. The boys on the field began to holler and laugh as the girls tried to break them up.

Brooke got on top of Niyah trying to pull her off of Lexus. "Niyah, stop! Get up!"

The girls lifted Niyah on her feet. She was still swinging her fists as Lexus held on to her ponytail.

Stephanie grabbed Lexus around the waist trying to get her to release Niyah's hair. "Lexus, let go! Let her go!" she said.

Lexus finally let go of Niyah's ponytail, holding a few strands of hair in her hand.

Niyah pushed Brooke away as the coaches ran towards the girls. "Get off of me!" Niyah said.

Coach Dana ran to Lexus whose nose was bleeding. Niyah jumped up, wiped the blood from her lip and ran off to the other side of the field. She grabbed her backpack and stormed off the track towards the parking lot.

Coach Dana yelled after her, "Niyah! Niyah!"

Brooke, Carmen and Stephanie looked at each other. They ran to grab their stuff and ran after Niyah before anyone could stop them.

Niyah ran to the student parking lot towards her car.

Brooke ran up behind her and grabbed her door. "Niyah, wait just talk to me!" she said.

"Talk? Talk to you? I don't want to talk to you! Everyone's done enough talking behind my back! How could you not tell me!?" Niyah yelled.

"We were going to tell you. I didn't know when the right time was!" Brooke said.

"The right time would have been when they did it! Someone could have called me, texted me, wrote me a letter, something! You could've called me and said, 'Hey, Niyah. How are you today? Oh by the way the love of your life just fucked one of your best friends!'"

"Nini, we didn't do anything! Don't be mad at us!"

Niyah looked at them. "You're right," she said. "I'm not mad at you. I know who I'm mad at. I'm going to that game!" Niyah pushed Brooke off the door and got in. Brooke jumped out of the way as Niyah fiercely drove off.

Brooke called after her, "Niyah! Niyah, Wait!" She looked at Carmen and Stephanie. They were standing there speechless and scared.

"Yo, she is going to kill them," Carmen said.

Brooke pulled her keys out of her backpack and shouted, "let's go."

The girls ran to Brooke's car, hopped in, and sped off.

The sun had set as Niyah hightailed down the freeway towards the high school where Caleb's basketball game was taking place. She honked her horn at anyone moving slowly in front of her. "Come on! Let's go! Get out of my way!" she yelled.

She swerved in and out of the lanes trying to reach the school as fast as she could. She got stopped by a red light. Her tires screeched as she hit the brakes. She closed her eyes trying not to cry. "Why the hell would they do this? I hate both of them!" she screamed, hitting the steering wheel. A car behind her honked its horn. Niyah opened her eyes and screamed, "Okay I'm going!" She sped through the green light speeding towards the school.

Niyah drove up to the parking lot to the basketball game. She pulled up to the side of the school and quickly parked the car. She dropped the keys in the seat and got out. Pulling another hair tie from her wrist, she put her hair back in a ponytail after the first one was ruined by Lexus. She said to herself, "I swear, I'm going to kill him if he did it!" A car pulled up behind her. Carmen, Stephanie, and Brooke hopped out. They ran after Niyah trying to stop her, but Niyah was determined to get inside.

Brooke screamed at her, "Niyah, what are you doing? He's not worth it."

Niyah yelled, "No! I'm going to punch both of them dead in their faces!"

Brooke grabbed Niyah's shoulders. "Nini, listen to me! You cannot just go in there acting all crazy! There's a game going on!"

Niyah slapped Brooke's hands off her shoulders. "Watch me!" She stormed towards the school.

As they walked in, the girls spotted the boys' varsity basketball team running into the locker room. The girls all saw Caleb.

Stephanie looked at Caleb and then to Niyah. "Oh shit. Here we go," she said.

Niyah walked toward Caleb full speed. She said to herself, "These motherfuckers think they can have sex and smile in my face? Who the hell do they think I am!?"

Caleb spotted Niyah and noticed the enraged look on her face. He frowned and walked towards her. "Baby, what's wrong?" he said.

Niyah slapped Caleb so loud that it echoed down the hallway. Everyone around jumped in surprise at the sound.

Caleb grabbed Niyah and pinned her against the wall. "Niyah, are you out your fucking mind?"

Niyah hit Caleb over and over, trying to get him off of her. Everyone hopped in the middle trying pull the two apart.

"You stupid lying asshole!" Niyah screamed, partially choking on the words.

Niyah's friends finally restrained her as Caleb's teammates pinned him against the wall.

"What the hell is wrong with you, girl? Have you really lost your damn mind?" Caleb said, rubbing his face.

"Let go of me!" she said, rushing past the basketball team and her friends. She bolted towards the gym door in search of Destiny. Niyah's blood boiled in her veins as she charged for the bleachers ready to question Destiny. Brooke and Carmen ran after her. Stephanie tried to run after them as Caleb grabbed her arm.

"Yo, what the hell is wrong with her? What the hell happened?" he asked.

Stephanie snatched her arm away from Caleb and looked at him irritably. "She found out about Destiny, asshole."

Caleb's eyes opened wide with surprise. "Oh shit!" Caleb said. He and Stephanie both ran into the gym after Niyah.

The JV boys were playing their game on the court when Niyah swung the gym door open. The sound of the door hitting the wall sounded like a bomb and made everyone jump up in surprise. Niyah walked right in the middle of the game into the bleachers. The players on the court all stopped running. The referees and parents watched in awe as Niyah walked right through the game. As her heart throbbed, Niyah pushed through everyone in her way as she ran up the steps to Destiny. Destiny looked at her baffled.

"Nini, what's wrong?" Destiny asked.

Niyah caught her breath. The thought of Destiny and Caleb having sex sent Niyah over the edge. She closed her eyes and inhaled deeply. "I'm going to ask you this one time. Des, did you have sex with Caleb?"

Destiny laughed apprehensively. She looked around her and gulped.

Looking at Niyah right in her brown eyes and with a straight face, she replied, "No, I did not sleep with Caleb."

Instantly Niyah attacked her. She hopped on top of Destiny, choking her. Destiny punched Niyah in the stomach causing Niyah to stumble back in the bleachers. Destiny hopped on top of Niyah. She struck her in the face. Niyah hit her back in the face. Destiny screamed out in agony. The girls scratched and punched each other until the crowd separated them.

"I swear, I'm going to fuckin' kill you, Des! I swear!" Niyah yelled, her arms being held behind her back by a man from the crowd.

Destiny spit towards Niyah's face. "I can't believe you hit me! You psycho!" she screamed.

Niyah bent down and picked up an unfinished cup of soda and threw it at Destiny's face. The warm, dark soda and melted ice smacked Destiny across her face. Her hair and clothes were soaked.

Caleb got through the crowd and picked Niyah up. He carried her outside as she tried to resist him, kicking and screaming the entire way to the parking lot. The parents and students in the school were all confused and fired up. They all piled out of the crowded gym into the parking lot to finish watching the uproar.

Niyah was trying her best to get out of Caleb's grip, but he held her tightly. Barely able to get the words out through her tears, Niyah bawled, "Let me go, Caleb!"

Caleb put Niyah down as the crowd began to form outside. "Calm your little ass down! Listen to me!" He grabbed Niyah's shoulders. "I made a mistake!"

"A mistake? When did you realize it was a mistake? After your nut?" she said.

"We were drunk!" he said. "We were dancing, she kissed me. One thing led to another. We went to the bathroom and... you know."

"No I don't know! I'm the last one to know!" she yelled.

"Listen I'm sorry! But what did you expect me to do? All you care about now is track! You barely talk to me. I barely see you! We barely do anything anymore! What did you think was going to happen?" he asked.

"Are you kidding me?" she said. "First of all, you know why I barely want to have sex now! That's not an excuse! Are you serious? And with one of my best friends? Is this why you were saying all that shit about us not working in college? Because you can't keep your penis in your pants? I can't believe you! And you wanna smash me with no protection after you fucked her ass! Asking me do I trust you! After everything you've put me through, everything I did for me and you! Fuck you!" Niyah walked away before she started to cry in front of Caleb.

Caleb yelled after her, "That's the problem. You're stuck on the past. If you would open your legs more this would have never have happened."

Niyah stopped walking, turned around and walked back toward Caleb. "What did you just say?"

"You so focused on running! Maybe you should focus on me," he yelled at her.

She walked closer up to him and kicked him hard in the prostate. Caleb yelled and fell to the ground. The crowd reacted yelling out, "Ooooh!"

"Focus on that, motherfucker." Niyah ran to her car, grabbed her keys from her seat, and drove off.

Niyah pulled up to her high school track and parked. The pain she felt was unbearable. She sobbed hysterically as she grabbed her track backpack, got out of her car and slammed the door. She walked to the track with her backpack, more tears falling harder from her face with each step. She hopped over the fence and threw her backpack to the ground. Pacing back and forth, she walked over to the fence and started to vigorously kick it. She plopped down on the ground in frustration and opened her backpack, throwing off the shoes she had on and putting on her track spikes. She got up and sprinted angrily up and down the track. She stopped suddenly to lay on the ground. She closed her eyes and let her tears flow. "Why would they do that to me?" she thought. She sat up with her eyes still closed and imagined her parents fighting in the house, kicking and screaming at each other. She imagined herself as a little girl running out of the house and down the street trying to get away from all the fighting.

She imagined the happy relationship she had with Caleb.

"Niyah." Niyah's daydream was interrupted as Brooke walked up behind her. She jumped up in fright at the sound of Brooke's voice. Brooke smiled and sat next to her on the track.

"I'm sorry. I didn't mean to scare you. Everyone is worried and looking for you. You don't have your phone so everyone is calling me."

"I don't feel like talking anyway," Niyah said, burying her head in her knees.

Brooke rubbed her back. "Nini, I've told you about Destiny plenty of times."

Niyah looked up at her. "I thought you were just being jealous," she said.

Brooke laughed saying, "A little bit. You started hanging out with her a little too much."

Niyah wiped her tears away. "I try to give people chance after chance. It's my fault. My mama always told me to never let females around your man," she said.

"Nini, you are a track star. You are about to go to college and meet thousands of people. You will be fine. Forget both of them!"

"But everyone knew! And that asshole really came to my house afterwards like nothing happened. They both just were with me like everything was okay! I don't understand. I don't blame you guys but I'm just like, what the fuck? Really, Brooke. Everything I've done for him," Niyah said as the drops of tears fell on her lips as she spoke.

Brooke grabbed Niyah's face saying, "Listen to me. You will be fine. I promise. This will pass. Watch, you're going to marry some football star because you know you like football players anyways. And I'm going to marry Drake, and we're all going to be one big happy family. What did that quote say earlier? That we can't focus on our past. Well let's look to our future with J.J. Watt and Drake."

Niyah smiled, and Brooke rubbed her face. "There's that pretty smile," Brooke said.

"Shut up. How did you find me?" Niyah asked as she dried her face with her shirt.

"As your true bestie, I know where you go when something is wrong."

"You know me so well."

"Because I love you."

"I love you too." They stared at each other for a while and smiled. Brooke kissed Niyah lightly on the lips. Niyah gazed into Brooke's eyes shocked.

"And, Nini, you can't go around hitting everybody. Especially a man," Brooke said. "What if he would have hit you back? Then we would all be in jail. You can't do that."

"I know. I was just so mad. He meant a lot to me, Brooke. You know that."

"I know. I'm sorry."

Niyah looked at the charm bracelet on her arm and took it off. She threw it on the track and sighed.

Brooke smiled and stood up. "Okay, enough of this. You a thug. Thugs don't cry. Let's go. I'll get you something to eat." Brooke held her hand out for Niyah.

Niyah finished wiping her face and grabbed Brooke's hand. Brooke helped Niyah up. She wiped her eyes and looked down at her knuckles. "And some ice for my fists," Niyah exclaimed. They laughed and the two walked off the track to the parking lot, leaving the charm bracelet behind them.

6

Can't Run Away

Niyah sat in class with her friends going over the events from the night before. The teacher passed back the graded tests. One of Niyah's classmates asked her, "What you get up there, Mayweather?"

Niyah laughed and turned her test around. It read A-.

As the students were comparing their test scores, the principal of the high school hastily walked into the classroom. "Ms. Johnston, I need to see Niyah please."

The class stopped and stared as Niyah lifted her head from her desk. She dropped her pen and walked to the principal.

"Ooooh!" The classroom chimed in as Niyah made her way to the door.

Niyah laughed, but the principal was not smiling. They walked out into the hallway.

Niyah nervously bit her blue painted fingernails. "Ms. Stiles, if this is about last night…"

"This is way more serious than what happened last night, Niyah," Ms. Stiles said.

Niyah walked down the hallway, confused as to what Ms. Stiles wanted with her.

Finally they reached the front office. Niyah spotted Destiny in an office crying, talking to a couple of officers. Principal Stiles turned to Niyah. "Wait right here," she demanded. The principal walked into her office as Niyah stood there not taking her eyes off Destiny. Destiny spotted Niyah. As soon as their eyes met, Niyah charged towards Destiny.

"Niyah!" Principal Stiles yelled for her from her office door.

Niyah stopped walking toward Destiny and walked into the Principal's office. Principal Stiles closed the door. "Have a seat," she said. Niyah sat in the chair. There was a knock at the door. "Come in," Ms. Stiles said. In walked a police officer and a nicely dressed man in a black suit. He looked like a detective from an old black and white movie with his long mustache and thick, black hair combed to perfection. Principal Stiles left the room and closed the door behind her. The man in the suit sat in the chair across from Niyah and pulled out a notebook. The officer stood behind him looking directly at Niyah.

"Good morning, Ms. Nayah," said the man in the suit.

"It's Niyah," she uttered as she shot the detective an irritated look.

"My apologies. It is nice to meet you, Ms. Niyah. I've heard a lot about you. I'm Detective Williams and this is Officer Davis. We just want to ask you a couple of questions."

Niyah looked around the room uneasily. Her palms became sweaty. She wiped the excess sweat on her blue jeans and restlessly squirmed around in the chair.

"I'm here on behalf of the Pearland ACU," he said.

Niyah's eyes widened as she stopped breathing.

Detective Williams noticed her nervousness. "I'm just going to let you know, we already talked to Ms. Destiny. So when I ask you these questions, I advise you to tell me the truth," he said.

Niyah looked at the cop and then back at the detective.

Detective Williams continued, "There was an incident where someone put Chuck E. Cheese tokens in the coin machine at the ACU Bank and apparently received money for them. Do you know anything about this?"

Niyah took a deep breath and responded with a simple, "No."

Detective Williams frowned at her. "Niyah, I already told you, I know what happened. You're a good student. I heard you have college scholarships lined up. You actually raced against my niece in the 400-meter dash. She would love to know I arrested her biggest competitor right before the district track meet. We know you and Ms. Destiny technically robbed that ACU with Chuck E. Cheese coins. And if you continue to lie to me, we can just end this conversation right now. Then Officer Davis can put you in handcuffs and take you into custody, and I can go home and go to sleep. I don't think jail time would look too good on college applications. I'm trying to help you here," he said.

Niyah looked at him with her mouth wide open. "I didn't rob no bank," she said.

"In the eyes of the law, you did," he replied. "You are looking at about five years in a federal prison. And I must tell you, Ms. Coleman, there is no track team in a federal prison."

Niyah looked at Detective Williams and Officer Davis with tears in her eyes without saying a word.

Detective Williams continued, "The owner of the bank, because of your ages, does not want to press charges. She just wants her twelve hundred dollars by four thirty p.m. today. Now I'm going to ask you again, Ms. Coleman, do you know anything about those Chuck E. Cheese coins?"

Niyah looked at him and sighed. The tears rolled down her face. She closed her eyes tightly. "Can I call my mom, please?"

Niyah rushed into the school bathroom. She ran to the sink and began washing her face and crying. Destiny walked into the bathroom. "Niyah, can I talk to you?" she asked.

Niyah dried her face with her shirt and looked at her saying, "I'm sorry. I can't understand you without Caleb's penis in your mouth."

"Niyah, please just talk to me. We are in this together. Did they tell you I didn't tell on you at all? They caught your letterman on tape and asked everyone in the office who you were. I almost went to jail for not telling on you!" she said.

"So what, you want me to thank you for not snitching? Thanks! But they found me anyway."

Destiny tried to console Niyah but Niyah pushed her hands away. "Don't touch me, Des!" Niyah shouted.

"Listen, my dad just called saying your mom called him. Our parents are going to pay. We're not going to jail," she reassured her.

"It's not about jail! If colleges find out about this, I'm done! These people know who I am! Everything I do is watched!" Niyah screamed.

Destiny tried to console Niyah once again and hugged her. Niyah pushed her hard while crying. "Don't touch me! I already told you not to touch me! It's taking everything in me not to punch you. I'm in enough trouble," she said.

Destiny slightly pushed Niyah back and began to cry. "Nini, I'm so sorry. If I could take it back, I would. I was drunk and upset at a lot of things going on."

"That's when you call me and talk to me! Not fuck my boyfriend!" Niyah yelled.

"He was just there. I was drunk!"

"Classic." Niyah said, trying to walk out of the bathroom, but Destiny grabbed her arm.

"Niyah, please just tell me you forgive me!"

Niyah was beyond angry now. She faced Destiny. "You were one of my best friends, Des! I took up for you! Anything you needed, I was there! I would fight for you! And you had the nerve to smile in my face afterwards? I would never think you would do something like this to me! You can have him. I don't want him, and I don't need you. Now please, get the hell out of my face!"

"I really am sorry, Niyah," Destiny said as Niyah rushed out of the bathroom. Destiny was left there in tears when the bell rang.

That evening, Niyah was sitting on the couch sulking as both of her parents were yelling at her. David and Tammi paced their hardwood floors as their daughter sat there speechless.

David asked, "What the hell were you thinking?"

Tammi chimed in saying, "I had to leave work!"

"You think we have money to pay for that kind of stuff?" David said. "You are almost eighteen years old and about to graduate. You can't be acting like a kid no more!"

"You have colleges watching you! You can't be messing up like this. We should have let you sit in jail!" Tammi said.

Niyah sat there with her head hanging. Tammi scratched her head and sighed. "I shouldn't even let you run at all anymore," she said.

Niyah looked at her mom in tears. "Mom, no! Please! I'm sorry!" she begged.

David replied, "Give me your car keys. We'll talk about it later."

Niyah took her keys out of her pocket and handed them to her dad. Tammi stared at her daughter. "Go to your room before I kill you. I don't want to hear a sound either," she said.

Niyah ran up the stairs upset. Tammi and David sat on the couch next to each other shocked at what just went on. Tammi looked at her husband saying, "I can't believe she robbed a bank with Chuck E. Cheese coins."

David looked at Tammi and laughed. "If you really think about it, it was kind of cool though," he said.

Tammi laughed. "Yeah it was," she said. "We still have to punish her ass though. I'm too mad at her right now I can't even laugh about it. That was so stupid! We don't have money to just be wasting like that. We have bills too."

"We sure do. We got some Chuck E. Cheese coins around here?" he said. Tammi laughed at her husband as he smiled.

The next day, Coach Dana was sitting behind her desk in her office looking over paperwork. There was a knock at the door. "Come in," she said.

Niyah popped her head from behind the door. She tried to smile but Coach Dana just looked at her with a blank face. Coach Dana motioned for

Niyah to come all the way inside the office.

"Have a seat," she said.

Niyah nervously walked in the office and over to the desk chair. She sat down across from Coach Dana. Coach Dana put the paperwork down and stared at Niyah.

"So what happened?" she asked.

"I walked into the house of hell last night. My parents yelled at me for what seemed like an eternity. I got my car and my phone taken away and I can't go anywhere. I had to plead with them to continue to let me run track, and live."

"Well there was no way I was going to let your mom take you off the track team."

Niyah giggled a little and said, "This I know."

Coach Dana clasped her hands together. "So how much did you guys take?" she asked.

"About twelve hundred dollars."

Coach Dana gave her a surprised look.

Niyah laughed. "I know! I know!"

Coach Dana finally cracked a smile. "It was kind of smart though."

Niyah smiled a little relieved that Coach Dana wasn't yelling at her.

Coach Dana's smile quickly vanished. "But Nini, you are too close to the end," she said. "Fighting with Destiny at a basketball game? You know how many calls I got that night? Then you're fighting Lexus and robbing banks. You have to be smarter than this. You *are* smarter than this and I don't know what's going on with you. There are always scouts looking at you. They are calling me telling me that you're a bad kid, and that they don't want you at their schools. I tell everyone that you're coachable and you have a great attitude. You're ruining it for yourself! I even got a call from the athletic director this morning saying a mother called him anonymously talking about how you hit teachers and rob banks, and you're malicious and shouldn't be allowed to run anymore."

Niyah jumped up out of the seat angrily. "What? Are you kidding me?"

Coach Dana motioned for Niyah to sit back down. "Calm down," she said. "But this is exactly what I'm talking about. Some jealous parent trying to get her daughter on varsity. Don't worry. I'm going to handle that. But you have to stop drawing this kind of attention to yourself, Niyah. Now a lot of scouts have stopped calling about you. I'm sure they have heard one thing or another. But there are still some schools that are interested in you, especially Bay University. You just have to run and stay out of mess. Do you understand me?"

Niyah wiped her tears away.

"Hey, hey stop that crying. Do what you have to do. You hear me?" Coach said.

"Yes, ma'am." Niyah wiped her face, laughed and gave Coach Dana a hug.

"I got your back don't worry."

Niyah rubbed Coach Dana's back saying, "I know."

They let go of each other and Coach Dana chuckled. "Now take your ass to the field and get ready for practice," she said. "But you know there is a punishment coming. You will not be fighting on my field and going all crazy and think you're going to get away with it. You and the hill outside are about to be best friends. Plus to keep you from being suspended, you will be in ISS for about two weeks. You got me?"

"Yes, ma'am," Niyah said, sighing as she walked out of the office.

"And you better know the quote of the day!" Coach Dana yelled before returning to her paperwork.

It was an unbearably sweltering afternoon on the track. The crowd was screaming as Niyah and her opponents were about to run. As Niyah was warming up, one of her opponents walked up to her. "Glad to see your mom let you come out and play today," she said.

Niyah stared at her and laughed. "You might want to stop talking so you can have some energy at the end when you have to catch up with me."

The girls stepped on the track as Niyah kneeled down to pray. "Dear God thank you for this day. Please guide my feet around the track…"

7
Last Resort

Niyah's parents, Coach Dana, and the athletic director from Bay University were sitting in Niyah's living room. Coach Tatem was looking through some of Niyah's paperwork. When Niyah entered the room, Coach Tatem stood up and shook Niyah's hand.

"Hi, Niyah! I'm the head athletic director, Coach Tatem. Coach Jones couldn't be here personally today," he said.

Niyah shook Coach Tatem's hand and smiled. "It's okay. I've met him before," she said.

"Good! First off I would like to congratulate you and your coach on all your wins these past couple of weekends."

Coach Dana clapped her hands saying, "Thank you! We try!"

"It was God-given," Niyah added.

Coach Tatem continued to flip through the paperwork. He added, "And your SAT scores. You will have no problem getting into Bay."

"So tell us more about the school," David said.

"Bay University is a private school. We are the number five ranked business school in the country," Coach Tatem said.

Coach Dana replied, "I know all about the track team. Tell them a little more about it."

"Small. About thirteen girls. Your friend Brooke just signed with us as well."

David asked, "What will she have to pay? After recent events, a lot of schools have stopped offering full scholarships."

"Thanks Dad," Niyah said as she lowered her head.

"Yes, we have heard a couple of things. The bank robbery and fights on the track…"

"When did you have a fight?" David asked looking at Niyah.

Tammi chimed in, "On the track?"

"When was I going to hear about this?" David asked.

"Hey, parents. Don't be rude the man is talking," Niyah said, wanting to change the subject.

Tammi shot Niyah an evil look. Niyah sat back on the couch and turned all of her attention back to Coach Tatem. Coach Tatem cleared his throat and continued.

"We are willing to offer you a partial scholarship," he said. "That will pay for most of your schooling, and we will help you get grants. I understand you will be getting some academic scholarships?"

Niyah nodded her head. "Yes, sir."

"Well, with those scholarships and grants, you will be required to maintain a 2.8 GPA. If you do well in class and help us win the Outdoor National Championships, we will give you a full scholarship for the remainder of your time at school. If you do not do well, we will take away your partial scholarship and if you want to stay at Bay you will have to pay the tuition yourself. This is just our way of making sure you stay on track. Literally."

"And how much is tuition if she doesn't do what she is supposed to do?" David asked.

"Since this is a private institution, about forty five thousand dollars."

"For all four years?" Tammi asked, straightening in her seat.

"Per year," Coach Tatem replied.

Tammi and David looked at each other and both said, "Shit!" at the same time.

David replied, "If she messes up, she will be coming home."

"Niyah will be fine," Coach Dana said.

"Niyah, I'm going to level with you," said Coach Tatem. "Bay has been placing low in the National Track Meets. We must win the Outdoor National Track Meet this year in order to keep the track and field program period. We think you and the new girls we signed can help save the program."

Niyah puffed her chest out and pondered on the thought of going to Bay.

Coach Dana looked at her and said, "Your best friend will be there."

Tammi turned to her and said, "You will get a good education from an elite school."

David added, "You don't have to pay for anything right now."

Coach Tatem stared at Niyah and asked, "Well, Niyah, what do you say?"

Everyone turned to Niyah. She stayed silent while looking at her lap before she finally looked up and playfully asked, "Are the boys cute?" She smiled.

8

New Starting Line

Niyah and her family pulled up to Bay University. Niyah looked around the large, bright university campus. People were walking all around with their families, carrying suitcases and furniture. All the freshmen were so excited to be moving in. Niyah and her family found her dorm building and lugged all her things to the curb.

Rochelle accidentally dropped a bag, tripped over it and fell to the floor. Niyah and her brothers laughed as David helped Rochelle up. She picked up Niyah's bag and continued walking as she said, "Dang, did you bring everything you own?"

A couple of guys walked past them smiling at Niyah. Tristan noticed and stared at them. "I don't like this co-ed living," he said.

"Yeah, I'm not feeling this either," said Junior, walking toward the elevator and watching all the guys, making sure they were not staring at his little sister.

They piled in the elevator to the third floor. They finally reached Niyah's new front door. She unlocked it and they all walked in with Niyah's boxes and suitcases.

The dorm room seemed smaller to Niyah than her room at her parents' home, but she was excited. The room was painted beige, reflecting the sunlight. Two wooden desks sat side by side on the wall closest to the front door. One of the desks already had a laptop on top of it surrounded by boxes.

On the other side of the room were two twin beds that took up the majority of the space. One was positioned against the side wall, and the other was adjacent to the only window in the room. Out the window was a view of the school's track and field stadium in the distance. The bed closest to the window had sheets and clothes already on it. Two small closets were across from the beds. In the back of the dorm was a door leading to a bathroom. The white tile on the floor matched the snow colored walls and tub. The room smelt like a vanilla scented candle.

Niyah took a deep breath, getting a whiff of the vanilla smell. "This is it!" she exclaimed. She pointed to the empty bed and jumped on it. "Guess this is mine." The hard mattress that came with the bed hurt Niyah's butt as she hopped on it. "Ouch!" she shouted. "I'm going to need a new mattress. This hard thing won't do."

Tammi dropped the boxes she was holding. "This is nice!" she said.

David walked around and inspected the room. He asked, "When is coach going to be here?"

Niyah excitedly leaped off the bed saying, "Tomorrow. We have our first practice in the morning."

Tristan placed Niyah's television on the dresser and stared out the door. "So, where the girls at?" he asked.

Rochelle smiled and rolled her eyes at her brother. "Can we be here five minutes without you thinking about college girls? And you talking about college boys looking at me and Niyah," she said.

Her family put down all her boxes just as a young lady walked in. She was tall, and had short blonde hair and green eyes. Her skin was tanned and she was wearing a shirt that read "Bay RA." She turned to the family and smiled. "Hi! I saw you guys walking in. I wanted to come introduce myself," she said. "I'm Melissa, your R.A."

Tammi reached out to shake Melissa's hand. "Nice to meet you," she said.

Melissa turned to Tammi and shook her hand. "Welcome to Dorm Briar. You're going to love it. This is mostly an athletic dorm, coed. Do you play a sport?" she asked.

Tammi looked around the room. "Who me?"

"Yes! You are my new resident right?"

Tammi smiled as the rest of the family rolled their eyes. "Oh, honey!" she said. "I graduated college twenty years ago."

"More like thirty," whispered Rochelle under her breath. The family heard her and laughed.

Tammi pointed to her family saying, "These are my children and husband."

Melissa looked at her shocked. "Wow you look so good!" she said.

Niyah walked up and stood in front of Melissa. "Please don't get her started," Niyah replied. Everyone laughed. Niyah extended her hand and introduced herself. "I'm Niyah, and I'm your new resident. And yes I run track."

Melissa shook Niyah's hand. "Great! Hi, Niyah! Let me let you get settled and I'll see you tonight at the mandatory building meeting!" Melissa said before walking out of the room.

David looked around the room and then back at his daughter. "Okay, you have your bags, groceries, and you know everything from your visit. You have money?" he asked.

Niyah shook her head no. He pulled out a wad of cash. He gave Niyah three hundred dollars.

Niyah smirked at him and giggled, "Thanks, Dad."

Tammi looked at her cell phone at the time. She turned to Niyah and said, "Okay, come on everybody. Tell Coach sorry we missed him."

Junior walked over to Niyah and gave her a hug saying, "Run fast so you can get this scholarship."

Tristan hugged her next and added, "Don't be afraid of these girls."

Rochelle wiped the tears from her face as she hugged her sister. "I love you," she cried out.

Niyah closed her eyes and hugged her sister tightly. She replied, "I love you too."

David came up next and hugged Niyah. "I love you," he said. "Do well. Call us if you need anything."

"I will, Dad," she said.

He smiled. They walked out leaving Tammi and Niyah in the room. Niyah tried to hold back her tears.

"You sure you're going to be okay?" Tammi asked.

"I'll be fine, Mom."

"You have to keep that scholarship, Nini. Do what you have to do. Don't let no one throw you off track." Tammi said fishing through her purse before pulling out a fifty-dollar bill which she handed to Niyah. "I know it's not much, but you will be okay for now," she said. "I will send you some more money when I can. Run fast."

Niyah smiled and replied, "Turn left."

They laughed. Tammi hugged Niyah and kissed her on her forehead. "I love you," Tammi said.

"I love you too, Mama."

"Don't use all that money up. And we're only letting you keep your car here so that you can get around. Coach told us athletes shouldn't have their cars here freshman year. No drinking and driving. And don't be speeding and getting tickets or we will come take the car."

Niyah smiled saying, "I know, Mom."

"And if I get mad at your daddy, I will just come stay here!" Tammi said.

Niyah bowed her head and frowned. Tammi lifted Niyah's head and hugged her. "Don't worry about us," Tammi said. "We'll be fine. Worry about doing what you have to do here."

Niyah couldn't hold her tears in anymore. They ran down her face like a river. She wiped them away quickly, hoping her mother didn't catch them. Tammi let go of her daughter. She looked at her and smiled. Tammi walked out of the dorm.

Niyah stood at the door waving to them. "I love you guys," she said. "Bye!"

They waved back at her and walked down the hallway. Niyah let out more tears when her family was out of her sight. She closed the door behind her and looked around sighing.

"Home sweet home," she said.

9

Burnt Rubber

Niyah was unpacking her boxes when a very jolly, athletically fit girl ran in the room. She was mixed with Puerto Rican and Black. She had beautiful long, curly brown hair. She was about 5'2" with dark brown eyes. She rushed towards Niyah excitedly.

"You're finally here!" the girl said. "Hey! I'm Laurie, your roomie!" Laurie ran and gave Niyah a hug.

Niyah hugged her back overwhelmed and excited. "Hi, Laurie, I'm-"

"Niyah Coleman. I know. Coach told me I would be rooming with you. I can't wait to see what you got on the track."

Niyah went back to unpacking. "So I take it you run track?" she asked.

"Yes! And I'm fast too."

Niyah smiled at Laurie saying, "You better be!"

A very tall Caucasian girl, Alyssa, walked by the open door. Laurie noticed her and called out, "Alyssa! Come here!"

Alyssa peeked her head through the door. Standing at 5'9", she stood over Niyah and Laurie like a giant. Her light blue eyes reminded Niyah of the ocean. She entered the room smiling and stumbling over boxes. She closed the door behind her.

"Niyah, this is my friend Alyssa."

"Hi, Alyssa! I'm Niyah or Nini, as a lot of people call me."

Alyssa walked over and hugged Niyah. Her sandy blonde hair hitting Niyah in the face.

"Hey, girl! Nice to meet you," she said.

"Well heeeey! You guys love hugs," Niyah laughed.

Laurie laughed and looked around the room at all the boxes on the floor. "You're not done unpacking yet?"

"I brought my entire life with me," Niyah said as her cell phone began to ring. She ran over to it on her dresser and answered it. "Hey where are you? Okay! I'm in the Briar Dorm Room thirty four B. It's right when you turn on campus, right across from the track. Okay. Bye." Niyah hung up the phone. She smiled exhilarated. "My bestie, Brooke, is on the way! She runs track too!"

Laurie thought for a moment before saying, "Brooke? I think I've met her. Track girls in this thang!"

Alyssa pulled up her shirt and grabbed the fat on her stomach saying, "I wish I could run track. Or workout. Look at this fat."

Laurie walked over and grabbed Alyssa's stomach. "Yeah you are getting a little chunky," she said.

Alyssa laughed and hit Laurie on the shoulder.

Niyah looked Alyssa up and down saying, "Well you're tall. You could have definitely done hurdles. What do you do?"

"Party and look cute."

Niyah responded while smiling, "I like that too."

They all laughed. Laurie went to her bed and lay on it.

"I'm excited for this year though," Laurie said.

Niyah went back to unpacking her boxes saying, "Me too! I can't wait to start this season."

"Our first practice is tomorrow at six in the morning."

"Oh no that is too damn early! I will be asleep in the bed, hopefully with a new guy," Alyssa laughed.

"Well I don't know about a different guy. But I would like *a* guy," Niyah said, clapping her hands in agreement.

Alyssa checked herself out in the mirror and grinned saying, "Yeah I have a boyfriend. I just like to flirt."

"So what's up with you, Laurie? You single too?" Niyah asked.

"Single and ready to mingle… on one of these football guys. They are so cute!" she retorted.

They all laughed. There was a knock at the door. Niyah ran and swung it open.

"Brooke!" she shouted.

"Nini!" They hugged for a long time. Brooke ran inside the room. Niyah closed the door behind her.

"Brooke, why are you here so late?" Niyah asked.

"Girl, they are over booked on dorms! But I'm staying in a campus apartment by myself, so I'm not complaining."

"Dang, how did you get that?"

"You know how my mama is! She called coach and the school. They were trying to do credit checks and talking about we had to wait to get approved. My mom was like my baby isn't staying in the streets so you guys better do something. That's what took me so long. My mom wanted to come by and see her Nini-baby but we have been dealing with this all day and she had to get back on the road."

"It's cool. She is going to call me. Oh, I'm so sorry I'm being rude. Brooke, this is my roommate Laurie, and this is Alyssa."

Laurie walked over and hugged Brooke. "Brooke! We met on your visit!" she said.

Brooke looked at her and smiled when she remembered who Laurie was. "Oh yes. Hey, girl! You got me drunk on my visit."

They both laughed.

"And tonight will be no different," Laurie said, pulling a bottle of clear liquor from her dresser. She opened the bottle and took a swig. "So glad this is a wet campus."

Alyssa turned to her asking, "Wet campus?"

"Yeah. Meaning if you're of age you can have liquor here. But we're just going to let the age part slide for right now," said Laurie taking another shot of liquor.

"Oh that's what you meant. I thought you were talking about another type of wet," Alyssa said.

They all looked at Alyssa and laughed. Brooke asked, "Do you run track too?"

"I party and go to class."

Brooke gave her a high-five. "Well shit, let's get this party started!"

Laurie took another shot of liquor saying, "I love you girls already!"

Niyah looked at the time on her cell phone.

"Crap! We have that mandatory meeting in a little bit," she said.

Alyssa said, "Well, let's go and then turn up! I know there's a back to school party tonight. One of the Kappa's is throwing it. But it's like an hour away though at that school Quinn, up north."

Niyah looked at Alyssa shocked. "And you're down with the Greek men too? Oh you are too cute," she said.

Laurie agreed, "She is! Shit! How are we going to get to the party?"

Niyah replied, "I have my car."

Laurie smiled saying, "Thank you, Jesus. Freshman with a car. You're going to have a lot of friends."

Brooke playfully hit Niyah on the shoulder. "What? Mama Tammi let you bring your car after everything that happened this year and last year?"

"Yeah she did, thank God. I just have to be good that's all."

"As your best friend, we both know how hard that's going to be."

Niyah laughed and looked at the time. "Okay, let's go to this meeting. But seriously guys if we go to this party we have to be back at a decent time because we have practice in the morning."

Brooke grabbed one of Niyah's shirts from her box. "Deal. We will be back," she said. "I'm going to go to this meeting with you, and I'm going to borrow this shirt. I forgot to bring some clothes."

"I see! But who told you that you could spend the night though?"

They all laughed as Brooke switched shirts.

"Alright let's go," Niyah said and they all walked out of the room.

The girls entered the front room of the dorm building. Everyone in the building was gathered around ready to hear the speeches from the R.A. The girls took a seat in the back. They noticed a couple of football players walking in. Laurie stared at the guys in admiration. "I like what I see," she said with a delighted look on her face.

Niyah looked in the direction of where Laurie was looking. "We stay in here with them? I'm loving this," Niyah said.

"Why they ain't put me in here?" Brooke said, looking at the guys.

The guys walked to a corner and started talking to each other. Niyah took a closer look at one of them.

"Hold up," she said, recognizing one of the football players. "That's my cousin!"

Niyah jumped up and ran to her cousin. He was 6'2" with a chocolate colored complexion. His gym shorts and fitted shirt showed off his massive football arm and back muscles. His white teeth shined bright when he smiled. Niyah jumped on him. He turned around shocked and smiled. "Nini!" he said as they hugged for a long time.

"Gary, what are you doing here? I thought you signed to Florida?" Niyah asked.

"Changed it at the last minute," he said. "Look at you, superstar. You came to take over the track? Because they need some help."

"You already know I'm here to shut it down. I'm too excited to see you, and we are in the same dorm."

"I'm not excited."

Niyah frowned and stared at him. "Why?"

"Because now I'm going to have to hurt someone if they do you wrong here."

Niyah laughed and pushed him playfully as Gary looked around the room. "Where your friends at? You always have all the baddies," he said.

Niyah laughed and pointed to her girls. "I'm sitting over there," she said.

"Well after this come to the basement. You have my new number?" he asked.

"Yeah I have it."

"Okay! We are going to drink and pre-game and then head to this party tonight. Well, you know I don't drink but there will be liquor there. You are going to ride with me, so I can make sure you're safe."

Niyah laughed appreciative of the love from her cousin. "Okay, bet," she said. "I have my car too so if someone wants to drive my car we can do that."

"Alright cool! We'll figure it out tonight. Come down when y'all get dressed."

"Cool," Niyah said before running back over to her friends.

Laurie grabbed her arm saying, "Hey! So your cousin is fine as hell. Tell him I said hey!"

Brooke stared at Gary then looked back to Niyah. "Why have I never met him before?" she asked.

Niyah turned to her friends and laughed. "Can you guys stop? I am not going to play with y'all! But he did say come to the basement after we get ready. They are going to drink and stuff and then we are all going to go to the party. You guys want to do that?"

"Sounds like a plan," Brooke said.

Melissa the R.A walked in saying, "All right let's start our meeting."

Niyah whispered to Brooke, "wake me up when she is finished." Brooke laughed as Niyah lay in her lap and closed her eyes.

Brooke, Alyssa, Laurie and Niyah walked into the basement after they were all dressed. Niyah had on a tight, spaghetti-strapped red dress with V-Cut exposing her cleavage. She had on three-inch black, open-toe stiletto heels. Her hair was in a big and curly afro. She had her make-up done, and her silver jewelry matched her shoes. Inside the basement, there were washers and dryers in a small room on one side and on the other side there were couches and televisions. In the middle of the room was a foosball table and a pool table. Gary was playing pool with one of the guys and two girls standing nearby. Two other guys were relaxing on the couch watching television. Music was playing and everyone seemed to be having a good time. There were liquor bottles on the table and everyone was holding a red cup. Niyah and her friends walked over to Gary. Niyah hugged him.

"See I'm going to have to watch these fools around you," Gary said as he looked at her outfit. "I already know I'm going to have to beat up someone."

Niyah laughed as she said, "Well I guess that means I look cute."

The guys on the couch got up to talk to the girls. Everyone surrounded the pool table. The guys introduced themselves as Dante, Kevin, and Sean. The two girls introduced themselves as Renae and Kayla. Dante was a star senior on the football team. He was 6'1", brown skin with a fade. He was the eye candy of every girl on campus and was destined to go to the NFL. Kevin was shorter than the rest of the guys with long black and blonde dreadlocks. He was the wide receiver on the football team. Sean was a 6'3" freshman and a corner back on the football team. He was muscular with a smile that could light up the room. His light brown skin and hazel eyes made him one of the most attractive men on campus. Renae was 5'3" and thicker than most of the girls. She was light-skin with light brown hair. Her chubby cheeks were always red. Her curly hair stopped at her shoulders and she was very conceited about her looks. Kayla was 5'6" on the basketball team. She was muscular and friendly and had a short haircut with a tattooed arm.

Renae stepped up to the girls saying, "Hey, ladies! Nice to meet you!"

Niyah gave her a hug saying, "Nice to meet you too!"

Gary looked at all the ladies. "Well all you ladies looking extra nice right now," he said.

Dante looked at all the ladies as well. He stopped and stared at Laurie saying, "Yeah, they do look nice."

Laurie noticed and blushed. She had on a tight green skirt with a half black top exposing her six pack stomach. She went into her purse and pulled out a bottle of liquor. "Well we didn't come empty handed," she said, placing the bottle on the pool table.

Sean looked at Laurie then focused his eyes on Niyah. "I like them already," he said. Niyah noticed Sean staring at her and smiled at him.

Kayla grabbed the bottle and poured some of the liquor in her red cup. "That's what I'm talking about," Kayla said.

Brooke walked over to grab some of the remaining red cups. She set them on the table. "Who's ready for shots before we go to this party?" she asked.

Gary passed out the cups to Niyah and the girls. "Let's do it! I'm going to take a shot of juice," he said as he laughed and poured some fruit punch in his cup.

"So what's the driving situation?" Niyah asked, cup in hand.

Gary put his arm around Niyah saying, "Well, since I don't really drink you want me to drive your car? Some people can ride with us and Dante can drive everybody else. Is that cool with everyone?"

Dante smiled and said, "That's fine with me."

Brooke grabbed a bottle and poured everyone besides Gary a shot.

Kevin lifted his cup in the air and said, "Cool. Now that we got that out the way, let's make a toast."

"To what?" asked Renae, lifting her cup.

Niyah followed suit and lifted her cup in the air. "How about to new friends, new freedom, and to just having some fun while we all kick ass in our sports this season!"

Brooke smiled at Niyah saying, "That was so cute, Niyah."

Sean lifted his cup and said, "I like your toast, Niyah." He winked at her. Niyah smiled as everyone raised their cups high in the air.

Gary shouted, "Toast to fun!"

They all yelled, "Toast to fun!" They clinked their cups together and took their shots. Gary finished his shot of juice and looked at everyone ready to go. "All right. Party time!"

The crew entered the loud party. A sign read "Welcome Fresh Meat," referring to the incoming freshmen, hanging on the front wall of the building. The music was blaring as the group took shots and danced the night away. As the girls were on the dance floor, Sean walked up to Niyah.

"Ms. Nini, getting down I see."

Niyah smiled at him drunk and replied, "I does what I can with my no booty."

Sean laughed hysterically at her comment.

"It looks nice to me."

Niyah staggered towards him and grabbed his shoulders.

"Well come dance with me then and stop staring."

Sean smiled and positioned himself behind Niyah. He grabbed her waist as she grinded on him. They continued to dance with each other the rest of the party.

It was three o'clock in the morning as Niyah, Sean, Gary, Brooke, Alyssa and Kayla were in Niyah's car as the rest of the group were in Dante's car driving back from the party. Gary was driving as Alyssa was in the front passenger's seat asleep. Niyah was sitting on Sean's lap in the back with Brooke and Kayla next to them asleep as well. Gary looked in the rear view mirror at Sean and Niyah. "Y'all better be good back there," he said.

Niyah laughed saying, "just keep your eyes on the road, sir. Y'all already got me riding in the back seat of my own car." She leaned down and lay her head on Sean's chest. "I'm a little tipsy. Sorry, are you okay?"

Sean laughed. "Yeah, you good?" he asked.

"Yeah. I'm not too heavy, am I?"

"Nah, you like fifty pounds."

Niyah playfully hit Sean on the shoulder as he laughed. "Hush up. I'm one hundred and fifteen pounds."

Sean smiled and said, "You're a great size. You looked great tonight."

Niyah blushed and covered her eyes. "Don't make me blush."

"No, you did though. Still do."

"Thank you."

"You're welcome. Did you have fun tonight?"

"I really did. I didn't get as drunk as these fools. But I had too much fun. As long as we get home soon." Niyah lifted herself up and grabbed Gary's shoulder. "How much longer we have?"

Gary looked at his GPS on his phone. "Like thirty more minutes," he said. "We already going fast as hell, but your car is doing some crazy stuff."

"Yeah, I know. It's been tripping lately. I didn't want to say anything to my mom and dad because then I wouldn't have it. I was going to wait until I got that financial aid check and go get it looked at."

"Well, it's been tripping, so I'm trying to chill."

Niyah looked over Gary's shoulders and said, "Gary, why do you have the car in third gear? Is that why it's tripping?"

"Oh shit I didn't even see that."

"Well slow down. There's a cop!" Sean said spotting one out the window.

Gary pressed on the brakes. "Oh shit!" He shifted the car from gear three into drive. Suddenly, there was a loud pop sound. Gary swerved to the shoulder of the road. Everyone in the car woke up as smoke rose from underneath the car.

"Oh my God! What the hell just happened?" Niyah asked.

Everyone got out of the car, seeing fire coming from underneath it. Dante had stopped his car on the shoulder ahead. The police officer pulled up behind them. As the flames grew bigger under the engine, they heard a ticking sound.

Sean yelled, "Yo, we have to go!"

Everyone quickly grabbed their phones and purses out of the car. Niyah was looking for her purse when Sean grabbed her. "Niyah, let's go!" The group of kids ran towards Dante's car as Niyah's car burst into flames. The car made a loud BOOM sound! The group of kids jumped back in fright.

Brooke screamed, "Oh my God! Did the car just blow up? What the hell just happened?"

Niyah began to cry. "How the hell did the car just catch on fire?"

The police officer pulled up to the kids. "Are you all okay?" he asked. The group of kids panicked and tried their best to console Niyah as she watched her car go up in flames. Everyone was freaking out thinking about their near death experience.

Firemen and police officers surrounded the car as the firemen put out the fire. After talking to the firemen and cops, Niyah walked back over to her friends. Gary walked over and hugged her. "Nini, I really don't know what happened."

"It's okay Gary. The fireman said that it looked like it was something wrong with the engine. He said it's not the first time something like this has happened with that brand, so I don't know what the hell happened."

Brooke yelled, "We should sue their asses! Like the car literally caught on fire! We were in there!"

"Did you talk to your parents?" Gary asked.

"Yeah. They are just happy I'm okay. They said they will take care of it and don't worry about it. You know my mom is like freaking out right now."

Gary hugged Niyah again. Dante exclaimed, "Damn, man. The car really just blew up. Like a movie!"

They all looked at each other and sighed. Niyah said, "Well, two of the cops said they will get us back to the campus so I guess some people go with Dante, and we will ride with the cops. That damn fire sobered my ass up."

Sean grabbed Niyah's hand and said, "I'll go with you."

Brooke rubbed Niyah's shoulders and asked, "You sure you okay?"

Niyah smiled through her tears. "Fine. Just a little shaken up. Let's just get to the dorms." The group of friends went back to the car to witness what was left of it. The car was charcoaled and destroyed. The group all dispersed and went to different cars to leave.

Gary and the guys walked Laurie, Brooke and Niyah to Niyah and Laurie's dorm. They were covered in soot from the fire and smelled like burnt barbecue. They hugged the guys as Laurie and Brooke went inside the dorm room. Gary kissed Niyah on the cheek and left with Dante and Kevin.

Sean and Niyah stood in front of the door. Niyah was still in shock and a little shaken up. Sean grabbed her hands and put them in his. "Are you sure you're okay?" he asked trying to calm her shaking hands.

"Yeah I'm sure. We just literally had a near death experience and I haven't even been at this school an entire day yet."

"I'm sorry about your car."

Niyah shrugged and said, "me too. But I'm just happy I'm alive. My mom and dad are good about replacing stuff for me, so we'll see. I'll just have to take the bus and train or something for now."

"Well, you know what they say. Couples that have a near death experience together last a long time."

Niyah smiled big. "But we aren't a couple, Sean."

"Not yet."

"You don't even know me."

"No. But I'm already intrigued. And I can't wait to get to know you. I'm just glad I was there tonight to get you out of the car," he said.

"Thank you for that, by the way. I don't know what I was thinking."

"I'll always have your back," he said. Niyah giggled as Sean kissed her on the cheek.

"Goodnight, Niyah. Get some sleep. And take a shower. You smell like ribs."

Niyah giggled. "So do you!"

Sean began to walk away.

"I'll see you tomorrow."

"Goodnight, Sean."

Sean smiled and walked down the hallway. Niyah watched him until he disappeared around the corner. She looked down at her dress which was now ruined from the soot and the smell.

"Well, there goes this outfit," Niyah sighed and walked inside her dorm.

10

Track History

The next morning, Laurie, Niyah and Brooke were laying on the floor in the dorm. Niyah woke up slowly. She wiped the drool off of her face and attempted to look around. She squinted her eyes as the sun peered through the window right into her face. She looked around for her phone and realizing the time she jumped up. They had ten minutes until they had to be at track practice. "Oh shit!" she said. "Y'all wake up! It's 5:50! Get up!" She hopped up and ran to the bathroom trying to rush and get dressed. Laurie and Brooke started getting up slowly looking at Niyah run around like a chicken with her head cut off. Niyah ran in with her toothbrush in her mouth and clapped her hands loudly. "Hello! Wake up, drunkies! It's 5:50! We are about to be late!"

Laurie took a look at her phone and saw the time. She screamed and jumped up. "Oh shit! We have to go!"

Brooke finally woke up and started to throw on some clothes. "I mean we should get a pass after the shit that went down last night. We almost died!"

Niyah came running out of the bathroom still brushing her teeth and trying to put on her track shorts. "Yeah, well we still have to run to practice," she said, toothpaste running down her face as she tried to find her shoes. "I told you guys we shouldn't have stayed so late anyways!"

Brooke continued to get dressed. "Hey, we will just tell him our alarm clock didn't go off and about the car!"

Laurie ran into the bathroom. "Better late than never!" As soon as all of the girls were dressed, they grabbed their track bags and ran out the door.

Brooke, Niyah and Laurie were racing to the track. The other girls on the team were sitting down listening to coach, including Renae. Niyah, Brooke and Laurie walked up behind their coach. Niyah stepped closely behind him. "Sorry we're late, coach. Last night was crazy," Niyah said.

Coach Jones turned around and stared at his late athletes. "Yes, I already know," he said. "Renae told me. Yet she was still able to make it here on time."

Brooke stepped up next to Niyah and said, "Our alarms didn't ring."

Coach Jones rubbed his beard and said, "Funny. Mine did. And so did theirs." He pointed to the team.

Brooke, Niyah and Laurie stood there in embarrassment as their other team members laughed. Coach Jones motioned for the girls to sit down. "I'm glad you're okay," he said. "Now take a seat."

The girls walked over and took a seat in the back of the group of girls. Coach Jones continued his speech. "Like I was saying before I was so rudely interrupted, we have four new freshmen. Only one of them knows how to be on time."

Laurie, Niyah and Brooke lowered their heads in shame.

"Renae introduced herself to the team already," Coach continued. "She runs the 400 meter hurdles. My ladies that were late, tell us your name, where you're from and what you run."

Laurie stood up and said, "I'm Laurie Carter. I'm from Florida. I run the 100 meter hurdles, all relays and long jump."

Laurie sat and Brooke stood up. "I'm Brooke Maxwell," she said. "I'm from Houston, Texas. I run all the relays, 200 meter dash, 400 meter dash and the 100 meter dash."

Coach Jones turned to Niyah. "And you, Niyah."

Niyah stood. "I'm Niyah Coleman," she said. "I'm from H-Town. I run relays, the 400 meter dash, 200 meter dash, and the 800 meter dash."

Alisha, the senior team captain, stared at Niyah with her green eyes. She was very light skin with her brown, sandy hair touching her right below her neck. She was a beautiful sight to look at, but had a nasty attitude. She smacked her lips as Niyah was talking.

Niyah looked and recognized who Alisha was. She smiled and said, "Well well well! Nice to see you again, Alisha." Alisha rolled her eyes as Niyah sat down smiling.

Laurie whispered to her, "Y'all know each other?"

"Yeah, we have some history." Niyah waved at Alisha then looked back up to Coach Jones.

Coach Jones finished talking to the team, ignoring the evil stares between Niyah and Alisha. "We are going to be a great team this year. We have an indoor meet coming up soon so today we're going to do ninety second runs. I want to see where everyone is condition wise. That orange cone..." Coach pointed to an orange cone at the curb of the track. "After ninety seconds everyone should be at that cone or further. Let's warm up and get started. Let's go!"

The girls got up to warm up. Alisha walked over to Niyah. "I prayed you wouldn't sign here," she said.

"Oh, Alisha. You nervous I'm going to take your spot... again."

"Listen, Niyah, this is my track team."

"Is that a threat? Damn! I haven't even run yet and I got you all scared."

"And this is why I don't like you."

Niyah shrugged her shoulders and said, "Well, I hope you like how my ass looks because you're going to be seeing it until the day you graduate. Nice seeing you again." Niyah smiled and ran away.

Alisha glared at Niyah on the track. She began to ruminate on a track meet where she first raced against Niyah four years ago. Niyah was just a freshman in high school, running on varsity. Alisha was senior at her high school. They were running at the regional track meet. Eight girls were standing on the track getting ready to run the 200 meter dash, including Niyah and Alisha. The announcer came over the intercom. "Ladies and Gentleman! This is the regional track meet. We are now ready for the women's 200 meter dash. The top two will advance to the state track meet. This is going to be a good one! In Lane one, Shirl Lacey. In Lane two, Kyla Torres. Lane three, coming in with the fourth fastest time in the state, Freshman Niyah Coleman. In lane four coming in with the second fastest time in the state this year, Senior Alisha Watkins. In lane five coming in with the fastest time in the state ran this year, Senior Gabby Lawrence. Lane six, Rebecca James. Lane seven Nicole Young and in lane eight Denise Hardy. As you can see, this is a packed race." The crowd cheered loudly. The shooting official blew his whistle. The announcer shouted, "quiet at the start please." The stadium grew silent.

The shooting official stood on his podium. "Ladies, stand behind your blocks." All eight girls stood behind their starting blocks ready to run. "Runners, to you mark." The ladies all did their starting routines and got in their starting blocks. No one moved or made a sound. The shooting official lifted his gun. "Set." The girls rose up in their blocks, pushing their feet on the pedals. The starting official shot his gun. The girls took off.

The announcer came back over the intercom. "And they're off!" The crowd was cheering, going wild. "Gabby Lawrence is in the lead followed by Alisha Watkins followed by Niyah Coleman."

The three girls were out in the lead. They came around the curve and were now at the last 100 meters from the finish line. Gabby began to make a small gap between the other competitors as Niyah and Alisha were battling. "Gabby still is in the lead followed closely by Alisha and Freshman Niyah Coleman." Niyah and Alisha were neck and neck. They caught up to Gabby as they all pushed their legs to the limit, wanting to finish in first place. They were fifty meters from the finish line. The crowd got on their feet. "Who wants it!? Who wants it!?" The three girls crossed the finish line at what seemed like the exact same time. The announcer breathed in deeply excited. "That was close. The clock doesn't even know who won!" The rest of the girls finished as Niyah and Alisha looked at the scoreboard above the field to see who was going to state. "Only the top two will advance." Finally, the board showed that Gabby was the winner followed by Niyah in second place and Alisha in third place. The crowd went wild. Niyah and Gabby hugged and celebrated as Alisha began to cry. From that moment, she hated

Niyah's existence. Niyah walked over to congratulate Alisha. Alisha pushed her away and walked off the track.

Alisha was still standing on the Bay University field reminiscing about that track meet. She stood there staring at Niyah with hate in her eyes. Coach Jones blew his whistle. "Alisha, let's go!" he shouted. Alisha ran over to her coach and her teammates. Coach Jones stepped next to the girls. "All right, let's go give me three people on the track." Everyone looked at each other, not wanting to go first. "Fine since no one wants to move, give me Alisha, Janet and Niyah. Come on! Let's go!"

The three ladies stepped on the track. Alisha rushed to lane one. Niyah stood next to her in lane two and Janet in lane three. "Alright ladies after the first 100 meters, you can cut over," he said.

Brooke leaned over to Laurie and whispered, "This is going to be good."

Alisha sighed as Niyah settled herself next to her. Niyah laughed and said, "Calm down, Alisha. I won't embarrass you too much."

Coach Jones grabbed his whistle. "All right, remember ninety seconds. Be at that second cone. On your mark." The girls bent down ready to run. "Set." Coach Jones blew his whistle. The girls sped off on the track. Niyah and Alisha were in the lead followed by Janet. They got to the 100 meter mark. Niyah was trying to cut over, but Alisha wouldn't let her. She ran right next to Niyah, shoulder to shoulder, not allowing her to get in lane one unless she slowed down. Niyah got extremely frustrated. They rounded the first cone headed towards the second cone.

"Come on, Nini! Come on!" Brooke cheered for her best friend on the sidelines.

Coach Jones looked at his stopwatch and shouted, "You're at a minute and fifteen seconds! Pick it up!"

Niyah and Alisha were right next to each other with Niyah still in lane two. Suddenly, Niyah picked up massive speed. She quickly cut in front of Alisha causing Alisha to slow down. Niyah passed the second cone as Coach Jones blew his whistle followed by Alisha and then Janet. Niyah put her hands on top of her head breathing in and out slowly. She walked over to Alisha who was gulping down water. "So you wasn't going to let me cut over?" Niyah said.

Alisha stopped drinking from the water bottle and wiped her mouth without looking Niyah's way. "No I wasn't."

"You're so childish. You always want to beat me at something. It's just practice. Damn!"

"It wasn't about winning."

Niyah smiled at Alisha. "It's all good. Your jealousy is going to run you crazy. I can't wait to watch you self-destruct, so worried about me."

Alisha glared at Niyah. Coach Jones blew his whistle and yelled at the girls from across the field. "Hey! Y'all ready to continue practice or no?" Niyah smiled at Alisha and ran off.

Coach Jones blew his whistle for the last group. The girls began to walk off the track now that practice was over. Coach Jones walked past Niyah. "Good Job, Niyah," he said.

"Thanks, Coach."

Coach called out to the girls. "All right, ladies, good job. See y'all tomorrow at three o'clock at the pool."

Brooke yelled out, "Not the pool!"

"Yes, the pool." Coach Jones walked up and grabbed Niyah as she was walking away. "Niyah, let me talk to you for a second."

Niyah turned to her friends signaling them to go ahead and go on without her. "I'll meet you guys in the cafeteria," she said.

Brooke, Renae, and Laurie nodded and continued their way towards the parking lot. Niyah and Coach Jones walked down the track as coach picked up the equipment from the day. Niyah looked at him nervously.

"Am I in trouble, Coach?" she asked.

"No, I just needed to talk to you. First things first, are you okay? With the car?"

"Yeah, we're okay. It was scary but we're fine."

Coach Jones turned to her and put his hand on her shoulder. "I'm glad you're okay." They continued walking down the track. "Niyah, I need you to be a leader on this team."

"I'm trying, Coach."

"Yes, running on the track you are. I'm talking about being on time and going to class. Now I know what happened last night wasn't your fault, but you don't need any negative attention right now. Coach Tatem is watching you closely. I had to fight to get you here. You have to perform at the highest level in everything you do. Don't give him or anyone else a reason not to give you the full ride you deserve. You have to show up. You got me?"

Niyah smirked and nodded her head. "Yes, sir."

"I'm serious, Niyah."

"I know, Coach. I got you. I promise."

"So what's this issue with you and Alisha?"

"What do you mean?"

Coach Jones stopped walking and stared at Niyah. Niyah stopped in her tracks and smiled at her coach. "What?"

"You know what I mean. I don't want any fights on this team. Y'all have to work together if we are going to win these meets. She's the captain, and if you do what you have to do you will be captain." Niyah's eyes brightened when Coach Jones said she could be captain. "But there will be no track team if we don't improve and win some meets. So if my two best athletes can't work together, there will be no team for you to be a captain on. So fix whatever problem there is between you two. Okay?" Niyah nodded her head yes. "I need to hear you say you got it. Do you have it, Niyah?"

"Yes, sir. I got it."

Coach Jones patted her on her back. "All right, go ahead." Niyah smiled and began to walk off the track. "And, Niyah…" Niyah stopped and turned around. "You owe me for being late. I don't care if aliens abducted you the night before. Be here on time. Don't do it again."

Niyah snickered. "Yes, sir." Niyah ran off as Coach Jones continued to pack up.

Inside the Bay University student cafeteria, people filled the tables eating and talking. Music played and the loud chatter from the cafeteria echoed outside the building. Sean, Gary, Kevin, Dante, Renae, Brooke, Alyssa and Laurie were sitting at a long table in the back of the cafeteria eating, laughing and talking.

Renae took a big gulp of root beer and turned to Dante. "So, Dante, a girl that doesn't give you head is not your type?" she asked.

"Hell naw," he replied. Everyone at the table started laughing.

"I don't think that's any man's type," Gary said.

Brooke gagged on her French fries. "You guys are so gross."

Kevin looked at the ladies and said, "We are grown. No time for childish women."

Laurie replied, "Not giving head is childish?"

All the guys look at each other and say, "Hell yeah" in unison.

The group of kids all started laughing. Niyah walked in the cafeteria over to her friends. She sat across from Sean and next to Brooke. Everyone said hi to Niyah as she plopped down in her seat and dropped her backpack to the floor.

"Nini, you not going to eat?" Brooke asked.

"I'm not hungry."

Laurie reached across the table and grabbed Dante's piece of bread. "Nini, what's the deal with you and Alisha?" she asked. At the sound of Alisha's name, Dante sighed and looked away. No one noticed but Gary, who began to laugh.

Brooke looked at Gary. "What's so funny?" she asked.

"Nothing, I'm just thinking about something crazy. But yeah what happened with you and Alisha?" Gary said.

"Ain't she the senior you beat freshman year at regionals in the 200?" Brooke asked.

Niyah nodded her head yes again and smiled. "Yeah, she's a hater. Anyways, I'm going to go to sleep. After last night I need to sleep all day. Plus I have an eight o'clock class…Psych Intro, Professor Adaren. Heard it was a lot of work in that class. I would choose Criminal Psychology as a major."

Sean looked up from his plate excited. "I got that class at eight too!" he said. They gave each other a high five across the table.

Niyah screamed, "Yes, we have a class together."

Sean winked at Niyah. Kevin looked at Niyah then at Sean. He looked at his watch, ready to go.

"Well we have to go to this football meeting," Kevin said. The boys got up to walk out. Kevin stared at Niyah as he walked but she was too busy staring at Sean to notice.

Gary came over and gave Niyah a kiss on her forehead. "I'll see you later," he said.

"Okay, love you."

"Love you too."

Sean walked up behind her. "Do I get an 'I love you' too?" he asked.

Gary grabbed Sean's shirt. "Hey, man, too soon," Gary said.

Niyah laughed and waved to the guys as they walked out. She finally noticed Kevin staring at her but she ignored it. As soon as the guys were out of sight, the girls began to gossip.

"Sean is so fine," said Renae. "I want him."

Niyah rolled her eyes. Alyssa looked at Niyah.

"But he already has his eyes set on someone," Alyssa said.

Niyah shook her head no. "He does not like me. He's just a flirt"

Brooke laughed. "Stop being in denial," she said.

Niyah began to blush again. She rubbed her hands through her hair and grabbed a hair tie from her wrist to put her hair in a ponytail. "Whatever. He does not."

"See, look at you. You only put your hair in a ponytail when you nervous or mad. You nervous that he waaaants yoooou," Brooke teased.

"Stop thinking you know me!" Niyah laughed as she continued to put her hair in a ponytail.

Laurie shook her head saying, "No, you know who is fine? Dante is fine as hell."

Brooke hit Laurie on the back. "And his girlfriend is the captain of our track team," she said.

Laurie looked at her and said, "And?" They all laughed.

Renae leaned in and said, "Dante is cute. I want him too."

Niyah replied, "You want everybody."

Brooke spat out her drink laughing. Niyah's phone vibrated. She read it and started smiling. "Somebody likes Brooke for sure. Gary just text me and said, 'Somebody said tell Brooke to come outside.'"

All the girls screamed out "oooooh" and playfully hit Brooke.

Brooke tried to hide her smile and excitement. "What are we twelve years old sending messages through our homeboys and shit?"

Niyah pushed Brooke out of her seat. "Girl, go outside and see who it is. You know you want to."

Brooke rolled her eyes and got out of her seat. The girls all waved goodbye to her. She pointed the middle finger at them and walked out.

Renae took another big gulp of root beer and said, "I hope it's not Sean. Or Gary. Or Kevin."

Alyssa replied, "You're such a hater."

Laurie laughed.

"You're so cute, Alyssa, I swear," she said.

They all laughed and continued eating their food wondering who Brooke went outside to see.

11

Lust Is In the Air

The next morning Niyah walked into a big, well-lit classroom and spotted Sean. He smiled at her and tapped the seat next to him. Niyah smiled and walked up the stairs.

"Hey, crazy boy," she said, sitting down as the other students began to slowly pile in ready for their first day of class. She dropped her backpack on the floor and then looked at Sean in astonishment saying, "I never had a football player beat me to class before."

"I'm not your average football player. I brought you something," he said, handing her a plate covered with foil.

Niyah removed the foil and saw breakfast steak tacos with scrambled eggs, onions, potatoes and peppers. She looked at them happily and then at Sean.

"How did you know I loved tacos?" she asked.

"I have my sources," he replied.

"Yeah and I bet those sources are named Gary," Niyah said, giggling.

Sean smiled as he pulled out a bottle of apple juice. She took the apple juice and stared into his eyes with appreciation.

"You really went all out huh? You have really made my day," Niyah said.

Sean smiled. "I made them myself. I thought you would be hungry this early in the morning. My source told me you don't like to eat breakfast when you're in a rush, but that you would love some tacos and apple juice. I know you love skittles too. I got you later."

Niyah smirked and took a big bite into the taco. She closed her eyes and moaned, "This is so good. I love a man that can cook."

"Next time you're going to have to let me make you breakfast in bed," he said.

Niyah blushed and continued to eat.

Sean stared at her and smiled as the professor walked in.

"Good morning class. Welcome."

Coach Jones was sitting down behind his desk working on the computer when Niyah walked in.

"Bad time, Coach?" Niyah asked.

"No come on in, crazy girl," he said.

Niyah laughed as she walked over to the desk chair and sat down.

"Why I have to be all that?"

He smiled. "How was your first day of college?"

"It was good. It's been fun. I have like three papers already," she said. "And my Spanish class. Don't even get me started."

"That's college life for you."

"And I met a boy I really like."

Coach Jones stopped typing and looked over at Niyah.

"Already? Let me guess. It's a football player," he said.

"Coach, you're so smart!"

"I know this. But is everything okay though? Really?"

"Yes! I just came in here to mess with you! And talk to you about the season."

"Well, we have a lot of big meets both indoor and outdoor. I'm thinking of putting you on that 800 meter dash for the first meet."

"Coach! I hate the indoor 800!" Niyah yelled.

"It will help you with the 400 meter dash. You know that."

Niyah sighed and put her head down.

"This is my punishment for being late, isn't it?" she asked.

Coach Jones laughed saying, "Yes, this is your punishment."

Niyah smiled and got up. "As long as I'm on the mile relay I'll run everything."

"We shall see!"

Niyah laughed and started to walk out.

"Let me go get ready for practice before I'm late, and you put me on the two mile indoor," she said.

"Actually that's not a bad idea."

Niyah laughed hysterically and started to walk out as Coach Jones called out to her.

"Hey, Niyah. Just some advice. Don't let these guys throw you off your game. You don't know how many girls get caught up with a man and get pregnant while in school or something. And if you need anything you know you can come to me right?"

"I know, Coach. I won't let anything distract me. I promise."

"Okay. Now get out of here."

Niyah smiled and walked out of the office, still thinking about what coach had just told her.

Shortly after Niyah left Coach Jones's office, Coach Tatem walked in.

"Was that Ms. Coleman?" he asked.

"It was," Coach Jones replied.

"How is she doing so far?" Tatem asked.

"She's killing it, like I knew she would. Like I told you she would."

"I trust you, Malcolm. But she does have a tendency to mess up," Coach Tatem said.

"T, you have to trust me. She'll be fine. We'll be more than fine. We're going to bring home that trophy," said Coach Jones smirking.

"We'll see!" Coach Tatem replied as he walked out of the office.

Coach Jones sighed and went back to working on the computer.

Niyah, Brooke and Laurie were about to walk into the locker room when the girls spotted Alisha kissing Dante. Laurie rolled her eyes as they went inside the locker room. They started to undress at their lockers and get ready for their pool workout. Laurie was quiet as she got dressed. She looked around the locker room and pulled out a flask from her backpack, taking a long drink. Brooke and Niyah stopped dressing to stare at her. Laurie put the flask back in her backpack and into her locker.

Brooke nervously laughed saying, "Laurie, what the hell is wrong with you? Why do you have a flask of alcohol just ready to go like that?"

"Because sometimes I get stressed and I just need a little stress reliever. Seeing Alisha kiss Dante just pissed me off," Laurie said.

Niyah uttered, "Ugh, seeing Alisha kiss anybody makes me want to vomit."

Laurie replied, "Well… I hope she likes the way I taste cuz' Dante was all in it last night."

Niyah looked up at her shocked.

"Wait a minute. You mean to tell me. Noooo… you're…" she said.

Laurie whispered, "Yup. He's like a lizard."

Niyah covered her ears.

"I cannot listen to this nastiness!"

Brooke and Laurie gave each other a high five. Niyah turned to Laurie.

"You lucky I like you, and hate Alisha or else I would tell on you," Niyah said.

The girls laughed as they continued to get dressed.

The track team was sitting in their bathing suits shivering from the cold air inside the indoor pool building. They were talking as Coach Jones walked up. "I hope everyone is feeling like Michael Phelps today," he said. The girls all let out a sarcastic laugh. Coach Jones clapped his hands. "Come on! This is going to be fun!"

Brooke patted her head saying, "I just put my new weave in."

Coach Jones turned to her. "Should have gotten wet and wavy."

The girls all started cackling at Coach's joke.

Brooke replied, "I'm mad you know about that."

"I've had plenty of girlfriends back in my day before Mrs. Jones."

The girls started teasing him by singing the song, "Me and Mrs. Jones."

Coach Jones clapped his hands.

"All right, let's go. We are doing sprints in the pool back and forth. Six down and six back. And I want you running. Knees and arms up! I'm giving you guys the day off tomorrow. You will be sore!" he shouted.

All the girls moaned.

"Who needs floaties?" Coach Jones asked.

All the girls raised their hands. Coach sighed and took some floaties out his bag. The girls put them on and got in the water. The cold pool water hit the girls' muscles like ice. They all shivered as they tried to get their bodies used to the water temperature. Alisha and Niyah were right next to each other.

"Y'all ready?" he yelled.

Niyah and Alisha looked at each other. Coach blew his whistle. The girls took off in the cold pool water.

Niyah, Laurie and Brooke were in the locker room drying off and changing back into their street clothes. Niyah was shivering hard as she dried herself off with a towel. "I'm cold as hell," she said.

Brooke looked at her.

"You still look good though," she said.

Niyah looked at Brooke and smiled.

"That was random but I'll take that compliment. Made my day," she said.

Laurie looked at the both of them saying, "I swear y'all are gay."

Niyah shook her butt at Laurie.

"She just likes what she sees," Niyah said.

Laurie snickered.

"She likes someone else. Someone named Kevin."

Niyah turned to Brooke in shock. "What? You hooked up with Kevin and didn't tell me? That's who called you outside you little punk!"

Brooke laughed and blushed. She then shook her butt too. "I was going to tell you! Laurie only knows because her and Dante came to his house last night," she replied. "We haven't done anything yet but kissed."

Niyah shook her head. "Y'all fake. Both of y'all. Man I need to catch up!"

Laurie smiled and closed her locker saying, "Well I have to go hook up with someone too."

Brooke waved her hand at Laurie. "We know! We know!" she said.

Laurie replied, "Okay see you guys later." Laurie ran out of the locker room.

Niyah looked at Brooke.

"So Dante still dates Alisha right?"

Brooke shook her head yes. "Yeah!" she said. "You know that! And we saw them all kissing today. I thought they had broken up, but I guess they back together. Somebody told me that they have been dating since high school."

"Damn that sucks. I know how that feels to have a cheating man," Niyah said.

Niyah spotted Alisha across the locker room. Alisha was laughing and smiling until she spotted Niyah looking at her. She rolled her eyes at Niyah and went back to her conversation with her friends.

Niyah shrugged. "Too bad I don't like Alisha's ass. It's none of my business. Let's go."

Niyah and Brooke closed their lockers and walked out of the locker room.

Niyah and Brooke walked out into the hallway right into Sean, Gary and Kevin. Gary walked up to Niyah and gave her a big hug. "What's up, big head!" Gary said, giving Niyah a kiss on the forehead.

Kevin walked over and kissed Brooke on the cheek. He then walked over to Niyah and gave her a long hug.

"How you doing, Nini?" he asked.

"I'm fine, Kevin. Thanks for asking," she said.

Kevin hugged Niyah for a little while longer making Niyah uncomfortable as she tried to let go of him. He finally let her go. Niyah caught Sean staring at her and quickly started to smile. Kevin stared at them with jealousy in his eyes before grabbing Brooke and pulling her close. Niyah walked over to Sean and gave him a hug.

"And what are you about to do, Mr. Sean?" she asked.

"I'm about to go home to make me some spaghetti," he said.

"Spaghetti, huh?"

Brooke laughed saying, "Nini, loves spaghetti. That was her dad's specialty back in the day."

"What you mean back in the day? It still is! But I want to try Sean's spaghetti."

Sean grinned saying, "You're welcome to come with me."

Brooke grabbed Niyah's arm.

"Nini, we have class."

Niyah turned to Brooke and said, "One missed class ain't gone hurt."

Brooke smiled and let go of Niyah's arm.

"Okaaaay hot stuff," Brooke said. "Just meet me at study hall later. We have to get ten more hours this week."

Niyah turned back to Sean. He reached out his hand as they walked off.

Gary called out after them saying, "Y'all better be good!"

Sean and Niyah were sitting in his dining room eating spaghetti and drinking wine. Sean's apartment was extremely clean and smelled of cinnamon candles. Niyah was truly enjoying his company. They were laughing as she told the story about her and the Chuck E. Cheese coins.

"You really robbed a bank with Chuck E Cheese coins?" Sean asked.

Niyah laughed saying, "I don't consider it robbing a bank. I didn't go in there with guns! But technically yes, me and my ex best friend did!"

Sean continued eating and laughing.

"That is sexy," he said. "You gangster and athletic!"

Niyah sipped on her glass of wine.

"I mean. We really didn't mean to. I really just noticed the glitch and we went from there."

"Man so what happened after? Did y'all get in trouble?"

Niyah smiled while rolling her eyes.

"My parents and her parents had to pay the money back. We got in so much trouble!" she said.

"I bet! But that's kind of cool though. Not everyone can say they robbed a bank."

"Hey I got some new clothes and shoes out of it!"

They both laughed and continued eating.

"So why do you keep referring to this girl as your ex best friend?" Sean asked.

Niyah looked up at him.

"Who Destiny?" she said. "Well she had sex with my boyfriend at the time. Everyone knew except me. When I first asked her she lied to me about it. I hate being lied to in my face. That is a really big deal to me. If you did it, you did it. There is nothing I can do about it. If I'm asking you I already know. So don't lie to me!"

Niyah began eating her food angrily. Sean put his fork down.

"I'm sorry. I didn't mean to upset you," he said.

Niyah realized she had upset herself. She took a deep breath and calmed herself down. "I'm sorry," she said. "I didn't mean to get angry. It just sucks you know. Having someone cheat on you. And with someone who you've been friends with for five years. Me and my ex, Caleb, were dating since we were like ten. So it was horrible. It's all good. Brooke is my bestie anyways."

Sean shook his head in agreement saying, "I know what you mean. I hate cheaters. And liars. I would never do that to you. I'm sorry you had to go through that."

Niyah looked up at him and smiled.

"Thank you for that."

He smiled back at her. "You're welcome."

Niyah continued eating the spaghetti loving every bite.

"You really can cook. Where did you learn?" she asked.

"My mom. I use to stay in the kitchen with her. She told me food was a way to a woman's heart, but that I shouldn't cook too much she would think I was trying to make her fat," he said laughing as he thought about his time with his mother. He frowned as he continued to stroll down memory lane. "I used to love spending time with her in the kitchen. I use to spend a lot of time with her. Before she ran out on us."

Niyah stopped eating. "I'm sorry to hear that."

Sean poured himself another glass of red wine and took a big gulp. "It's all good," he murmured. "She didn't appreciate my dad struggling for us. All they did was fight. She was selfish. She left us for a man with money. But now my dad is beyond successful and happy."

There was an awkward silence for a while. Niyah tried to lighten the mood by smiling and saying, "I would never run out on you. Especially if you keep cooking like this. I won't think you're trying to make me fat."

Sean looked up and smiled at her. "I would hope not," he said. "I really like you, Ms. Niyah Coleman, and I hope to spend a lot more time with you."

Niyah looked up and started blushing. "I really like you too, Sean," Niyah said taking another sip of wine. "Whew! This wine got me a little tipsy."

Sean chuckled saying, "You're a lightweight. You only had one glass."

"Remember what you said! I'm like eighty pounds right?"

"Nah. Fifty pounds."

They both laughed and looked into each other's eyes. Sean put down his fork and got out of his chair. He walked slowly towards Niyah. Niyah watched him as he got closer to her. She began to breathe in deep. She held her breath as Sean grabbed her face and kissed her lips. She grabbed his face pulling him in closer and deeper. Niyah stopped kissing him to exhale and Sean grabbed her face gently. "Spend the night with me," he said. "I don't want to do anything. I just don't want you to leave."

Niyah smiled and said, "I'll spend the night with you."

"Good."

"But there's a problem."

Sean looked at Niyah puzzled. "Yeah? What's that?" he asked.

"You do want to do something."

Sean smiled and replied, "Yeah. I mean we been spending so much time together. It's crossed my mind a time or two. But I would never disrespect you and Gary is my boy and…"

Niyah grabbed Sean's neck and pulled him in closer. They kissed passionately. She looked at him and smiled. "Then a booty rub will do."

Sean laughed as he picked her up and carried her to his bedroom. They continued kissing as Sean laid her on the bed. He wrapped his arms around her tightly. He began to rub on her booty. He then slid his hands inside her panties. He felt her wetness and moaned.

"Oh my God. Somebody wants me."

She laughed as she pressed her butt against the bulge in his pants. "And someone wants me. In due time."

Sean smiled as he slightly pulled her pants down. He stopped himself. "I'm sorry. I got excited."

Niyah laughed. She turned over to kiss him. "Well then we can stop playing games and do what we both want."

He climbed on top of her and took her shirt off. He unsnapped her bra and began caressing her breasts. She moaned as she wrapped her legs around his back. She took off his shirt as they caressed each other. Sean slowly took off Niyah's pants and boy shorts. He kissed her neck as he took off his pants. He took out a condom from his dresser and quickly put it on. He thrust inside Niyah slowly as she moaned loudly. He suddenly began to go faster as Niyah screamed. He caressed every inch of her body. He finally stopped and lay on top of Niyah breathing heavily. They both were sweating profusely. He kissed her on the lips before he lay next to her. She wiped the sweat from her forehead as Sean wrapped his arms around her and smiled.

"You might be the one Niyah. I swear," he said smiling.

She laughed as she kissed his arm. "Ditto."

Sean kissed her back as they both closed their eyes and lay in silence before they both drifted into a deep sleep.

12

Mixed Signals

Niyah was laying in Sean's bed. Her alarm on her phone rang loudly, waking both her and Sean. She grabbed her phone with her eyes still closed. She turned the alarm off and fully opened her eyes. Sean rolled over and kissed her on the cheek. He tried to kiss her on the lips. Niyah pushed his face back. "Ew! Morning breath," she said.

He laughed and stole a kiss. "Got my kiss anyway!" he said. "It's been two months and you still can't kiss me early in the morning. Shame on you."

Niyah laughed as she got up and put on her boy shorts. She walked into the bathroom. She grabbed her toothbrush and began brushing her teeth. "I kiss you all the time in all the right places. You'll be fine."

Sean laughed as he got out of bed. He put on his sweatpants and walked into the bathroom. "What class do you have again?" he asked.

Niyah spit out toothpaste into the sink. "You know I have business algebra with Brooke," she said.

"Why do you have to go?"

Niyah looked at him and smiled. "Because I've been with you and haven't been to class," she said. "You complain every time I leave you."

"You can skip one more day."

Niyah looked at him and rolled her eyes saying, "Sean, I can't keep missing class. I have to keep my grades up."

Sean walked out of the bathroom angrily.

Niyah look at him baffled but continued brushing her teeth. She walked into the bedroom to throw on her clothes. "Hey, why do you have an attitude?"

"I don't. I promise."

"Seems like you have a little attitude over me choosing to go to class."

"No, you need to go to class. I just don't have a class until this afternoon. Wanted to spend some more time with you."

Niyah smiled and walked over to give Sean a hug. She sat on his lap and kissed him on the cheek. "I'll see you later," she reassured. "I promise."

Niyah tried to give him a kiss on the lips, but he moved his head out of the way. "Oh, so now you don't want to give me a kiss?" she said, sighing. She got up from his lap. "Fine then, be that way." She threw on her blue jean shorts and a halter top. She began to put her hair up in a ponytail ferociously. She pulled out a few strands of her own hair. She gritted her teeth at the pain from pulling her hair out. She noticed Sean looking at her blue jean shorts. "Are you looking at my ass or my shorts?" she asked.

"I'm looking at both," he said. "Why do you have to wear those?"

Niyah looked at him confused. "Are you serious right now? What's wrong with them?" she asked.

"I can see your ass if you bend over."

Niyah looked down at her shorts then at her butt. "You're being over dramatic. You cannot see my ass," she exclaimed.

Sean walked over and rubbed his hand under her shorts. "I can feel your ass under your shorts. Can you put on some pants please?"

Niyah gave him a dirty look saying, "No, Sean, I can't. This is what I wore last night when we went to the movies."

"Yeah but you were with me!"

Niyah turned and stared at him. "You need to calm down. I don't have any other clothes over here which is why I have to run to go to my dorm before class. Relax," she said.

"Don't tell me to relax, Niyah! I'm just saying those shorts make you look trashy. You seeking the wrong attention."

Niyah playfully replied, "it got your attention though."

Sean looked at her angrily. Niyah rolled her eyes. She grabbed her backpack and phone.

"I'll see you later," she said, storming out of the apartment.

Niyah walked into the classroom. She spotted Brooke and walked over and sat next to her.

Brooke noticed the frustrated look on Niyah's face. "You okay?" she asked. Niyah sat there deep in thought. Brooke shook her shoulders. "Niyah, are you okay?"

Niyah jumped up and looked at Brooke saying, "Yeah, I'm fine."

"Where in the hell have you been? You been missing class," Brooke said.

"I know. I know. I been with Sean's ass. Everything seemed good, but this morning he started tripping out of nowhere."

"What happened?"

Niyah turned around in her seat fully facing Brooke. "Well first, he started tripping because I was getting ready for class," Niyah said. "Talking about he wanted me to stay there with him. Then he started tripping about my shorts."

Brooke looked down at Niyah's clothes. "What's wrong with your shorts?" she asked.

Niyah shrugged her shoulders. "I had on some blue jean shorts just like these earlier," she said. "He talking about they too short and he could see my ass." Niyah lifted her legs to show Brooke her shorts. "They were the same length as these."

Brooke looked at the shorts up and down. "They look fine to me. We live in Texas. It's hot as hell."

"Thank you!"

Brooke started laughing saying, "He better not be on that controlling shit."

Niyah shook her head no. "No. He's usually not like that," she said. "He is just cranky this morning I guess. Maybe because we haven't had sex since the first time."

Brooke began to laugh. "Woah!" she yelled. "Y'all have been talking for like two months and he only been in that thing once?"

Niyah laughed hysterically. "No," she said. "We just chilling right now. That's all. We just cuddle and go to sleep."

"Well that's why he cranky as hell!" Brooke said. "Got you putting your hair in a ponytail. Oh yeah he definitely made you mad." They both laughed as the professor walked into the classroom and stood in front of her students.

"Okay, before we start, I'm going to pass back your tests from last week", the professor said. "Some of you will need to study more. There is a test next week and there will be no curve." The professor started passing back the tests.

Niyah and Brooke got their tests back. Brooke got an eighty four.

"Nini, what you get?" she asked.

Niyah put her hands on her head frustrated. She turned her test around. It read sixty two.

Brooke looked at the test shocked.

"Nini, what the hell?"

"I know. I know! I don't know what the hell is wrong with me."

"Because you haven't been coming to class or studying."

"I told you. Sean be like having me hostage."

"Yeah but you know what you have to do, Niyah, to get this full ride. Can't let no man take you off that."

"I know, Brooke. I just like attention. You know I be falling in love fast," Niyah said.

They both laughed.

"But I will get back on it I promise," Niyah said.

Brooke smiled at Niyah. "You better," she said. "You know I have to watch you."

The professor walked back to the front of the class and began her lesson for the day.

Niyah was in her dorm room on her computer before track practice. She was typing and giggling, reading aloud when there was a knock at the door. She quickly shut her computer.

"Hang on!" Niyah said, throwing on her practice shorts, running to the door. She swung it open to Sean standing there.

He smiled at the sight of her. "Hey, cutie," he said.

Niyah sighed and moved to the side allowing Sean to walk in. She closed the door behind them.

Sean grabbed her arms saying, "You not happy to see me?"

Niyah finally smiled a little bit. "I'm always happy to see you," she said. "You just was being mean this morning."

"Who were you talking to?" he said. "Were you on the phone when I knocked?"

"No," Niyah said, moving her computer from her bed to her desk.

"I heard you talking and laughing."

"I was on skype with my friend from track back in the day."

"What friend?" he asked.

"You don't know her."

"As long as you're not already talking to another guy," Sean said.

Sean hopped up on the Niyah's bed and pulled her in between his legs.

"And I wasn't being mean this morning," he said. "I just don't want you walking around looking like a hooker."

Niyah rolled her eyes and tried to get away from Sean. She pushed him in the chest, but he wouldn't let her go.

"Niyah, stop," he said. "You know I care about you and like you a lot. I just don't want anyone looking at you like that."

Niyah looked him in his eyes. "Well, I guess it's kind of sweet," she said.

Niyah walked away and continued getting dressed. "I gotta go," she said. We have a track meet this week and I cannot be late."

"Will I see you later?"

"Yes you will, Sean."

"Are you going to put some sweats on over them shorts?"

Niyah smacked her lips and pointed towards the door. "Bye, Sean. I'll talk to you later," she said.

Sean got up and walked out of the dorm. Niyah grabbed her backpack and ran out of the door.

13
Run Fast, Turn Left

Niyah and her track team pulled up to the indoor track meet on a bus. Teams were practicing on the field and the crowd was piling into the stadium. Coach Jones quieted his team so he could speak to them before they got off the bus.

"Alright, listen up," Coach Jones said. "Let's get out there today and do what we have to do. You all know what you're running already. Make sure that you check in by second call, so you don't have to worry about it later. Make sure you stretch, stretch and stretch. This should be a good indoor meet. Eighteen teams are here today. That's not bad at all. Alright, get your stuff. Let's go."

Niyah and Alisha were on the field warming up as Coach Jones watched. He walked up to the both of them.

"Y'all ready?" he asked. They both shook their heads yes.

"Funny, they would put both of you in the first heat together," he said.

Niyah and Alisha looked at each other then looked away without saying anything.

"Alright, so run this 200 like you guys do at practice and you will be fine. Do not let up. Get out the blocks and run the hell out the curves. They have long straights on this track so run that last one hard. Okay?"

They both replied "Okay."

"Good luck. Okay. Get out there," said Coach Jones. He then smiled and walked off.

Niyah and Alisha walked to the starting line when they heard the Announcer say, "Last Call. Women's 200. Last call. Women's 200."

Niyah began taking off her sweats as Alisha watched her.

"You ready to get your ass whooped?" Alisha asked.

Niyah turned to Alisha and laughed. "Are you serious?" she said.

"I mean, you are in lane one and I'm in lane five. You have to come get me," Alisha laughed.

Niyah stood up tall saying, "Well, that shouldn't be too hard. Trust me. I'm going to catch you."

Alisha took off her tights and threw them down saying, "We'll see." Alisha put her tights in her backpack and walked off.

Brooke walked up behind Niyah and smacked her on the butt saying, "Please kick her ass!"

Niyah put on her track spikes and laughed. "You know I got this, bestie," she said. "She so scared, she don't even know it."

Brooke balled up her fist saying, "Run fast."

Niyah balled up her fist and pounded Brooke's fist.

"Turn left," Niyah said.

Brooke smacked Niyah on the butt again.

"Let's go, Nini!" she said.

Niyah laughed and walked to the starting line.

The starting official cleared the track as Niyah and her seven competitors stretched, getting ready for the race. Niyah looked down at Alisha and waved playfully. Alisha shot her the middle finger.

"Alright, ladies, on the track," the official's voice boomed. Alisha, Niyah and their competition all stepped on the track in their lanes. Niyah grabbed her blocks and began to set them up. She looked in the stands and saw Dante, Kevin, Gary and Sean cheering them on.

"Let's go Niyah! Let's go Alisha!" they shouted.

Niyah caught Sean's eyes. He smiled at her and she smiled back. Sean blew her a kiss. She laughed and continued setting up her starting blocks. As soon as she was done she knelt down to pray. "Dear God, Thank you this day. Thank you for letting us get here safely. Please guide my feet and legs around the track as fast I can. Please let me use the talents you gave me to the best of my abilities. Amen." Niyah got up and blew a kiss to the ceiling.

The starting official blew his whistle as the crowd got quiet. "Runners, to your mark," he said. The ladies got down in their blocks. "Set." The ladies rose their butts and legs in their blocks. The official shot his gun and the ladies sped off. Niyah passed her first three competitors at the start with ease. She caught up to Alisha and the competitor in lane six. The three girls rushed around the track pumping their legs as sweat fell from their foreheads.

"Let's go, baby!" Sean yelled from the stands.

"Come on, Niyah!" Gary yelled.

Niyah and Alisha rounded the first curve of the indoor track as the competitor in Lane six moved ahead of them on the straight. They came around the second curve and into the home stretch. The crowd cheered as the girls on the track pushed their legs harder aiming for the finish line. Niyah, Alisha, and the competitor in lane six all finished within milliseconds of each other leaning in with their shoulders. They looked up at the scoreboards. It showed that the competitor in Lane six came in first place with the time of 27.3 seconds, Niyah came in second place with the time of 27.94 seconds and Alisha came in third place with the time of 28.04 seconds. Niyah congratulated the first place winner. She tried to congratulate Alisha by putting her hand out to shake it.

"Good job, Alisha," Niyah said.

Alisha looked down at her hand and slapped it away before storming off. Niyah shook her head, smiled and walked off the track towards her friends.

Niyah, Brooke and Laurie walked into the stands to Gary, Kevin, Dante and Sean.

Kevin stared at Niyah as she walked over to them and was the first one to get up and congratulate her. "Congrats, Niyah!"

"Thank you!"

He hugged Brooke next as Brooke sat on Kevin's lap. Niyah sat next to Sean as Laurie sat next to Dante. Laurie tried to give Dante a kiss.

Dante pushed her off saying, "Come on now. You know Alisha here. Chill out."

Laurie backed up and turned toward the track in embarrassment.

Sean grabbed the silver medal around Niyah's neck saying, "So you think you fast?"

Niyah smiled. "Just a little bit," she said.

Gary grabbed the medal from Sean. "Next time I need a first place," he said.

"First of all, y'all are killin' my neck snatching this medal around. Second of all, that's the fastest girl in the state right now!" Niyah laughed.

"So! Beat her next time!"

Niyah cackled as Brooke chimed in, "As long as she beat Alisha."

They all laughed.

Dante replied, "Not too much on my baby though."

Laurie looked at him angrily when he referred to Alisha as his baby.

Gary tried to change the subject saying, "So what we doing tonight? Party?"

"Can we get through the track meet first," Niyah responded.

They all started laughing when Alisha walked up.

"Dante, can you walk with me to my check in please?" she asked.

"Well hey to you too, baby," Dante said, getting up to walk towards Alisha.

Laurie watched him as he walked off with her.

"Why the hell do I keep seeing him? He gone be with that stupid broad," she said.

Brooke hugged Laurie.

"You have to stop talking to him, Laurie. He has a girl," Brooke said.

"He told me he was going to leave her."

"They've been together since high school. He not leaving that," Kevin replied.

Gary leaned over to Laurie saying, "I'll take you with your fine ass."

Laurie smiled and got up. "No thank you, Gary. You too ruthless for me," she said.

Gary laughed.

Laurie continued, "I'm going to go back to the tent to get ready for these hurdles."

Brooke hopped up saying, "I'll go with you. Walk with me, Kevin."

Kevin and Brooke got up and walked off. Gary looked at Sean then at Niyah.

"I guess I'll go get me a burger or something," said Gary as he kissed Niyah on her forehead and left.

Sean stared at Niyah as she sipped from her water bottle.

"So you and Gary are that close, huh?" he asked.

Niyah looked at him annoyed. "What do you mean?" she asked.

Sean moved closer to her.

"He is always kissing you on the forehead and shit," Sean said.

Niyah rolled her eyes saying, "Sean, that's my cousin. Chill. That's just how he is."

"I'm just saying. Maybe I don't want him kissing all over you."

"Well one day when you officially make me your girlfriend you can have some kind of say so. Until then, you just have to deal with it. That's why you're not getting any more goodies either!" Niyah laughed as she watched the track meet.

Sean put his arm around Niyah.

"One day I really am. One day. You have to be good and do some things before I can though," he said.

Niyah moved in closer to Sean.

"Like what?" she asked.

"Like maybe think about erasing all of your social media."

Niyah turned to Sean shocked at his remark.

"Excuse me?" she asked.

"I mean. We know you're a sexy girl, but you always posting too much. I wouldn't want my girlfriend posting pictures like that."

Niyah removed Sean's hand from her shoulder.

"What pictures?" she asked. "Pictures like what?"

Sean pulled out his phone and went to his pictures. He showed Niyah and her teammates posing in a picture on the track. They are in their sports bras and shorts. The caption read, "Time to beast."

Niyah stared at the picture and then to Sean saying, "Are you kidding me? I just put that picture up this morning because we were at the track meet."

"But why do you have to post pics like that?"

"That's not even that bad. At all! I've seen worse."

"But look at all these guys commenting and shit under the pic though."

Niyah rolled her eyes saying, "So what?! There are guys commenting and girls. Girls tell you that you look good all the time."

"Yeah but I don't post pictures of me with my shirt off."

Niyah put down her bottle and moved away from Sean.

"You're annoying the hell out of me right now. You don't even get on twitter and I didn't put that on any other social media. How did you even get that picture? Are you just stalking my twitter?" she asked.

"I have my ways."

Niyah got up and started to walk off. "You're not going to do this. Not in front of all these people at a damn track meet," she said.

Sean grabbed her hand so hard she almost fell to the ground. She turned around quickly.

Sean loosened his grip saying, "I'm sorry. Just wait. Sit down. Please."

Niyah sighed but reluctantly sat back down. She rubbed her hand as it throbbed with pain. The people around them turned to look. Sean lowered his voice so that only Niyah could hear him.

"Listen, I'm not calling you a whore or anything," he said. "I'm just saying I wouldn't want my baby seeking attention from other guys. I told you that when you wore them shorts."

"Yeah but I'm not your girlfriend. It's just a damn picture."

"But you're trying to be. Are you or are you not?"

Niyah lowered her head.

"Not if it comes with all these rules and this crazy stuff," she said. "I know I'm crazy but I'm not going to fight with you about what pictures I put on my social media and you're not going to tell me what I can and can't wear. I respect you and I always have, and you're not even my boyfriend. But you grabbing and yelling at me every five minutes is not necessary."

"I'm just saying. I want you all to myself. My eyes only."

"Well then just say that. Don't upset me while I'm at my place of peace at a track meet. I have to focus on running."

Sean kissed her on the cheek then said, "I'm sorry. Forgive me?"

Niyah stared at him without answering him.

"Hold on," Sean said as he went into his backpack. He pulled out a pack of Skittles.

Niyah slightly smiled at the sight of the skittles.

"Really, Sean?" she said.

"You love these more than anything. You can't be mad at me now. I'm sorry, Nini. Let's just start over, okay. No rules. I just really like you. That's all. You can't blame me."

Niyah smiled and snatched the skittles from Sean.

"You just need to chill, that's all. I loved the Sean I met before. I'm not going to do anything to hurt you. Just relax. For real," she said and kissed him on the cheek as she opened the skittles.

Sean smiled at her and then turned his attention to the track as Niyah lay down in his lap eating her Skittles.

14

Halloween Face-Off

Niyah and Sean were walking down the hallway towards Niyah's dorm carrying their backpacks. They passed Halloween decorations on the walls as they almost reached Niyah's door.

"Thank you for walking me home from study hall. My grades been slipping lately, so I need to be in there as much as I can," Niyah said.

Sean put his arms around Niyah's waist.

"You should start going to class!" he said.

Niyah looked up at him and responded, "If you recall, I'm always with you."

"And I like you being with me."

As they continued walking, a very handsome, tall basketball player walked towards them. It is Thaddeus, one of the point guards on the Bay University basketball team. He walked up to Niyah and Sean. Thaddeus held his fist out to dab Sean up. "What's up, man," he said.

Sean stared at him before dabbing him up. "Sup."

Thaddeus hugged Niyah as she smiled. "What's up, Nini."

Niyah replied, "Hey you! What's going on?"

Thaddeus let Niyah go before responding, "What's up on them notes from Economics though?"

Niyah laughed hysterically. "You must have failed that last test. I told you to sit up there with us and come to the study group."

"Man that class hard and she don't like me. I stay far away from her. That's why she failed me," Thaddeus said.

Sean stared at the two of them jealously. Niyah and Thaddeus continued their conversation.

"I got you. I have some good notes. I'll give 'em to you later," Niyah replied.

Thaddeus smiled. "That's why you my potna'! You going to the party tonight?"

Niyah laid her head on Sean's shoulder. "We'll be there."

Sean moved his shoulder and Niyah turned to him confused.

Thaddeus looked at them and awkwardly smiled. "All right, I'll see y'all there then. Later, man." Thaddeus held out his fist to dab Sean up again. This time Sean didn't move. Thaddeus looked at him confused then smiled. "All right then. See you later, Niyah."

Niyah frowned at Sean then turned back to Thaddeus. "Bye, T."

Thaddeus took one more look at Sean then continued walking down the hallway.

Niyah turned to Sean frustrated. "Why you was being like that?"

Sean looked at her. "I see you just friendly with every damn body huh?"

Niyah rolled her eyes. "Stop it! He is in my class. And as you saw, he is coming out of that dorm right there. His girlfriend's dorm." Niyah pointed to the dorm Thaddeus came out of. "You need to stop trippin'. My goodness." Niyah walked off angrily before reaching her door.

Sean ran up behind her and grabbed her from behind. "I'm sorry, baby. I just gotta protect you from the fools on this campus."

Niyah turned around. "You the only fool I see, if you can't see I only want to be with you."

Sean smiled. He grabbed Niyah's face and leaned in. They were about to kiss when Niyah's dorm room door flew open. Renae stepped out of the room, scaring Niyah and Sean.

"Renae! How in the hell did you get in my room?" Niyah asked.

"Laurie let me in. You told me to come over, so we can find something for the Halloween party," Renae said. "Hey, Sean," she said biting her bottom lip, looking him up and down. Niyah glared at her.

"What's up, Renae," he said.

"Did you eat that cake?" she asked.

"Yeah it was good. Thanks."

Niyah looked at Renae and then Sean.

"What cake?" Niyah asked.

"I took Sean some cake I made. I took it to his apartment the other day."

Niyah turned around and looked at Sean angrily, "Oh, okay I see. You get mad at me about some dude asking for notes, and you have people bringing you pie."

Renae smugly smiled. "Cake."

Niyah turned to her quickly with a mean look.

Sean hugged Niyah.

"Stop looking like that," he said. "It was just some cake. And she just brought it over and dropped it off. I'll see y'all later at the party."

Sean then walked off.

Renae yelled after him, "Bye, Sean."

Niyah frowned at him then walked into her dorm room followed by Renae. Renae sat down at the desk.

"That is one fine man," Renae said.

"And your ass bringing him food."

Renae laughed at Niyah's frowned up face.

"Why you mad though?" Renae asked. "You knew I liked him."

"You like everybody! I thought you would at least respect the girl code. You just gone try to take him from me?"

Renae got out of the chair and started to fix her hair in the mirror. "Have we been friends long enough for that rule to apply?" she asked. "We just teammates, honestly. I mean we cool and all, but it is what it is. I've been to his house and everything. Besides, he's not yours to take. You're not his girlfriend."

Niyah stepped in Renae's face, saying, "I think you need to leave." Niyah scowled at her.

Renae cracked a smile.

"I guess you don't want me to borrow anything now. I'll see you later then," she said then walked out of the room.

Niyah stood there glaring as Renae walked down the hallway.

"Not this shit again," she said to herself. "Reasons I can't trust nobody!"

Her eyes filled with tears as she closed the door and lay on her bed. She started to pull her hair when she pulled a few strands out. She looked at the strands and sighed before closing her eyes and going to sleep.

Later that night, Laurie, Niyah, Alyssa and Brooke were walking up to the club for the Halloween party. The girls were dressed in sexy Halloween costumes. Laurie was dressed as a seductive mermaid. She had on turquoise eyeshadow with a sea shell bra top. She had a long, tight turquoise skirt on that resembled a mermaid fin. Niyah was dressed as Jasmine from Aladdin with her hair in a long single braid down her back. She had on exactly the same outfit Jasmine had on in the movie. Alyssa was dressed as a cute cat with whiskers on her face and cat ears. Brooke wore a cheerleader costume that was made up of a short skirt and a half top with red pom-poms in her hand.

Niyah looked at all her girls as they walked through the parking lot up to the party.

"I'm glad to be out with you guys tonight," Niyah said. "I feel like we haven't had a good turn up in a minute."

Brooke smiled at Niyah and said, "Let's enjoy this. We look good, and we need a night to turn up!"

Alyssa looked down at Brooke and Laurie.

"Well I'm glad to see the both of you," Alyssa said. "One of you is all under Dante and the other one is all under Kevin."

Brooke laughed as Laurie pulled out her phone to check her messages.

"Speaking on Dante," Laurie said. "This fool did not call me yet. He told me to meet him here."

Niyah laughed and said, "Shit, I don't know if I'm going to be able to turn up. I'm going to be too busy taking care of Laurie when Alisha find out about her and Dante and goes ham."

They all laughed. Laurie put her phone back in her bra.

"Oh you got jokes!" Laurie said. "Please, I'm not worried about that bucket headed ho. Besides, I know you got my back if she tries anything."

Niyah smiled and said, "You're being presumptuous."

They reached the front of the building of the party. Laurie spotted Dante and smiled.

"There he is," Laurie said and dashed off to him.

"She lucky Alisha don't like to come to parties that much," Brooke said as they walked up to the front. She put her arm around Niyah and screamed, "Time to party!" They all walked in the door ready to drink.

The party was loud, and the music blared from the speakers. The lights were dark as everyone danced and drank. The DJ yelled over the speakers, "Let me see ya dance! Twerk somethin, ladies!"

Niyah, Alyssa and Brooke were dancing together when Gary and two of his teammates walked up. Gary hugged the girls. Niyah pulled him down to speak into his ear.

"Where's Sean?" she asked loudly so that he could hear her over the music.

Gary pulled Niyah close saying, "I'm not sure! He said he was going to get a drink."

The group continued to dance.

Niyah pulled Brooke in close to her and said, "I'm going to go to the bathroom."

"Want me to go with you?"

Niyah shook her head no.

"No keep dancing," she said. "I'll be right back."

Brooke smiled and gave her a thumbs-up as she kept dancing with one of the football players. Niyah walked off, pushing her way through the crowd trying to get to the bathroom when she noticed Renae sitting on Sean's lap at the bar. Niyah stopped walking and stared at them for a long time. Renae kissed Sean on the cheek as he took a shot of whiskey and rubbed Renae's butt.

Niyah rushed over and stood in front of them.

"Hi, guys," she said.

Sean and Renae both looked up, startled. Renae smiled maliciously.

"Hey, Nini!" she said. "You look cute."

"You guys look cute too," Niyah said.

Sean stayed silent.

Niyah frowned at him. She then forced a smile and said, "Well I guess I'll see y'all later." She stormed off.

Renae waved after her, laughing. Sean pushed Renae off, got up, and ran after Niyah.

Renae yelled after him, "Sean, where are you going?"

Sean caught up to Niyah and grabbed her.

"Why you walk off like that?" he asked.

"No reason, Sean," Niyah said and tried to walk away, but Sean grabbed her harder.

"Don't be like that. I don't like her at all. She just..."

"It's just funny how you complain about my pictures and all that but you sitting here feeling on my fake ass friend," she said. "But it's all good. No need to explain anything to me. I'm not your girl. Can you let go of my arm, please? You're hurting me."

Sean pulled her up to his chest and said, "But I want you to be. This is so cute. Don't be jealous."

"I'm not jealous. I'm territorial. And that shit is disrespectful!"

"She just came over and started dancing. I'm a little drunk. It's not that serious."

"You're right. It's not. I just thought we had something."

"We do!"

Niyah stared at him with tears in her eyes. Sean moved in trying to kiss her. She moved her head out of the way, denying the kiss. He grabbed her arm harder. She snatched her arm away from him. "Just get back to your dance, Sean," she said, then ran off to her friends.

Sean yelled after her, "Niyah! Niyah! Damn!"

He hit his hand on his forehead and walked off back toward the bar as

Niyah reached her friends. She grabbed Brooke and pulled her to the side. "Brooke, I'm going back to my dorm. I'm going to take the train."

Brooke looked at Niyah, concerned.

"Why? We just got here," Brooke said. "What's wrong? Why would you take the train by yourself this late? No ma'am!"

"I'm fine. I'll be fine. I just wanna go. Call me later." Niyah said then ran out of the club before anyone had a chance to stop her.

Brooke called after her, but Niyah was gone.

It was cold and dark outside as Niyah walked to the track. She had her track back pack now and hopped the fence to the field. She still had on her Halloween costume. She threw her backpack and started screaming.

"Every time I like someone, some bitch goes after him! I swear I hate them!" she yelled. She opened her backpack and pulled out some shorts. She took off her costume bottoms and threw her shorts on. She then pulled out her track spikes and put them on. Niyah was sprinting on the track angrily. She ran over to the trash can and puked in it. She took her spikes off and threw them across the track. She fell to the ground with her eyes closed. Her eyeliner and mascara ran down her face as she lay on the track. Niyah's phone began ringing. She ran over to see Brooke calling. She ignored the call and turned her phone on silent. She sat on the track and started crying loudly as a figure walked up behind her.

"Niyah?"

Niyah jumped up, scared for her life. She turned around to see Kevin standing behind her.

"Holy shit, Kevin! You scared the shit out of me!"

"Sorry. I thought that was you walking here earlier. I heard screaming. You okay?" Kevin asked as he walked up to her and sat his backpack down.

Niyah wiped her face, unable to stop the tears from falling. "Yeah, I'm fine. Running off some steam."

Kevin walked up to her and wiped some tears from her face.

"Hey. All that screaming and crying. Something is wrong," he said. "You can talk to me."

Niyah looked at him and moved his hand from her face.

"I'm fine," she said. "I promise. I'm just a little drunk and upset right now. Why aren't you at the party?"

"Didn't feel like going. Don't try to change the subject. I'm not letting you off that easy. What's wrong?"

Niyah sighed trying not to give in.

"Long story," she said.

"I got all night. And I got something that will help relieve some of that stress."

Kevin walked over to his backpack. He unzipped it and pulled out a full water bottle and smiled.

"This ain't no water in this bottle," he said. "I learned from Laurie. You down to drink?"

Niyah and Kevin were sitting on the track drinking liquor from the water bottle, looking up at the sky. The moon was shining and the stars glistened in the sky. Niyah and Kevin were both drunk.

"But seriously, Kevin, Am I wrong for being mad? I mean me and him been chillin' for a while, and everyone knows I like him. Renae just a bitch. I'm surprised I didn't hit her. I'm trying to be good," Niyah said.

Kevin took a gulp from the water bottle and passed it to Niyah.

"He likes you, Nini, but he's a known ho. You need someone that knows your worth. You're beautiful, smart, and athletic. You need someone that's going to love you right."

Niyah took a drink and looked at Kevin.

"You're just trying to make me feel better," she said.

Kevin put his arm around Niyah.

"No, I'm serious. Any man would be lucky to have you."

Niyah brushed Kevin's arm off her shoulder.

Kevin sighed, "What's the problem? We just talking. I can't put my arm around you?"

"No. I appreciate you talking to me. It just makes me a little uncomfortable to have you put your arm around me and stuff, being that you talk to Brooke."

Kevin smiled and said, "Hey, like I said, we're just talking. I just want to make sure you're okay."

Kevin and Niyah stared at each other. They were both now extremely drunk. Kevin grabbed the back of Niyah's head and pulled her in close. He kissed her slowly. Niyah's breathing picked up as she kissed him back. Suddenly, she realized what was happening. She pushed him off and wiped her lips.

"Kevin, what the hell are you doing? You're with my best friend! What the hell is wrong with you? Oh my God that did not just happen! That did not just happen!" she said.

"I'm sorry. I've been wanting you ever since I first saw you. You were too wrapped up in Sean to notice. I'm always staring at you. Always trying to be around you. I want you."

Kevin kissed Niyah again. Niyah tried to fight Kevin off but was failing miserably, too drunk to get up. Niyah finally managed to get him off of her. She jumped up before falling back down. She noticed Kevin staring at something behind her. She turned around to see Brooke standing there. Brooke was shocked and heartbroken after witnessing her best friend kiss the guy she liked.

Niyah was horrified at the thought of Brooke watching her and Kevin kiss. "Brooke!" she yelled.

Brooke looked at Niyah and began to cry.

"I thought you would be here," Brooke said. "I came to see if you were okay. I see why you didn't answer your phone." Brooke began to walk off.

Niyah tried to get herself together and stop Brooke.

"Brooke, wait!" Niyah yelled, chasing her.

Niyah finally reached Brooke and grabbed her arm.

Brooke pushed a drunk Niyah down.

"You know what, don't even, Niyah. Fuck both of you!" Brooke yelled before she ran off.

Niyah shouted after her, "Brooke! Brooke!"

She turned back to Kevin, still in shock, grabbed her stuff, and ran off. Kevin sat on the track smiling as he rubbed his lips.

Niyah rushed inside her dorm room, calling Brooke. She kept getting her voicemail. She threw her backpack down on the ground as she slammed the door and re-dialed Brooke's number. Again she got the voicemail. "Brooke, please call me and let me explain! I had nothing to do with that kiss! Call me back! Please!" She hung up the phone. Her phone then started to ring. She looked down at the phone, hoping it was Brooke. Instead it was Sean. She ignored the call and threw her phone shouting, "Fuck my life!" She looked over at Laurie's empty bed and ran over to Laurie's dresser.

She pulled out the alcohol bottle and went to the bathroom. She opened the cabinet and pulled out a bottle of pain killers. She put four of them in her mouth and swallowed them, followed by a gulp of alcohol. She sat down on the bathroom floor and continued to drink the alcohol while sobbing. She looked over at the tub and grabbed a razor. She cut her left wrist with the razor. She watched the blood trickle down her arm and onto the floor. She grabbed her wrist in pain as the blood from the cut continued to flow between her fingers unto the white tile floor.

Niyah sobbed silently holding her wrists. She sat there for thirty minutes before finally walking out. She put the alcohol bottle back in Laurie's dresser drawer and went to bed.

The girls track team was sprinting up and down the bleachers. Coach Jones stood at the bottom of the stands watching them. "Let's go, ladies, move your arms! Get them knees up!"

The girls were running and breathing hard. Coach Jones blew his whistle.

"Alright, go get some water," he said.

Niyah and Laurie ran down together as Brooke ran down in front of them.

Niyah turned to Laurie and said, "She still won't even look at me."

"She's hurt, Nini."

Niyah started rubbing her wrists when she noticed Laurie looking and moved her wrists out of view.

"What's wrong with your wrists, Nini?" Laurie asked.

"Nothing. Just sore. I'm going to go talk to Brooke," she sighed as she jogged up to Brooke.

Brooke didn't look at Niyah as she stepped in front of her.

"Brooke, can you please talk to me?" Niyah said.

Brooke took a sip from her water bottle, still not acknowledging Niyah. Niyah stood there watching as Brooke drank her water in silence. Then Brooke finally threw down her bottle and turned to Niyah.

"What is it, Nini?" Brooke said.

"Listen, I am so, so sorry you had to witness that. Kevin came at me while I was vulnerable and mad at the bitch, Renae, and Sean! I was drunk. It took me a minute to realize what was going on. I know that's not an excuse at all, but I would never hurt you like that. Ever! You know that."

Brooke looked sadly at Niyah.

"All I saw was you kissing him. What do you expect me to think?" she said. "I don't want to talk to you. Ever."

Brooke walked away leaving Niyah standing there alone.

15

Blast from the Past

The girls were getting ready to compete at the national indoor track meet. Niyah was sitting in the bleachers with her family.

"You ready?" Tammi asked.

Gary turned around and looked at Tammi.

"She better be," he said.

Tammi balled up a fist and said, "Run fast."

Niyah cracked a smile and made a fist as well. She pounded her mom's fist.

"Turn left," Niyah said.

Just then Sean walked up. Niyah hesitated for a second but then got up to hug him.

"Everybody this is my friend, Sean," she said.

David looked at Sean and said, "Just a friend huh?"

Tristan chimed in, "Let's keep it that way."

"For real," Junior added.

Niyah looked at her dad and her brothers.

"Be nice, guys," she said.

Tammi reached out and shook Sean's hand. "It's nice to meet you, Sean."

Sean smiled.

"Nice to meet you as well," he replied. "Niyah, can I talk to you?"

"Yeah, walk me to my check in," Niyah said.

She and Sean got up and walked toward the track. Sean pushed Niyah playfully.

"So I'm just your friend, huh?" he asked.

"We are friends, Sean," she said. "Look I've forgiven you and all that, but I'm not going to lie. I'm still salty. I do appreciate all the little gifts and gestures, but I just need some time to forget about it and move forward because I felt like that was a little out of line."

Sean stepped in front of her and stopped her from walking.

"Baby, you can't still be mad at me," he said. "I came to see you run!"

"I'm not mad at you okay? I just need some time. And I appreciate you coming to see me run. That's what friends are for!" Niyah stated.

Sean laughed saying, "You know you still want me."

He moved in closer to Niyah aiming to get a kiss. Niyah moved her head back and smiled.

"Maybe," she said. "Come on, I gotta go."

They continued walking down the stadium towards the field. As they were walking, a girl hastily walked up to them. She was dressed in a track uniform of an opposing team of Niyah's.

"So is this your new chick, Sean?" she asked.

Niyah looked at Sean then at the girl. Sean grabbed Niyah's waist.

"Vanessa, don't start no shit," he said.

Niyah stared at the girl.

"I'm sorry, but who the hell are you?" Niyah asked.

"Oh, he hasn't mentioned me huh?" Vanessa said. "I'm not surprised. He probably doesn't want you to know who he really is."

Sean let go of Niyah's waist and charged towards Vanessa. She stood still as Sean grabbed her shoulders and screamed, "Get the hell out of here!"

Vanessa pushed Sean off of her and backed up. She looked at Niyah.

"Whatever. Watch your back, new girl," Vanessa said then ran off.

Sean stood there angrily, breathing hard. Niyah walked up to him and touched him on the shoulder. He slapped her hand away. She jumped back shocked.

"Ouch! Why you do that?" she said.

"My bad."

"What the hell was that?"

Sean calmed himself down and turned to Niyah.

"That's just my ex being crazy," he said. "She runs for Tech. Just go out there and run and beat her ass for me! We will talk later."

"No, you need to explain this to me. This is the crazy shit I'm talking about Sean!"

Sean grabbed her shoulders.

"Hey! Calm the hell down!" he said.

Niyah pushed Sean's hands off of her shoulders.

"Don't yell at me!" she said.

Sean breathed in and out deeply. He grabbed the back of Niyah's neck.

"I'm sorry. She's nothing. I promise. Focus on your race. That's all you need to be worried about right now. Just calm the hell down." He gripped Niyah's neck harder.

Niyah hit his hand. "Sean, that shit hurt! Let go of my neck!"

Sean and Niyah started fussing with each other as Gary came from the side of the bleachers fast. He walked in between Sean and Niyah.

"Everything good?" Gary asked. He moved Niyah behind him as he stood facing Sean.

Sean stared at him as Niyah folded her arms and stared at Sean.

"We're fine, Gary," Sean said.

"It don't look like it."

"We're fine," Sean repeated.

Sean kept his eyes on Niyah. He walked past Gary and grabbed Niyah's arm. He pulled her in to kiss her on the cheek.

"Good luck," he said. "We'll talk later. I'll see you after your race."

He walked off to the bleachers. Niyah turned around and tried to smile before Gary could notice the troubled expression on her face. Gary was not smiling.

"What the hell was that? I caught the end of it," he said.

"Where the hell did you even come from, Gary?"

"I was going to the bathroom and heard y'all yelling. You all right?" he asked.

Niyah nodded her head yes.

"Yeah, I'm fine," she said.

"Do I need to handle this?" Gary asked.

Niyah grabbed Gary's hands.

"No calm down. I have to go warm up. I love you. I'll handle it. It's fine."

Niyah kissed Gary on the cheek and ran off.

Niyah was on the field warming up, getting ready for her 400 meter dash when she spotted Sean's ex, Vanessa, on the field warming up as well. She walked up to her.

"Excuse me, Vanessa is it?" she said.

Vanessa turned around quickly with an attitude. She put her hands on her hips and said, "Yeah what do you want?"

"Listen, I don't know who you are or what you and Sean had going on. I just don't like girls coming up to me like that."

Vanessa laughed and said, "Listen, little girl. I wasn't coming up to you. I don't even know you. I was Sean's girlfriend for three years. Trust me, you have no idea who he is. So why don't you back up."

"I'm not the enemy here! And I also ain't no punk. So don't talk to me like that."

"Or what? I'm just trying to help you. You will find out sooner or later."

Brooke walked up and stood next to Niyah glaring at Vanessa.

"Nini, you okay?" Brooke asked.

Niyah replied, "Yeah, I'm fine."

Vanessa rolled her eyes. "Y'all both are dumb," she said. "Don't come up to me at all. I have to get ready for my race. Have fun with Sean."

Vanessa walked off towards her teammates, and Niyah turned to Brooke.

"Thank you for having my back," she said.

"Don't get excited," Brooke said. "Just didn't want you fighting and getting the entire team disqualified. We worked too hard to get here. As you were."

Brooke jogged to the other side of the field as the starting official announced, "Ladies 400 meter dash on the track."

Niyah stepped on the track in lane 4 viciously putting her hair in a ponytail again. She calmed herself and kneeled down to pray.

"Dear God, Please guide my feet around this track…"

It was late in the afternoon as Bay's campus was starting to die down with activity for the day. Niyah and Gary were having lunch in the school cafeteria. Niyah was wearing her gold and silver medals from the indoor national track meet. Gary grabbed her medals.

"Do you have to wear those, you little show off?" he asked.

Niyah looked down at her medals.

"What these little gold things?" she joked.

Gary began laughing hard. "You are so cocky."

"Runs in the family."

Niyah played in her fruit salad not eating it as Gary continued talking.

"Did you handle that little situation at the track?" Gary asked.

"Yeah, that ho is crazy."

Gary put his fork down.

"You sure she's crazy and not him?" he asked.

"I don't know. Me and Sean are barely talking right now anyway. Besides, you know I can handle myself."

"Yeah well, I don't want to have to kill him. Be careful."

Niyah smiled and said, "Like I said, this is why I love you. But I'm fine."

Niyah continued eating. Gary was smiling at her until he took a look at her wrists. He noticed her scars.

"What the hell is that?" he asked.

Niyah looked up at him confused.

"What the hell is what?" she said.

"Those marks on your wrists. What the hell is that?"

Niyah started fidgeting.

"Oh, I fell at track practice and scraped my wrists," she said.

Gary dropped his fork on the table.

"Do you think I'm stupid?" he asked. "Let me see."

Niyah tried to move her hands to her lap. Gary got up and sat next to her. He grabbed her wrists. Niyah tried her best to hide them, but Gary was too strong.

"Niyah, don't play with me let me see," he said.

Gary took a look at Niyah's wrists as tears welled up in her eyes. Gary pulled Niyah closer.

"Have you been cutting yourself?" he asked.

"No, I haven't been cutting myself!"

"Then why are you about to cry?"

Niyah shrugged her shoulders as she wiped tears from her face.

"Nini, what is the problem?"

"Nothing. I'm fine, Gary."

Niyah snatched her arm from Gary and wiped her face. Gary sighed as he went back to his seat across from Niyah.

"Nini, that is not okay," he said. "You better not be cutting yourself at all. You can come to me or something. Do not do that again, and I'm serious."

Niyah nodded her head yes while wiping the tears from her face.

"If you have a problem or need anything, you come to me. I'm literally downstairs from your dorm. Don't let me see that again," Gary said.

Niyah nodded her head in agreement.

"So what's wrong?" Gary asked.

"I just get depressed sometimes. That's all."

"No, that's not all. That's scary. Do I need to call your mom?"

Niyah shook her head no.

"I'm not going to do it again," she said.

"And don't think I haven't noticed that you've barely been eating too."

Niyah lowered her head ashamed.

"I'll be fine," she said. "I promise."

Gary forced a smile and got up and walked over to Niyah. He bent down and gave her a long hug.

"I love you, okay," Gary said. "I'm here for you."

"I love you too."

Gary grabbed his tray and backpack.

"Are you going to class, crazy girl?"

Niyah giggled a little bit and shook her head no.

"I don't feel like it today," she said.

"Alright, bad girl. I'll see you later. I'm coming to check on you after practice. I see, I really have to keep my eyes on you. I can't let anything happen to you. I'll call you after I leave practice and we will talk about this."

Gary kissed Niyah on the forehead, and put his tray on top of the trash can and walked out.

Niyah continued playing in her fruit salad when someone came and sat down in front of her.

"Hey, baby."

Niyah looked up to see Kevin sitting there. Niyah sighed and threw her fork down.

"Please, Kevin, not today. What do you want?" Niyah asked.

"I tweeted you yesterday. Why you didn't reply?" he said.

Niyah took a sip of her drink and looked out of the window.

"I was asleep," she said.

"Do you miss me?"

"Listen, Kevin. I like you as a friend. You cool as hell. But you were with my best friend, and I don't get down like that."

"We aren't together anymore. So what's up?"

Niyah slammed her hands down on the table.

"That's my best friend! And that stupid kiss ruined my friendship and damn near my social life here! I got people looking at me crazy when I walk around this school like I'm some ho or something!"

"Well, so fuck them! What's the big deal? Y'all aren't friends anymore, so we can do our own thing. And who cares what these dumb ass people think anyways!"

"No, Kevin, we can't do our own thing! We can't! We will never!"

Kevin got up and went to sit next to Niyah. She sighed but scooted over to allow him to sit to avoid arguing with him.

"Listen, Nini. I really like you. I told you that. I don't care if the entire school hates me. I want to give us a try."

Niyah looked at Kevin.

"But I do care," she said. "I care if everyone is calling me a whore because they think we're sleeping together. I care if my best friend is heartbroken over this. I care if it starts affecting my life! I care!"

Kevin stared at her.

"At least tell me you like me, and I'll leave you alone," he said.

Niyah looked into Kevin's eyes.

"You're awesome, Kevin. You really are. And you're great to talk to. I can see why Brooke really liked you, but I'm not that kind of girl. That kiss should have never happened. We were drunk, and I was vulnerable. I am sorry if I led you on, but we will never be together. I'm trying to at least not hate you. But if you keep Facebooking me and following me to class, people are going to keep thinking we are together when we both know that's not the case. So let's just end this. We can be cordial, but that's as good as it's going to get."

Kevin replied, "I understand" and kissed Niyah on the cheek.

Just as Kevin kissed Niyah on the cheek, Renae and Brooke walked into the cafeteria and saw them. Brooke ran out of the cafeteria as Renae stood there smiling. Niyah hit her head against the window.

"Fuck! You see what I'm saying!" she said.

Kevin laughed carelessly.

"That shit is not funny, Kevin! You know what, get out of my way. Move!" She screamed as she pushed him out of the booth. "I have to go!"

She grabbed her backpack and ran out of the cafeteria.

16

Slippery Fingers

The girls were on the track running 200 meters for practice. As they finished, the team walked over to Coach Jones.

"All right, ladies!" he said. "I am so proud how we ended the indoor season. Now it's time for outdoor!"

The girls cheered excitedly at the thought of outdoor season.

"Everyone go to the weight room except for Niyah, Brooke, Laurie and Alisha. Your workout is on the wall so start on it and I'll be in there soon. And do all of the sets," he said.

Everyone ran off except for Laurie, Brooke, Niyah and Alisha. Coach pulled a baton out of his bag.

"I want to do some four by one handoffs," he said.

Niyah, Laurie and Brooke got excited. Alisha was angry.

"Coach, really?" Alisha said. "Three freshmen on the four by one-meter relay? Why?"

"Because I'm the coach, and this is my team. I can put who I want on the relay. Brooke at first leg, Laurie at second, Niyah at third and Alisha you're anchor."

"But, Coach, I'm always first leg!"

"And now you're the anchor, Alisha. If you don't like it, you can leave. On the track. Niyah and Laurie are up first."

The girls ran to their spots. Niyah and Laurie stepped on the track to set up their steps as Coach handed Laurie the baton. Alisha stood on the side upset. As Niyah was setting up her steps, she turned to see Alisha's angry face.

"You mad or nah?" Niyah taunted.

Alisha looked back at Niyah. "I'm never mad," she said.

"Then go set up your steps."

"Don't tell me what to do!"

Coach Jones walked up behind Alisha.

"Alisha, go set up your steps," he said.

Everyone laughed, even Brooke. Alisha rolled her eyes and started to walk off.

Niyah called after her, "Hey, Alisha."

Alisha turned around.

"What?" she asked with an attitude.

"You might want to give me twenty steps. I might be coming in a little hot for you."

Alisha rolled her eyes and walked away as Niyah snickered at her remark. Coach Jones stepped on the track next to Niyah.

"Ready, Nini?"

Niyah bent down preparing to receive the baton from Laurie.

"Always," she said.

Coach blew his whistle. Laurie took off towards Niyah.

Teams piled in the first outdoor track meet of the season. Girls and guys were on the track practicing their handoffs, getting ready for the first race of the day, the four by 100 meter relay. Niyah and Laurie were practicing their handoffs as Coach Jones watched. Laurie came flying down the straight away. As soon as she hit Niyah's mark, Niyah took off running. Niyah heard Laurie shout, "Stick!" Niyah put her right hand back to get the baton. Laurie placed the baton in her hand perfectly. Niyah grabbed it and sprinted fifteen meters around the curve before stopping. Coach Jones cheered from the side of the track.

"Yes!" he shouted. "That's what I'm talking about! That was perfect!"
The girls ran over to coach and gave him a high five.

Laurie said, "We on it! We have to win today! Set our mark!"

Coach Jones smiled and turned to Niyah.

"Nini, I didn't see you and Alisha's handoffs. How were they?" he asked.

Laurie looked at Niyah, knowing that Niyah and Alisha hadn't practiced yet.

Niyah responded saying, "They were good."

"Good. Put your sweats on and go check in. Find your other two teammates."

Coach Jones walked off. Laurie and Niyah began putting on their sweats and their regular tennis shoes. Laurie sat on the field and looked up at Niyah.

"So are you guys really going to do handoffs or what?" Laurie asked.

"I'm perfect. She needs to practice. Instead she over there with Dante," Niyah said as she pointed to the side of the track.

Alisha and Dante were all hugged up. Laurie became agitated that Dante was over there with Alisha.

"But he was with me again last night," Laurie said.

Just then, Brooke walked up. "Here's your water, Laurie," she said. "I'm going to go check us in."

Brooke did not look at Niyah as she walked away. Laurie opened the bottle and took a sip of the water. She noticed Niyah's sad expression as she stared after Brooke.

"She misses you. She's forcing herself to be mad now," Laurie said handing Niyah her bottle of water.

Niyah grabbed the bottle and shrugged.

"Let me go get Alisha." She handed the bottle back to Laurie.

Niyah walked over to Alisha and Dante wiping sweat from her forehead.

"Coach wants us to practice handoffs before they close the track," she told her.

"I told you we should practice earlier," Alisha responded.

Niyah folded her arms aggravated.

"No you did not," Niyah said. "Besides, I don't need it. You the one that needs to practice. I'm trying to help you out."

"Girl, please! Get out my face," Alisha said, putting her hand up in Niyah's face.

Niyah slapped her hand down.

"First of all, I was just playing with you. Second of all, you don't have to put your hand in my face like that."

Alisha turned around angrily.

"Don't touch me!" Alisha screamed.

"Don't put your hand in my face then."

Dante stepped in between them.

"Baby, just go ahead," he said.

Alisha glared at him.

"No, she ain't the boss of me."

Niyah yelled, "Yo, come on before they close the track."

Alisha got in Niyah's face.

"Try me," Alisha said.

Niyah balled her fists. Dante pulled them apart as Laurie ran up.

"Niyah, let's go!" Laurie said.

Niyah ran off, upset. Laurie and Dante stared at each other for a second. Alisha caught them and cleared her throat. Dante looked away, and Laurie ran off.

"I saw that, D," Alisha said.

Dante pretended to act like he did not know what Alisha was talking about.

"Saw what?"

"Don't play with me, Dante."

"Stop trippin'. Go run your race. That's what I came to see."

He gave her a kiss and walked off.

Alisha watched him as he walked away. She whispered to herself, "Love you too."

She walked over to Niyah and Laurie. Niyah was sitting on the ground. Her legs were shaking angrily.

"I hate her. I swear," Niyah said.

"Calm down, Nini," Laurie said.

Niyah pulled a hair tie from her wrist and started angrily putting her hair in a ponytail. Brooke walked up to the girls carrying their hip numbers. She saw Niyah putting her hair in a ponytail and noticed her legs were shaking. She knew she was upset.

"What's wrong?" she asked.

Just then Alisha walked up with Coach Jones behind her.

"Y'all checked in, ladies?" Coach Jones asked.

Brooke showed Coach Jones the hip numbers.

"Yeah, I checked us in," she said.

Coach Jones noticed Niyah's demeanor. She looked at him and stopped shaking her leg, but her face still looked upset. He looked at Alisha who was sitting down away from the group putting on her shoes quietly. She also looked upset.

"I don't know what's wrong here, but y'all better get it together," he said. "Now come on, let's win this. Fix whatever is wrong here. Understand?"

The ladies nodded their heads yes. Coach Jones walked off. Brooke pulled out the baton from her backpack.

"I guess we really need to pray," Brooke said.

The girls put their hands on the baton in order of their spots on the relay. Brooke with her right hand on the bottom of the baton, Laurie with her left hand on top of Brooke's hand, Niyah with her right hand on top of Laurie's hand, and Alisha with her left hand above Niyah's hand. Niyah and Alisha did not make eye contact as they bowed their heads and closed their eyes. Niyah began praying.

"Dear Lord, Thank you for this day. Thank you for letting us get here safely. Please Lord, let us get through this relay like we were trained to. Let our legs carry us around this track as fast as we can. And please Lord, please bless our handoffs since some of us didn't want to practice..." Laurie giggled as Alisha opened her eyes and smacked her lips at Niyah. Niyah continued, "Please just bless us and let us get this win. We love you. In Jesus name we pray, Amen."

All the girls said, "Amen."

Alisha let go of the baton and stared at Niyah.

"I know you wasn't referring to me in your prayer," she said. "That was petty."

"Well if the shoe fits," Niyah laughed.

Alisha began walking up to Niyah when Brooke stopped her.

"Hey! Let's just get through this race. Please. Y'all can hate each other later," Brook said.

"Fine by me," Niyah exclaimed.

Alisha looked at the team.

"Just get me the baton in a great spot, so we can easily win this thing," she said. "Comprende?"

"Comprende, bruja," Niyah responded as she put on her track spikes.

The girls were on the track in their spots. Brooke was setting up her blocks on first leg. Laurie had just finished setting up her steps and was stretching. Alisha was practicing sprinting out and throwing her hand back for the stick while Niyah was bent down praying.

"Dear God, please let us make it through this race with no problems. Please. Amen."

Niyah got up and looked around the track as she loosened her muscles. She caught Alisha's eyes, and they stared at each other for a couple of seconds before looking away. The crowd was loud and restless, waiting for the first race of the day to begin. The official blew his whistle loudly. The crowd grew silent.

"Ladies, stand behind your blocks," the official announced.

The girls on first leg stood behind their blocks. Coach Jones and the rest of the team were in the bleachers cheering.

"Let's go, Brooke!"

The starting official stood on his podium with his starting gun.

"On your mark."

The girls all did their block routines, jumping up and down loosening their muscles. They all bent down and crawled backwards into their blocks.

The competitors all bent their knees and their heads up with the batons in their right hands.

"Set."

The girls rose in their blocks. The official shot his gun. The girls pushed off their blocks and sped off. Brooke was off to a great start. She was in the lead as she ran around the curve full speed when she reached the orange tape Laurie had set up, and Laurie sped off. She threw her hand back and Brooke placed the baton in her hand smoothly. Laurie ran down the straight away like a horse in a race track. They handed the baton off first. The girls had a small gap in front of their competitors.

Niyah yelled to Laurie from her spot, "Let's go, Laurie! Let's go! Come on, Laurie!"

Laurie raced towards Niyah, lifting her knees and pumping her arms. As Laurie got closer, Niyah knelt down slightly ready to take off. Her fingers twitched but she kept the rest of her body still concentrating on Laurie's feet as they dashed down the track. Laurie hit her mark and Niyah scurried off. Laurie handed the baton off to her fluidly, and Niyah ran towards Alisha. They were still in first place with competitors coming for her around the second curve. Niyah's hair stuck to her forehead with sweat as she breathed in through her nose and out of her mouth, trying to make it to Alisha in a timely manner. Alisha clapped her hands signaling for Niyah to bring it in. Niyah flew around the curve of the track as the crowd cheered for them. She hit her mark for Alisha, and Alisha turned and ran towards the finish line. Alisha hit her second mark and put her left hand back for the baton. Niyah placed it in her hand when suddenly the baton dropped to the ground. The crowd reacted yelling "Oooooh!" as the baton rolled down the track. Niyah's heart sank as the sound of the baton hitting the ground clinked in her ears. Alisha screamed out as she tried to grab it. The other teams had caught up by now. The third legs of the relay handed off their batons, and their anchor legs took off while trying not to run into Alisha. Alisha finally gained control of the stick angrily as Niyah fell to the track upset. The other competitors raced to the finish line as Alisha came down the track in last place. Niyah looked at the board and walked off the track. She threw off her hip number and exited the field. She kicked a trash can as she walked out of the gate, knowing that they were disqualified.

Coach Jones was standing with Niyah and Alisha behind the stadium bathroom. He threw down his clipboard and paced the floor. He finally turned to the girls and yelled, "What the hell happened?"

Both girls hung their heads low, unable to answer their coach.

"Something happened! You don't drop the baton and then have no explanation! So what is going on?"

The girls stayed silent.

Coach Jones rubbed his head irately as he continued to pace back and forth.

"I don't understand how my two best runners can't get along!" he said. "Over some petty shit! Whatever beef y'all got going on needs to be cleared up immediately! You are hurting the team with this bullshit! Y'all are not running the four by four today. I can't risk it."

Both girls looked up shocked. Niyah called out, "Coach!"

Coach Jones stopped her before she could finish.

"I don't want to hear it! You're off until I say otherwise! And for dropping the baton I need thirty push-ups now. Let's go."

The girls dropped down and did the thirty push-ups. They stood up and faced their coach.

"This is not the only punishment either. Be prepared for practice on Monday. We are not done with this conversation. Alisha, go get ready for your 100 meter dash."

Alisha looked at Niyah and ran off. Niyah started crying.

Coach Jones stepped up to Niyah and grabbed her shoulders.

"Hey, look at me," he said.

Niyah looked into her coach's eyes.

"What is going on with you, Niyah?"

Niyah wiped her face.

"I'm fine, Coach."

"You need to get it together and fast. What did I tell you when you first got here, huh? You have too many eyes watching you. You cannot be messing up like this. Suck it up and get it together. Do you understand?"

"Yes, sir."

"Wipe your face before you go back to the tent. Go and get rested for your 400."

Niyah walked off fast as Coach Tatem walked up to Coach Jones.

"She's starting to slip, Coach," Tatem said.

Coach Jones picked up his clipboard.

"She'll be fine. Let me do the job you hired me to do," Coach Jones said.

Coach Tatem walked away, leaving Coach Jones standing alone thinking about what just happened.

Niyah was walking towards her team's tent when she heard a familiar voice behind her say, "Hey, beautiful."

Niyah froze in her tracks and turned around slowly. Kevin was standing there with a smile on his face. Niyah backed away from him.

"What the hell are you doing here?" she asked.

"I came to see my baby run," he said.

"Kevin, I am not your baby. Please don't do this. Not right now."

Niyah backed away as Kevin moved in closer to her.

"Can you stop stalking me please? You're starting to piss me off."

"You know you like it. I don't know why you fighting it."

Niyah rolled her eyes and tried to walk off.

"Niyah, just talk to me please. I love you!"

Niyah stopped walking and turned around.

"Wait, you love me? You barely know me! Because of you, I lost my best friend. Yes we kissed! I was drunk, and it was a mistake! Me and you will never happen! Get that through your fucking head! Stop following me and calling me! I told you that before! You're clearly delusional, and you're not hearing me. Stop it! I'm tired of having this conversation with you, and now this shit is getting creepy! We will never happen! Ever! Leave me the fuck alone!" Niyah said and ran off.

Kevin stood there upset. He turned to his side to see Brooke standing next to the bleachers listening. Kevin looked her up and down before walking off. Brooke stood there in silence before walking back into the bleachers.

17

Who Doesn't Watch Porn

It was early morning as the sun peeked through Niyah's dorm room window. As the sunlight hit her face, Niyah woke up slowly. She looked over at Laurie's bed. Laurie was fast asleep. She looked at the time on her cell phone and hopped out of bed. "No, I cannot be late today!" she thought.

Niyah ran to the bathroom to get dressed. When she tried to enter the bathroom, the door was locked. She knocked on the door confused. "Ummm, hello?" She heard the toilet flush and the sound of running water from the sink. The door swung open and out walked Dante. Niyah jumped back.

"Hey! I didn't know you were here," she said. "I didn't hear y'all come in."

"Yeah you a hard ass sleeper! You don't hear nothing," he said.

Niyah put her hands in her ears. "Stop! Stop! I don't even want to know."

Dante laughed as he grabbed his shoes and backpack. He walked to the front door and turned to Niyah before leaving.

"When Laurie wakes up tell her I had to go. She's a little drunk, so I didn't want to wake her up," he said.

"All right. I will. Bye."

Dante left the dorm room closing the door behind him. Niyah looked after him then went into the bathroom rushing to get dressed. Forty-five minutes later, Niyah was dressed trying to grab her books when her cell phone rang. It was Rochelle calling. She answered it happily. "Hey, my baby!"

Rochelle laughed.

"Hey I miss you! Mom told me about your track meet. You did great in the 400."

"Yeah but I've never dropped the stick in my life. How was your track meet?"

Niyah continued to gather her things holding her phone to her ear with her shoulder.

"I got a record in the long jump."

Niyah smiled, proud of her sister.

"That's my girl," she said. "And I heard someone is going to have their own award named after them at their middle school."

"Mama told you huh? I wanted to tell you! Yeah they're giving away the 'Coleman' award named after me every year to the person with great grades, a great attitude, and a beast at sports. So I have to go back every year to give it away."

"I am so proud of you! That is amazing! I'm gonna try to be back for your ceremony! So proud!"

"Thank you! Thank you! But are you busy, Nini?"

"Not really. I'm just trying to get to class on time. I haven't been in a while, and we have a test today. My professor gives us fifteen minutes to study, so I'm going to learn as much as I can in those fifteen minutes."

"Well, I know something that will put you in a good mood. Have you been on twitter today?"

"Not yet."

"Guess who has a viral sex tape?"

Niyah stopped gathering her things and grabbed her phone with her hand.

"Who?" she asked.

"Destiny!"

Niyah dropped her jaw in complete shock.

"What? Destiny? Like the one I robbed the bank with and went to the game to fight Destiny?"

Rochelle laughed really hard through the phone.

"Yes! I just emailed you the link!"

Niyah grabbed her laptop and logged into her email. She clicked on the link, and the sex tape opened up. Suddenly, her eyes widened as sounds of moans start coming through the speakers on the laptop. She saw Destiny on the screen having sex with a boy she'd never seen before.

"Oh my God!"

"I told you!"

Niyah continued watching the video in shock laughing at her ex best friend Destiny.

"You should not be watching this Rochelle. I can't stop looking."

Rochelle laughed uncontrollably.

Niyah looked at the time on her laptop.

"Dang!" she said. "I gotta go!"

Niyah shut her laptop without closing the video out.

"Okay, text me later. I love you."

"Love you too." Niyah hung up the phone. She put her laptop in her backpack, closed it and rushed out of the door.

Niyah ran into her classroom out of breath. Most of the class was already studying. Her professor looked at her.

"Nice to see you, Niyah," he said. "You have about ten minutes to study. All the slides are on the PowerPoints."

Niyah looked around for a seat. Sean motioned for her to come sit close to him. She ignored him and sat in the front row instead. He sighed deeply. The room was quiet as everyone finished reviewing their notes. Niyah quickly grabbed her laptop out of her backpack and opened it. Once she opened her laptop, the sounds and noises from the sex tape began to play. She suddenly became frantic as she tried to enter her password to get to her home screen. The entire class was staring at her as the sex tape continued to play in the background. Destiny's moaning and the slow music playing from the laptop filled the air. Niyah kept typing in the wrong password, mortified. She finally got her password right. Her screensaver went away as her home screen popped up. The sex tape was playing loudly. She quickly exited out of the screen, and the room once again became silent. Niyah turned to her classmates with an embarrassed smile.

"I am so, so sorry!" she said. "That wasn't what you thought it was. I do not watch porn. I swear!"

The entire classroom burst into laughter including the professor.

"We've all watched porn before," the professor said.

Niyah started to blush as the entire classroom continued to laugh. She looked up at Sean. He was smiling at her. She shrugged her shoulders and was shamefaced as she smiled back at him.

Coach Jones was sitting at his desk on the computer working as Coach Tatem walked in with a folder and handed it to Coach Jones.

"I came to tell you that Niyah needs to be off the team," Tatem said. "Have you not been checking up on this? I know you want her to run, but you have not been doing your job!"

Coach Jones looked at the paperwork. It displayed Niyah's poor attendance and bad grades. He threw the folder down on his desk and looked up at Coach Tatem.

"I am doing my job!" Coach Jones said.

"I need her off the team, effective immediately."

"I'm not going to take her off completely. Just until she gets her grades up. She just needs a warning. Just trust me!"

"You been telling me to trust you! I knew this was going to happen. Now, Niyah cannot run."

Coach Tatem stormed out of the office as Coach Jones stared at Niyah's progress reports upset. He threw the folder off his desk and sat there speechless.

Niyah and Sean were sitting at Sean's dinner table playing dominos. Sean slapped down a domino on the table and yelled out, "Five."

Niyah laughed as she took her pen and pad to mark down Sean's points. Niyah looked over her hand as Sean took a sip of wine and gazed at her.

"So, Ms. Niyah watches porn huh?"

Niyah busted out laughing.

"No I really don't! That was embarrassing. That was Destiny, the one I was telling you about. Apparently, her little sex tape went viral. I just wanted to see what was happening."

She laughed as she threw down a domino.

"That was funny as hell. Now everybody thinks you're a lesbian."

Niyah rolled her eyes laughing.

"I mean, I've experimented."

Sean looked up at her shocked and happy.

"Really? You still experimenting?"

She looked at him with a smirk on her face.

"No! Of course not, I have you."

Sean threw down another domino smiling.

"Honestly, I really thought you and Brooke had something going on."

"Why does everyone think that?"

Sean shrugged his shoulders.

"Y'all are just really close."

She lowered her head.

"Were really close," she sighed deeply.

Sean looked at her.

"Hey, you don't need her. I know you miss her, but if she can't forgive you and believe you then forget her."

Niyah looked up and smiled.

"Well you can be my friend."

"That's right. And you don't need anyone else. I'm your best friend, right?" Sean looked at her with a serious look on his face.

"Right," Niyah said and smiled.

"I'm serious, Niyah."

Niyah's smiled disappeared as she noticed Sean's very serious demeanor.

"I got you, Sean."

Sean nodded his head and smirked.

"All right, let's finish playing. Let's go!"

Niyah slammed down her last domino.

"Ten! Domino! You suck!"

Sean and Niyah laughed as Niyah tallied her score on her piece of paper.

"I told you I was going to beat you, Sean. I'm such a beast."

"I'm glad you finally came back around. I've missed you."

Niyah looked up from her piece of paper. She put the pencil down.

"I missed you too. My feelings were hurt because I thought we had something good going on."

Sean got up and walked over to Niyah. He got on his knees and grabbed Niyah's hands.

"I like you and only you, Niyah. I think I'm falling in love with you. I want you to be mine."

Niyah looked at him and leaned forward. "I think I'm falling in love with you too."

Sean grabbed her face and kissed her. He began rubbing on her breasts and her neck. Niyah moaned as Sean began kissing her neck. Sean stopped and stood up. He grabbed Niyah's hand.

"Come on," he said and led her into his bedroom. Niyah sat on the bed as Sean got on top of her. He leaned in and kissed her on the lips. Niyah took off his shirt. She pushed him onto his back as she climbed on top of him. She unzipped his jeans. She pulled his pants down and got back on top of him. He took off her shirt and unsnapped her bra. He put his hand in her shorts and inside her panties. He began rubbing her clit and sucking her nipples, making them hard. She moaned as she pulled her shorts all the way off. Sean flipped Niyah over unto her back. He kissed her stomach and began to go down on her. Niyah wrapped her legs around his back as she moaned and screamed. She gripped the sheets. Sean slowly began to kiss her stomach again. He then grabbed her face and kissed her lips as he pulled off his boxers. Niyah bit his neck as he slid his penis inside of her. Sean licked her neck as he stroked back and forth. He grabbed her breasts as she lifted her legs higher and higher. Niyah scratched his back as Sean moaned. Niyah screamed loudly, enjoying him. Finally, Sean finished and lay on top Niyah. They both were breathing hard. Niyah kissed Sean on the cheek. Sean rolled off of Niyah. He grabbed her by her waist and pulled her close. Sean kissed Niyah's shoulder as they both smiled.

"I love you, Niyah," he said.

Niyah smiled as she closed her eyes.

"I love you too."

18

Dumb Drunk

Later that night, Niyah and Sean were laying in the bed nude, talking.

"Girl, you going to give me a cramp," he said. "All this sex!"

Niyah laughed as she hit Sean's shoulder.

"You want it. Don't front."

"I really do," Sean said and bit Niyah's ear. "We even ran out of condoms."

Niyah looked at him shocked. "Oh my gosh, so that last time…"

Sean looked at her apologetically.

"I'm sorry, baby! But I got out in time. I promise."

Niyah put her hand on her forehead. "Oh my gosh, Sean! If I get pregnant or some nasty disease I'm going to kill you."

Sean looked at her. "You really think I have some disease or screwing around on you? Seriously?"

Niyah frowned. "I'm just saying…"

"I'm just saying. Nini, I would never put you in harm's way like that. And you act like this is the very first time we didn't use a condom."

"That was one time before this, Sean. It only takes one time."

"You know you want my babies anyways," Sean laughed and went in for a kiss.

Niyah laughed as she playfully hit Sean's chest.

He grabbed her hands laughing. "So violent!"

"I'm sorry. I've always been a little violent."

Sean's smile faded as he stroked Niyah's back.

"Why?"

She shrugged. "I don't know. I just have."

Sean grabbed her face.

"Come on. Talk to me. Something got you all violent."

Niyah stopped smiling and looked out the window. She closed her eyes and sighed.

"Ever since I was little. I was around a lot of fighting. I hated it. I used to run out of the house when my parents fought. I would run outside and just keep running. I couldn't listen to it. I think just hearing it, I always felt I had to protect myself or something. I know some friends that had boyfriends that hit them and all kind of craziness. I felt like I should learn how to fight, just in case. But I don't like to fight. Everybody thinks I do, but I really don't."

Tears rolled down Niyah's face. Sean turned Niyah around to face him. He wiped her tears away.

"People have problems, and your parents love you," he said.

"I know, and I love them too. It just, it just upsets me thinking about it."

Sean kissed Niyah on the lips.

"I would never put my hands on you, Niyah. I wouldn't say anything to hurt you. You're going to be okay. I'm here for you. Always. As long as you don't leave me. Ever. I don't like when people just up and leave. Reminds me of my mom. If your mom could just leave you, how can you expect other people to stay?"

Niyah grabbed his face.

"I will never leave you. As long as you just love me."

"I will. Just stop being so violent."

Niyah laughed as she kissed Sean and climbed on top of him once again.

Niyah and Sean were sleeping when Niyah's cell phone vibrated on the dresser. Niyah slowly woke up and grabbed her phone. She tip-toed into the bathroom and answered the phone. "Hello?"

Laurie was on the other end of the phone drunk.

"Nini, where are you?" Laurie said.

"I'm at Sean's, boo. What's wrong?"

"I lost my key. Can you come help me? I don't feel good."

"Okay. Let me call a taxi or something. I'm on my way."

She hung up the phone. She threw on one of Sean's sweatshirts. She put on her tennis shoes, grabbed her clothes and backpack and walked out the door.

Niyah walked down the hallway and saw Laurie laying on the floor in front of their dorm room door. She walked up to Laurie and laughed.

"Hey, drunkie!" Niyah said. "Come on get up!"

Niyah helped Laurie stand up.

"I'm oooonly a little drunk," Laurie said.

Niyah laughed and unlocked the door. She helped Laurie inside and laid her on her bed. Niyah started to undress her. Barely opening her eyes, Laurie squirmed as Niyah tried to get her shirt off. She finally looked at Niyah and smiled.

"And where were you, Ms. Thang?"

Niyah started smiling as she took off Laurie's shoes.

"I told you, drunkie, at Sean's."

"We all knew y'all liked each other. Brooke is going to be jealous."

Niyah stopped undressing Laurie and looked at her.

"Why you say that?"

"Don't try and fool me. I know y'all miss the hell out of each other."

Niyah laughed. She got Laurie down to her bra and underwear. She grabbed a big sleep shirt from Laurie's dresser.

"Whatever. Here put this on."

Laurie struggled to sit up. She slowly grabbed the shirt.

"Whatever my ass. Thanks for coming to help me, boo. I owe you one," Laurie said. "I need to go to the bathroom."

Laurie got up and staggered toward the bathroom. Niyah stared at her and her smile faded away.

"Why do you do it?" Niyah asked.

Laurie stopped, grabbed the wall to keep her balance and turned around. "Do what?"

"Drink. A lot."

Laurie looked at her speechless.

"I don't know. I just…it just eases my pain, I guess."

"Does it help you sleep with Dante when you know he's with Alisha?"

Laurie let out a sigh. Niyah got up and ran over to Laurie.

"I'm sorry, Laurie. I didn't mean it like that. You're my girl, and I love you. I just think you're playing with fire. And I don't want you to get hurt by him or hurt yourself."

"You think I don't know about how you hurt yourself?"

Laurie grabbed Niyah's wrists. Niyah looked up at Laurie.

"How did you know?"

"I'm not dumb, Nini. Look at these scars. You just haven't been around for me to talk to you about it, but it scares the shit out of me. And you pull your hair out too!"

"I won't do it again. We just have to look after each other, ya know?"

"Of course," Laurie said. She looked around the room nervously then back at Niyah. "I just…I really like him, Nini."

Niyah forced a smile.

"Yeah I know."

"Promise you won't tell."

Niyah nodded her head.

"I would never do that. I promise. I been keeping it a secret this long!"

Laurie forced a smile as well and hugged Niyah. She stumbled into the bathroom and closed the door. Niyah sat on her bed and pulled out her phone. She sent a text to Sean that read "Sorry, baby, I had to come let Laurie in the room. Call me in the AM."

She put her phone down and looked around the room. She looked at the bathroom door. Laurie could be heard peeing. Niyah walked over to her dresser and opened one of her drawers. She took out a bottle of pain reliever pills. She ran over to Laurie's drawer and grabbed a bottle of liquor. She ran back to her bed. She put three of the pills in her mouth and took a gulp of liquor. She hid the bottle in her dresser, lay in her bed and went to sleep.

The next day at track practice, the girls were warming up and stretching. Niyah kept staring at Brooke who was not paying any attention to her. Suddenly, Niyah ran over to the trash can to throw up. She wiped her mouth and drank some water. Renae noticed and started whispering about Niyah. Niyah went back and started stretching. Everyone was rolling their eyes at Niyah, and she was secluded from the group. Laurie noticed Niyah stretching by herself and walked over to her.

"Hey, you okay? Why you over here throwing up?" Laurie asked.

"I guess I'm just a little sick. And everyone is treating me like the red headed step child right now."

"You know the black community at this school is small. Apparently, Renae has been going around talking about the situation with you, Kevin and Brooke."

Niyah instantly got mad and started to walk towards Renae. Laurie grabbed Niyah's arm.

"Nini, she's not worth it. Don't get kicked off the team over her."

"So everyone knows about me and Kevin, but no one knows about you and Dante."

Laurie looked at her ashamed.

"Alisha is not my best friend, so no one would care. Brooke, however, is your best friend, so it makes you look bad. You need to fix it."

Niyah sighed. They continued to warm up. Coach Jones walked up to the girls. He looked at Niyah with disappointment in his eyes, but looked away to the rest of the girls.

"Alright, ladies we got 300's today," he said. "Let's get some water and start."

The girls ran over to their water bottles. Niyah walked by Alisha. Alisha snickered and said, "hide ya water. Hide ya backpacks. Niyah stealing everything out here!"

The girls laughed except for Brooke and Laurie. Niyah walked up to Alisha.

"Please don't speak on things you know nothing about," Niyah said.

"But you are a thief right? You steal your best friend's man and spots on the relay…"

"First of all, I didn't steal your spot, I took that! Stop worrying about me. I see why your man ventures off. You're annoying and bat shit crazy."

Alisha dropped her water bottle.

"Excuse me," she said.

"You heard what I said. Why don't you just tell everybody why you really hate me? You've been mad ever since I beat you at regionals like four years ago and you missed out on your chance at state. Get over it!"

Alisha burst into laughter.

"You know what? You ain't shit! I hate you because you're a cocky little bitch!"

"Like I said, Alisha, worry about yourself and your own man."

"Why, did you suck his dick too?"

Alisha and her friends laughed. Niyah rushed at Alisha. Alisha threw her water bottle at Niyah and punched her in the face. Niyah punched Alisha in her jaw, and they tussled to the ground punching each other. Everyone darted over to the girls to pull them apart. They were finally able to separate them. Coach Jones ran over angrily. The two girls continued to try to fight each other. Coach Jones tried to control Niyah.

"Stop it! Niyah, stop! Calm down!" Coach Jones said. "Niyah, to my office now!"

"I would never intentionally hurt Brooke ever. So everyone can kiss my ass!" Niyah yelled, still trying to break loose from her teammates.

"Niyah, go to my office!" Coach Jones yelled.

Niyah looked at Brooke, then Alisha before her teammates let her go. She ran to the athletic building. Alisha wiped blood from her nose with her shirt.

Coach Jones looked at Alisha and said, "Alisha, go to the trainer and get some ice. I'll be right back."

Coach Jones ran off. Alisha held her nose with her shirt as Brooke stepped in front of her.

"Alisha, that was so uncalled for," Brooke said.

"I was trying to help you out!"

"I don't need your damn help! You're just being messy because you hate Niyah. Mind your business for once!"

Brooke stormed off. Alisha noticed Laurie standing there laughing at her.

"Fuck off!" Alisha said and grabbed her backpack and ran off towards the trainer.

Niyah was sitting in a chair in the Coach's office. Her lip was busted and blood dripped from a cut above her eye. She was drenched with sweat. Her legs were shaking uncontrollably in the chair as she sat impatiently with her arms folded. She was breathing harder and harder as she awaited Coach Jones to enter. Eventually, Coach Jones stormed into the office and slammed the door behind him.

"You are a magnet for fucking up, aren't you?" he said. "What the hell was that?"

"She started it!"

"And you just had to finish it! You gonna' let what she said get you that mad? Huh? This is the same stuff you did in high school that got you in trouble in the first place! You can't fight everyone that says something to you that you don't like, Niyah! When are you going to get that through your head?"

"I know but…"

"But nothing! I fought to get you here you said you could fix your attitude. Everyone doubted you, and so far you're proving them right! Why should I stick up for you when you're making the both of us look bad?"

Niyah started to cry and buried her head in her hands.

"They hate me, Coach."

Coach calmed himself down and sat at the edge of his desk.

"No one hates you. You made a mistake."

Niyah looked up and tried to stop crying.

"Great. You know what happened too."

"I know mostly everything that happens with my athletes. But right now, I don't know what's going on with you!"

Niyah lowered her head. Coach Jones sighed. He walked around his desk and pulled a folder from his drawer. He tossed it toward Niyah.

"Today was going to be your last practice anyway."

Niyah looked up startled.

"What?"

"Those are your grades and attendance reports. You are on the verge of being on academic probation. You've been skipping class. I thought you would have straightened up by now after we've had numerous talks about this. What is the problem?"

Niyah grabbed the folder and looked at the paperwork. She put the folder down and looked into her coach's eyes.

"I'm just… I don't know."

"You're a student athlete. Student comes first. You're smarter than this."

Niyah stood up.

"Coach, Please! I'm sorry. Please just don't take track away from me. Not right now."

"Coach Tatem wants you off the team, indefinitely. I'm putting you on probation. One more mess up, and that's it. Get your grades up, or else. Until then, I don't want to see you at practice and you won't be at the meets. Go to study hall and to class."

Niyah looked at her coach as her tears continued to fall.

"Coach, please."

"There's nothing I can do, Niyah."

Niyah grabbed her stuff and walked out.

Niyah burst in her dorm room, crying and screaming. She ran to the bathroom and shut the door. She sat on the edge of the tub and sobbed. She ran to the toilet and puked again as her tears fell inside the toilet. She grabbed her razor and took off her shorts. She put the razor to the inside of her thigh to make long, deep cuts. She let out a loud scream but continued to cut. She dropped the razor and lay on the cold tile floor bawling her eyes out. "God, please help me!"

19

Stuck

Niyah was laying on her bed on the phone with her mom. Tammi could hear the desperation and sadness in her daughter's voice as they talked.

"You okay, baby?" Tammi asked.

Niyah quietly wept as she tried to disguise her sniffling as allergies.

"Yeah, mom I'm fine. I'm just tired. And my allergies are getting to me."

She wiped the tears from her face.

"We miss you. We were going to drive to your track meet this weekend, but your dad has to work."

Niyah broke down, still trying to keep her mom from hearing her.

"It's a small track meet anyway, Mom."

"Yeah, but you know I always come to see my baby."

"I know, Mommy."

"You sure you don't need me to come up there? You sound sad."

"No, no I'm fine. It's just been a long day."

There was an intense knock at Niyah's door. Niyah looked at the door.

"Mom, I have to go to class."

"Okay, baby, I love you."

"I love you too."

Niyah hung up the phone. She threw on some sweat pants to hide the fresh cut marks on the inside of her thighs. There was another big knock at the door.

"Coming! Give me a sec!" she yelled.

Niyah wiped her face and went to open the door. Sean was standing there mad.

"Sean. Baby, what's wrong?" she asked.

Sean pushed Niyah and rushed past her into the room. Niyah closed the door behind them. He began pacing back and forth.

"So you just leave and don't let no one know?"

"What are you talking about?"

"Last night, Niyah! Don't act like you don't hear me."

"No, I'm saying that I texted you!"

"Why didn't you wake me up?"

She gave him a bewildered look.

"I'm sorry, Sean, damn. You don't have to come in here screaming!"

"And where the hell you been all day? You didn't come to class! I haven't seen you!"

He grabbed her arm. She yanked it away.

"Don't grab me like that! I had a bad day, and I'm not in the mood!"

"You were with some nigga or something?"

Niyah gave him a perplexed look.

"What the fuck kind of question was that? You're getting on my nerves."

"I don't care. Grab some stuff. We're going to my place," he said.

Sean walked to the door.

Niyah stood there still. "I don't want to go anywhere with you right now. Not with you acting like that."

Sean turned around.

"Niyah Raychelle Coleman, do not make me have to tell you twice."

Niyah peered at him and saw the seriousness in his eyes. She wanted to avoid a fight so she grabbed some clothes and walked out the door with Sean.

Later that night, Sean and Niyah were sitting on the couch. Sean had calmed down and was trying to cuddle with Niyah, but she was still upset. She sat up next to him.

"What the hell is wrong with you, today?" she asked.

Sean pecked Niyah on her neck and put his arm around her shoulders.

"I just don't like feeling like you ran out on me! I told you my mom ran out on my dad. I have a hard time trusting people."

"I went to my dorm!"

"I'm sorry, baby. I just don't like you leaving me in the middle of the night, walking by yourself. My last girlfriend cheated on me, so I admit I get a little paranoid."

Niyah hopped off the couch.

"Well just say that! Talk to me! Like you really got that emotional from me walking out of the house."

"What would you have thought if I had sex with you and you woke up in the morning and I wasn't there?"

"I would have some questions, but I wouldn't burst into your house accusing you of everything under the sun!"

Sean grabbed her legs and pulled her back down on the couch.

"I'm sorry," he said. "Come here, baby."

He tried to kiss her on the lips. She backed up. He grabbed her hands tightly.

"Stop it. Don't back away from me," he said.

Sean grabbed her neck and went in for another kiss. She finally gave in and kissed him back. He grabbed her waist.

"I'm so sorry," he said. "Spend the night with me. Please. I need to wake up with you next to me."

Niyah sighed and laid down in Sean's lap. Sean kissed her on her forehead and turned on the television.

The sun had set as the moon took its place in the sky. Niyah and Sean were lying in Sean's bed sleeping snug under the covers. Niyah's phone started to vibrate, waking up Sean. He got up to grab the phone. There was a text message from Caleb that read, "Haven't talked to you in a while. Was just thinking about you and checking on you. I hope you're doing okay. I will always love you, Niyah."

Sean became enraged and threw the phone at Niyah. It hit her in the forehead and she hopped up quickly.

"Ouch! What the hell is wrong with you?"

She rubbed her forehead as a knot began to form.

"You stupid ho! Who in the hell is Caleb?" he yelled.

"Caleb?"

Sean grabbed the phone off the floor and threw it in Niyah's lap.

"In your phone! Don't play dumb!"

She grabbed her phone and read the text silently while rubbing her forehead. Sean began to tread back and forth.

"We just talked about cheating. You just like them other hoes!"

Niyah sprung out of the bed.

"Sean, calm down! That's my ex! I don't talk to him at all! I can't believe you just threw this damn phone at me!"

"You got your ex texting you now?"

Niyah put the phone in his face.

"As you can see it says 'I haven't talked to you in a while!'"

Sean walked up to Niyah and slapped the phone out of her hand.

"How do I know you don't still talk to him or anybody else? And why in the fuck is he texting you this late?"

"Because I'm telling you I don't talk to him! And he's in California. Might have forgot about the time change. Who fuckin' knows. I don't talk to him ever! Dang, my head hurts now. I have a knot on my head! What the hell is wrong with the boys at this school? Bunch of crazies!"

Niyah walked off to grab her clothes off the floor and started getting dressed.

"Where the hell you going?"

"To run off some steam."

"No you're not!"

Sean grabbed Niyah by her neck and pushed her up against the wall. Niyah tried to get away and pushed Sean.

"Are you fucking crazy? Don't ever put your hands on me like that!"

"You stupid, ugly ho! You're not going anywhere!"

Sean pushed her to the floor hard. Niyah got up. She began to cry and pushed Sean.

"Fuck you! Why are you saying that to me? What the hell is wrong with you?"

"Because it's true! I don't even know why I mess with your trifling, stupid ass. Running out on me. Talking to dudes behind my back! You're always on your computer, talking to some girl I don't know. You're probably lying about that too."

Niyah put on her sweatshirt, grabbed her phone, her bag and headed towards the front door.

"Fine if I'm so ugly and stupid, don't be with me then."

She tried to walk out when Sean grabbed her by her hair. Niyah slapped him in the face, and he threw her to the ground. Sean kicked her in the stomach and punched her in his jaw. Niyah screamed out in agony. Niyah punched Sean back in the face. Sean stumbled back as Niyah tried to run for the door. Sean chased her down and threw her across the kitchen table. The glass plates and cups on the table fell to floor, shattering. Niyah lay there in pain. Sean walked over and tried to kick her in the face, but she rolled over before he kicked her. She grabbed the back of the couch, attempting to lift herself up. Sean kicked her in her back, and Niyah fell back to the ground. She crawled to the side table by the couch.

Sean yelled at her, "You stupid bitch! You can't beat me! Come on, get up!"

Niyah grabbed the side table and lifted herself up slightly. She grabbed the lamp and threw it at Sean. He dodged it. The lamp hit the wall and it broke into a thousand pieces. Sean bolted towards her and grabbed her by her throat to choke her. He lifted her off her feet. She began trying to claw his face. He grabbed her hands and continued to choke her. Niyah kicked Sean in the prostate. Sean let go of Niyah's neck and fell down to his knees. Niyah fell to the ground as she gasped for air. Sean fell to the floor in pain. She crawled to her things and ran out the door.

It was early morning. The sun had barely risen as Niyah sprinted on the track. She stopped running and went into the bleachers. Her face was swollen, and her lip was busted. She had red marks across her neck and a huge knot on her forehead. She lay down, breathlessly.

Gary and some of his teammates were walking to the track to do some sprints. He noticed Niyah in the bleachers and ran over to her. He lifted her head and hugged her.

"Nini, what's wrong?" he asked.

Niyah looked at him and cried in his arms as Gary tried to console her.

"Hey, hey look at me! What's going on?"

"Everything! Everyone hates me! I don't run track right now! My grades are shit and Sean…"

Gary stared at her as Niyah stopped talking.

"What? Sean what?"

"He's just an ass."

Gary glanced at her face and noticed her busted lip and a knot on her head.

"Did he do this to your face? Did he hit you, Niyah?"

Gary stood up.

"Niyah, did that asshole hit you? Huh? Tell me now!" he said.

Niyah shook her head no.

"This from my fight with Alisha."

"All my life, I have never known you to let a girl beat you up, so don't lie to me! Did he hit you?"

"No. I wouldn't lie to you, Gary."

Niyah grabbed Gary's shirt and pulled him back down. She lay back in his lap and continued to cry.

Gary rubbed her back, trying to calm her down.

"You just gotta' get your shit together, cousin. You gotta' do what you came here to do. Everything is going to be okay. You just better not let me find out he put his hands on you, Nini."

They spotted Sean walking up to them. He stepped in front of Niyah and Gary with his hands behind his back. Niyah sat up. Gary did not take his eyes off of Sean. Sean looked to Niyah then to Gary.

"Gary, can I talk to Niyah please?" Sean said.

Gary looked at Niyah. He clinched his fists. Niyah shook her head no.

"It's okay, Gary. I'll be fine," she said.

"All right. I'll be right here on the track. You sure you're going to be okay?" Gary asked.

"Yeah. I'll be okay."

"Okay. Call me later. I love you."

"I love you too."

Niyah made a face as Gary kissed the knot on her forehead. Gary and Sean stared each other down before Gary walked off. Sean walked up to Niyah.

"There he goes again. Kissing you. You and Gary sure are pretty close."

Niyah rolled her eyes at the remark.

"You should not be jealous at all so don't start with that shit again. This is not the way to start a conversation with me! Matter of fact, why in the hell am I even talking to you?"

Niyah got up and Sean grabbed her hand. Niyah turned her head quickly.

"Don't you touch me!"

Sean let go of her hand.

"You're right! You're right! I'm sorry. Just please, talk to me. Please."

Niyah sighed and sat down. Sean stared at Niyah as Niyah looked out at the track.

"I'm sorry. Look, I didn't mean anything last night," he said. "I have a lot going on, and I took my anger out on you. I just get real insecure around you for some reason, and I don't want anyone to have you. I will never put my hands on you like that again. Ever."

"Why would you call me ugly and trifling? That was uncalled for, and that hurts. You played on my insecurities, and that's not cool. And you fucking hit me!"

"I know, and I'm sorry. Niyah, I will never do that to you again. I love you."

Niyah became silent as she took a deep breath and looked at Sean. Sean pulled a teddy bear from behind his back. It was dressed in track clothes and holding a pack of skittles.

"This is Teddy the bear. He is a track runner. All he does is run fast and turn left. Just like my baby. And the skittles because we all know you are obsessed."

Niyah did not smile.

"Niyah, I am truly sorry. I swear. It's killing me that I did that to you. I promise, that's not me. A man should never hit a woman and I never have. I need you."

Tears fell from Niyah's face down to her shirt. Sean wiped her tears with his hand. He grabbed her face.

"I love you so much, Niyah. I love you."

He kissed her again.

Niyah kissed him back. They looked into each other's eyes before Niyah cracked a smile. Sean smiled and gave Niyah the skittles and the bear. She took the gifts and said, "My sport is your sport's punishment."

Sean smiled and kissed her again.

"Come on. I have to get ready for practice with these guys. Let's go," he said.

Niyah got up and followed Sean down the bleachers and off the track.

20

Get Out

Niyah was sitting down in the campus cafeteria with a tray in front of her. She hadn't touched anything on her plate. She was wearing a sweatshirt and sweatpants. She had a black eye that she was trying to cover with her bangs and sunglasses. Laurie, Brooke and Alyssa walked in. Brooke and Alyssa walked toward the food, not noticing Niyah sitting at the table. Laurie finally looked Niyah's way and saw her sitting there not eating. She walked over and sat across from her.

"Nini! Where have you been?" she asked and hugged Niyah from across the table. Niyah stayed silent as she continued to play with her food. "You okay, Nini? You've been missing practice and track meets. That's not like you. Did you get kicked off the team or something? We need you. I mean we've been doing okay, I guess, but we do need you. Especially on the relays. And you haven't been to the dorm or any parties. Nothing!"

She looked at Niyah's clothes and hair.

"You look sad… Have you lost weight? Do you-"

"I just been with Sean okay!" Niyah interrupted. "Please, Laurie, enough with the questions! He doesn't like me to go to parties or hang out like that anymore. And I'm on probation from the team right now. I have to get my shit together."

"I mean have you been eating? What is going on with you? And what do you mean he doesn't let you party? Who the hell does he think he is? Does he..."

"Laurie, I am fine!" Niyah yelled as she hit the table. Laurie jumped back in shock. Niyah looked up at Laurie. "I'm sorry, Laurie. I'm just a little tired, that's all. All these questions. I'm fine."

Laurie looked over Niyah.

"I'm sorry. I just been worried about you," Laurie said.

Niyah sighed. "I know, Laurie." She looked over Laurie's shoulders and spotted Brooke sitting down with Alyssa. "I miss her."

Laurie turned around and saw that Niyah was talking about Brooke.

"She misses you too," Laurie said.

Niyah took off her sunglasses and rubbed her face. Laurie noticed Niyah's black eye. "Jesus, Niyah! What happened to your eye?"

Niyah tried to cover her eye with her bangs.

"Nothing."

"Oh hell no, Niyah, what the hell is that?" she asked. Laurie thought for a minute. "Did Sean do that? Did he hit you? Is that why you haven't been out?!"

"No! Laurie, please! Don't say anything okay. I have to go."

Niyah picked up her backpack and ran out of the cafeteria.

Brooke watched Niyah out the window as she ran down the sidewalk outside the cafeteria. Laurie rushed over to Brooke and Alyssa.

"Y'all something is wrong with, Niyah," she said.

Brooke rolled her eyes and started to eat her lunch.

"Tell me something I don't know," Brooke said.

Alyssa looked over to Brooke.

"Brooke, come on. You can't stay mad at her forever."

Laurie rolled her eyes at Brooke.

"You need to get over that!" Laurie said. "She made a mistake. She apologized. She's been publicly shamed for it. What else do you want?"

Brooke stopped eating and looked at Laurie.

"What would you do if you saw your best friend kissing your man?" she asked.

"Oh please! You barely liked him, and she said he came after her while she was drunk. She needs you right now. She has a black eye, and I think Sean did it!"

Brooke dropped her fork and looked at Laurie upset.

"A black eye? What?"

"Yes! And when I asked her about it, she freaked out and ran."

"She would tell someone if he was hitting her."

"I don't think she would. I think she's scared. I mean have you seen her? She wearing her hobo sweats. Her hair is a mess. She looks like she's sixty pounds."

Brooke picked up her tray and left without saying another word.

Alyssa called after her, "Brooke, where are you going?"

"I'm going to go see what the hell is going on."

Brooke grabbed her purse and walked out of the cafeteria.

Sean was walking on campus towards the parking lot when Brooke hurried up to him.

"Sean! Can I talk to you for a second?"

Sean turned to her and smugly smiled.

"Hey, Brooke. What's up? Long time no see."

"Yeah I need to talk to you. Niyah has a black eye. Do you know how she got that?"

Sean's smile vanished.

"No, I don't know. Why?"

"Because she's been with you a lot, and she looks a little sick. She hasn't been around. I just wanted to make sure everything was okay."

"We're fine, Brooke. You don't even talk to her, so why you worried about what we have going on?"

"Because that's my best friend."

"Was your best friend. Past tense. As in not anymore. She's my best friend now."

"Listen, Sean. I don't know what you're doing to her, but if I find out you've been putting your hands on her, we will have a problem."

Sean laughed hysterically.

"Was that a threat? Niyah is with me now. She's not going anywhere. She doesn't need to go anywhere. She doesn't need to party. Nothing. Just chill with me. What goes on in my house is no concern of yours."

"Just don't touch her, or I will see to it you spend time in jail, and Niyah will be staying with me."

"No. She's stuck with me. You might want to stay out of business that don't belong to you. Nice talking to you, Brooke."

Sean walked away as Brooke stood there watching him.

Niyah was in Sean's kitchen cooking dinner when Sean walked through the door. Niyah walked over to him.

"Hey, baby! I cleaned up, and the food is almost done."

She tried to kiss him. He put his hand up and pushed her face away. Niyah slapped his hand.

"What the hell did you do that for?" she asked.

"I ran into Brooke today. She asked me something real interesting about you."

Niyah lowered her head and then tried to explain.

"Look, Laurie saw my eye and started asking questions—"

"Oh, so you told her I hit you?"

"No! I didn't tell her anything."

"Well why does everyone think I hit you? That's from you falling on that chair!"

"Well, you head butted me. That's like the same thing!"

Sean grabbed Niyah and started choking her. She managed to slap him. He tossed her against the counter. A glass fell to the floor along with Niyah.

"You talk too much!" he said.

Niyah's hands started to bleed being cut from glass.

"Fuck you, Sean! I'm tired of this shit!" Niyah said, stepping up to push him.

"What you gone do, huh? You ain't shit, just like my mom," he said.

"No wonder she ran out."

Sean grabbed her by her neck again.

"You don't know shit! Nobody wants your ass but me, understand?"

Niyah gasped for air. Sean dropped her to the floor. Niyah got up to catch her breath.

"You think you're bad cuz you throw me around? You ain't shit. You're not a real man! You're a little ass boy, and I hate you!"

"I don't know what I'm doing with you anyways!"

"Fine! Then I will go! I keep telling you that!" Niyah said and grabbed her backpack, headed towards the door.

Sean put his arm up stopping her.

"I'm not done talking to your ass."

"I'm done talking to your bitch ass."

Sean grabbed her by her hair and threw her to the floor.

"See, this is why we have problems. You don't fuckin' listen, and you talk too much!"

Niyah got up and dropped her backpack.

"I don't want to fight you, Sean!"

"I don't care what you want. You're going to sit your ass down, and we're going to finish this conversation!"

"You're fuckin' crazy, you know that? Crazy!"

Niyah ran towards the door. Sean grabbed her and pushed her against the mirror hanging on the wall. Niyah dropped to the floor. Sean grabbed her by her hair and punched her hard in the stomach. Niyah vomited on the floor. She lost her breath and grabbed the back of the couch before finally falling down. Sean looked at the puke on the floor.

"You're trashy and disgusting," Sean said and grabbed her by her hair, dragging her through the vomit. "You can clean this up with your body then."

Sean dropped her in the vomit and let go of her hair. Niyah slowly got up. Her face was red, and her clothes were covered in her puke. She ran up to Sean screaming and hitting him.

"What is wrong with you?"

Sean laughed, making her even angrier. She punched Sean in the face. Sean laughed at her punch as he licked blood from his lip. He pushed her to the floor again. She sat on the floor weeping. Blood slid down her hand, and Sean knelt down in front of her.

"Is that all you got?" he asked.

Niyah spit in his face. Sean wiped the spit from his face and took a deep breath. He slapped her across the face. Niyah turned around and punched Sean again. Sean grabbed her by her neck. His grip was tight. He carried Niyah by her neck to the bathroom and threw her to the floor. He grabbed the plunger and dipped it in the toilet. He threw the toilet water from the plunger unto Niyah's face. He repeatedly threw toilet water on her. Niyah gagged at the toilet water.

"Stop Sean that's disgusting! Stop!"

"You're a dog so you get treated like a dog!"

Sean grabbed her by her neck again and carried her to the bedroom. Niyah's face turned red as her eyes rolled to the back of her head. Sean finally threw Niyah unto the bed. She coughed as she tried to breath. Sean grabbed her face.

"I'm going for a walk. Clean this shit up before I get back," he said.

He walked out and slammed the door. Niyah crawled from the bed onto the floor. She continued to cough. When she regained her breathing, she slowly got up and limped to the front room. Glass was all over the floor. The smell of throw up filled the air. Her clothes and hair were soaked with toilet water. She dropped to the floor and started to regurgitate. Her hands were bleeding from the glass. She was in pain. She limped to her cellphone on the floor. She pressed 9-1-1. Her hand started shaking as she hesitated to press dial. Her teardrops ran down her face, hitting the front screen of her phone. She threw the phone to the couch and sat down crying.

"God, what am I doing here? What the hell am I doing? Get up, Niyah! Get up and get out of here! You have to leave. Get up!"

She got up, grabbed her phone and ran out the door.

Niyah escaped down the street toward the track. She imagined herself as a little girl again, running away from her house when her parents fought. She hopped the fence to the field. She walked on the track. She took off her shoes and ran a couple of meters before falling to the ground. Her back was in pain, and her hands still were sore from the fight. She got up and attempted to run again. She tripped and fell back to the ground on her face. She lay there crying, "God, please help me! Please. I can't do this anymore. I can't live like this no more!"

A pair of hands grabbed Niyah's shoulders. Niyah hopped up and grabbed the hands. She turned around and saw Brooke standing there.

"Niyah, are you okay?" Brooke asked.

Niyah was shocked to see Brooke standing there.

"What are you doing here, Brooke?"

"I went to your dorm looking for you. I needed to talk to you. I saw you running over here when I was leaving study hall."

"You've done enough talking, Brooke! I don't want to talk!"

Brooke tried to hug Niyah, but Niyah pushed her hands away.

"Nini, please. I'm sorry I haven't been there for you. But you need to talk to me! Is he hitting you?"

Niyah sat back on the track.

"Why did you have to go and ask him questions, Brooke? We were okay. We were going to be okay. I'm fine."

Brooke sat down next to her.

"You're not fine! Look at you. The Niyah I know would never let this happen! Ever. Let me get you some help, please! You just need to tell me what's going on. Forget our little beef. I still love you and care about your well-being. I'm sorry, but I was just trying to help!"

"Well you didn't help! You made it worse! Look at my face! You haven't been here for me! No one has!"

"Because he made you feel alone, Niyah! Like you didn't have anybody! I know that's what he did because he kept saying that he was your best friend now! Niyah, please just talk to me!"

"Just leave me alone!"

Niyah got up, grabbed her things and ran to her dorm. Brooke hopped up, shouting for Niyah to stop, but she was long gone.

Niyah ran into her dorm room building and up to her room. She burst in the door. Laurie and Dante were sitting on Laurie's bed kissing when Niyah hurried in. She went straight to the bathroom. Dante and Laurie both hopped up. Niyah locked the bathroom door behind her as she sat on the floor and took off her pants. Laurie and Dante ran to the bathroom. Laurie tried to unlock the door. She knocked on the door hard. Niyah stayed silent.

Laurie started to panic.

"Niyah, are you okay? Open the door please? Niyah!" Laurie yelled.

Niyah looked at herself in the mirror and began to cry.

"I'm done. I'm so done," Niyah said.

She took her razor and started to cut herself on the inside of her legs again. On the other side of the door, Laurie and Dante looked at each other. Laurie continued to bang on the door, asking Niyah to open it. Niyah rested on the floor in a fetal position crying with blood running down her legs onto the ground.

Coach Jones sat at his desk handling some business over the telephone.

Niyah shyly knocked on the door and walked in.

"You wanted to see me?" she said.

She was wearing sunglasses and had covered her face with makeup. Coach Jones motioned for her to come in and take a seat. He hung up the phone.

"Hey there, speedy Gonzales! What's going on?" Coach Jones said.

Niyah remained silent. Coach Jones eyed her as she fidgeted in the seat.

"Take the glasses off, please," he said.

Niyah didn't budge.

"Niyah, take the sunglasses off."

Niyah removed her sunglasses. Even though she had on makeup, Coach Jones could slightly see her eye and scratches on her face. He jumped up.

"Niyah, what the hell happened to your face?"

"I got in a fight."

"With who?"

Niyah started to cry. Coach Jones ran over to Niyah very concerned.

"Talk to me, Niyah. This is a safe place."

"I got in a fight at the... club."

Coach Jones sat on the desk.

"Niyah, I took you off the team to get your act together. You have to stop fighting."

"That's just it, Coach! I've been acting out because I've been upset. Track is the only thing that keeps me sane. Please, Coach. I need to run! Please!"

Coach Jones sighed.

"You have been doing much better," he said. "That's why I wanted to see you. I'm going to let you run at the next meet only because I care about you, and I want you to get it together. I would rather you be around me and the team instead of out in the club somewhere fighting. I told you that if you got your grades up, I would let you run. You did that so be at practice."

She let out a sigh of relief and tears of joy.

"Thank you so much, Coach. Thank you!"

She got up and hugged him. She began to walk out the door.

"Niyah."

She turned around and looked at him.

"If something else is going on, you need to tell someone. Especially me. We can do something about it. But I can't do anything if you don't talk to me."

Niyah looked down at the ground and then back at her coach.

"I'm fine, Coach. Really. Just a little bar fight. I'll see you at practice."

"You can't run from your problems forever. Sooner or later they will catch up to you, and you will have to face them head on. I'm sure you know you have a lot of promise and a beautiful future ahead of you. If something is toxic in your life, you need to leave, and don't look back. Those types of situations never get better. They only get worse."

Niyah forced a smile.

"Thanks, Coach. Trust me. I'm done with bad situations. The only running I want to be doing is on the track. I'll see you at practice."

She walked out and closed the door behind her. Coach Jones watched her leave with a concerned look on his face.

21

Birthday Surprise

The relays in Texas were in full effect as thousands of people gathered in the stands to watch one of the biggest track meets of the season. Niyah and her teammates were on the track running the four by two meter relay. Laurie was gliding around the track towards Niyah. Niyah yelled to Laurie, "Come on, Laurie! Let's go! Pick it up! Let's go, Laurie! Let's go! Don't let her catch you! Come on!"

Laurie got to Niyah as Niyah took off. Laurie handed her the stick. Niyah hightailed around the curve and reached the straight. She and another competitor were inches apart from each other. Niyah began to distance herself from the rest of the competition. She was in first place as she blazed down the track towards the finish line.

Coach Jones stood to his feet as he watched the clock.

"Come on, Niyah! Get the record!" he shouted.

Niyah zoomed down the home stretch and leaned in at the finish line. She looked up at the scoreboard.

The announcer came over the intercom shouting, "And that's a new record for Bay University in the four by two meter relay!"

The crowd cheered loudly. Brooke, Laurie and Alisha ran on the track to Niyah. They all hugged and celebrated as the crowd cheered them on. The girls waved to the crowd and ran off the track excitedly. The girls were swarmed by reporters.

After getting their medals, the girls hopped off the podium, still excited. Coach Jones walked up to them smiling from ear to ear.

"I'm so proud of you guys!" he said. "Great run, Niyah! Now that's a comeback."

"Thanks, Coach!" Niyah said.

"You ladies ran your butts off today! Alright, cool down. Y'all still got one more race. Come back to the tent when you're done! Great job! That's what I'm talking about!"

Coach Jones walked off. The girls put on their warm ups. Laurie noticed the cuts on Niyah's thighs.

"Niyah, what happened?" she said pointing to the cuts.

"Oh, I scratched myself," Niyah told her.

"With what?"

"Dang, Laurie! Always a million and one questions," Niyah laughed nervously trying to change the subject.

Laurie laughed too.

"I'm just asking. Can't be scratching up your sexy legs. Need to cut your nails. My cousin cuts herself in her sleep. Probably what you doing. You do sleep bad as hell."

"I really do."

They both laughed as they finished putting on their warm ups. Niyah looked over across the field and spotted Vanessa jogging. She quickly put on her tennis shoes and jogged over to Vanessa.

"Hey... Vanessa right?"

Vanessa stopped jogging and stared at her.

"What the hell do you want?"

"Relax. I wanted to talk to you about Sean. Ask why you guys broke up?"

Vanessa chuckled, "Don't come at me with that back door shit. We both know what this is about. So... how many times has he hit you? Your friends know yet? How 'bout the coach? He ask about your bruises? Let me guess... you're telling them you're clumsy now."

"He hasn't..."

Vanessa pulled her bangs back. She revealed a nasty scar at the top of her forehead. Niyah's jaw dropped.

Vanessa exclaimed, "See my little souvenir? I told you to watch your back, new girl. Run while you still can, or he'll put you away."

Vanessa took off to join her team. Niyah watched her go. Brooke walked up to Niyah.

"What was that about? She messing with you again?" Brooke asked.

"Naw, it was nothing," Niyah said.

Niyah and Brooke stood there staring at each other silently. Niyah finally said, "Listen, Brooke, the other night I didn't mean to blame you. I was upset and hurt, and you were the only one there, so I just took all my anger out on you. Nothing was your fault, and I had no right to blame you. I'm sorry for everything."

Brooke smiled and replied, "No, Nini, I'm sorry. I've been such a bitch to you. I just didn't know how to react to seeing you and Kevin kiss. I was hurt. But I should have listened to you and heard your side of the story. You're my best friend, and I trust you. And I'm upset that I haven't been there for you over this petty bullshit. I love you, Nini."

Niyah smiled, relieved that Brooke was forgiving her. She grabbed Brooke's hands.

"No need to be sorry," Niyah said. "That thing with me and Kevin should have never happened. I just want you to know, I would never hurt you ever. I love you too much."

"You did hurt me. But the day you charged up Kevin, I heard it all. I know you wouldn't intentionally hurt me, and I love you too."

Brooke hugged Niyah. Then they laughed. Niyah kissed Brooke on the cheek.

"I've missed you so much!"

"Who you telling? I've been bored without you!" Brooke said.

Brooke walked up to Niyah close enough for no one else to hear.

"You know we need to talk about this Sean situation right?" she said.

Niyah frowned and replied, "I know we do."

Laurie ran up and hugged them both.

"Finally! Y'all were getting on my nerves!" Laurie said.

Brooke shoved Laurie as she hugged Niyah.

"It's good to see you smile again, Nini. Had me a little worried," Laurie said.

"I'm actually happy now that I've gotten rid of Sean. My grades are better, I'm running better than ever, and I'm eating. God is truly blessing me."

Laurie held her hands up over her head and started jumping up and down.

"And we're record holders now! Sixth street tonight to celebrate!" she said.

The girls laughed and walked off with their medals.

It was seven in the morning as Niyah slept peacefully in her bed. Laurie, Alyssa and Brooke woke her up, blowing horns and yelling, "Happy Birthday!"

Niyah opened her eyes slowly and smiled. She sat up in her bed, squinted her eyes, and tried to wake herself up.

"Y'all are so annoying! I just want you guys to know. Thank you, crazies! What time is it?" Niyah said.

Laurie jumped on Niyah.

"Time to get your ass up!" she said.

Dante walked out of the bathroom. Everybody looked at him then at Laurie. Dante grabbed his jacket and backpack.

"Laurie, I'm about to go," he said.

Laurie hopped off of Niyah and ran to Dante.

"You said you were going to stay!" she said.

"Alisha's been looking for me."

"So what!" Laurie yelled at him.

"Don't start, Laurie, damn!" he said. He turned his attention to Niyah. "Happy Birthday, Niyah. We partying tonight, right?"

Niyah nodded her head yes.

"Yup. We're all meeting up at Brooke's apartment to drink before we go to the club at nine thirty."

"Cool. I'll be there with Gary. See y'all tonight."

Dante walked out. Laurie rolled her eyes and walked back over to the bed.

"Anyway, let's start the celebration!" she said.

Laurie went to her dresser, pulled out a bottle of liquor from her drawer, and took a shot.

"Man, I can't find my other bottle so I had to buy another one!"

Niyah looked at her dresser where she had hidden the bottle of liquor she took from Laurie. Laurie handed the bottle to Brooke. Brooke put the bottle on the dresser.

"I swear, Laurie, you are an alcoholic. It's seriously like eight in the morning," Brooke said.

"It's never too early to drink," Laurie exclaimed.

They all laughed. Laurie suddenly fell to the ground holding her stomach. They all hopped up and helped her to her feet. Brooke grabbed her face.

"Laurie, are you okay?" Brooke asked.

"Yeah! I just feel a little sick."

Alyssa took the bottle of liquor from the dresser and put it back in Laurie's drawer.

"All right, no more drinking for you," Alyssa said.

Niyah's phone began to ring. She ran over to pick it up.

Alyssa laughed and said, "Nini, just so you know, your phone has been ringing off the hook since midnight."

Niyah laughed and answered. "Hello."

"Why you haven't been answering the phone? I called you like ten times."

Niyah looked at her phone and realized she answered the phone for Sean. She exhaled and put the phone back to her ear.

"Hi, Sean. Nice to hear from you too. I'm just waking up."

"Where are you?"

"Home, why?"

"I need you to come get your birthday present from me."

"Right now?"

"Yes, right now."

Niyah grew silent before answering him.

"Can you bring it to me tonight like everybody else?"

"Niyah, if you don't come get this present right now, I'm never speaking to you again and you will regret it. Come now."

Sean hung up the phone. Niyah sighed and threw the phone on the bed. She looked at her friends, trying to smile.

Brooke walked over to Niyah.

"What did that asshole want?" she asked.

"He said he has a present for me."

Laurie stood up slowly. "Is he going to bring it tonight?"

"He wants me to come get it now."

Brooke shook her head no.

"Don't go over there! We are about to take you to eat, get cute, take you shopping and get ready to party tonight. Don't let him ruin it!"

Niyah ran in the restroom and brushed her teeth. She ran out and threw on some clothes, grabbed her phone and purse. Brooke grabbed Niyah's arm.

"Niyah, please don't go over there. I don't have a good feeling about this," Brooke said.

"I'm just going over there to get his present. I'll be at your house at seven before everyone. Okay?"

Niyah hugged Brooke.

"I'll be fine. Promise. If anything goes wrong, I'll call you."

Niyah looked at her phone and saw that it was about to die. She grabbed her charger from the wall socket and put it in her purse.

"Well, it's about to die. I'll charge it over there. See y'all later," she said.

She ran out of the dorm. The girls looked at the door as it closed. Brooke sighed.

"Bet he doesn't even have a present," Brooke said.

Niyah hopped off the bus and walked into Sean's apartment complex. She got to Sean's apartment and knocked on the door. He answered quickly. She looked and saw he was a little upset.

"Sorry. I had to take the bus and my phone died," Niyah said. Sean just stared at her quietly. Niyah looked around inside the house. "So where's my present, so I can go?"

Sean moved aside and gestured for her to come in. Niyah hesitated before she walked in slowly. He closed the door behind them. He walked past Niyah.

"Let's talk first," he said.

Niyah looked at him. She felt like an argument was about to happen.

"Not today, Sean. It's my birthday."

Sean walked to his room and walked back with Niyah's laptop.

Niyah looked at him disappointed.

"Is that my present? My laptop? Why didn't you tell me you had it over here? I've been looking for it. I thought someone stole it."

Sean continued to stay quiet. He walked to the dinner table and set the laptop down. He opened it and began typing.

She stared at him suspiciously.

"How do you know my password?"

Sean still said nothing. He just continued to type. He finally stopped and turned the laptop facing Niyah. On the screen was a naked picture of Niyah. He pointed to the picture.

"What the hell is this?"

Niyah started to fidget. She became instantly nervous, certain that they were about to fight. She tried to move toward the door, but her legs wouldn't budge.

"I took that picture like ages ago! I was young and dumb. I just have them on my computer."

"You're such a liar. Who were you sending these pictures to?"

"I used to send them to this girl I met at a meet a long time ago."

"I knew something was up with you talking and emailing a girl from track. You're already too gay with all the girls on your team."

Sean turned the computer back toward him and began typing again. He turned the computer around and showed Niyah some emails. He pointed to the email.

"This email was sent two months ago. We were together two months ago. Kind of sexy actually."

"Sean, we're not together now, so you can't trip! And we were never together when I emailed her. I can promise you that."

Sean went to the kitchen, pulled out a knife, ran to Niyah and put it to her throat.

"You're such a liar and a cheater! I hate you! I trusted you."

Niyah started shaking, praying that Sean wouldn't cut her.

"Sean, please. Let's just talk okay?"

She dropped her purse and her phone. She put her hands on his chest trying to push him back.

Sean pressed the knife against Niyah's throat a little harder. Niyah could feel the knife cutting her.

"You were cheating on me the entire time. With a girl. Fuck you!"

Sean moved the knife away and threw Niyah to the ground. He wrapped his arm around her neck. Niyah bit his arm. He screamed and threw her across the table. He walked over to her.

"You are so pathetic!"

Niyah got up slowly. "I have never cheated on you ever! I talked to her when we weren't together and it was innocent! Look at the dates! I would never cheat on you!"

He kicked her back down. He grabbed her arm and bit her as she screamed.

"You like how that feels, stupid bitch?" he said.

Niyah snatched her arm away. She slapped him in the face. He grabbed her by her face and head butted her and knocked her down. Sean grabbed her by her hair and dragged her across the room as she tried to get away.

Niyah screamed, "Get off of me! Get off of me!"

Sean ripped some of Niyah's hair out. She let out a loud yell. She grabbed a chair and hit Sean with it. Sean fell to the ground. Niyah ran over and kicked him in stomach. As she tried to kick him in the face, he grabbed her foot, and she fell to the ground. He grabbed her by her hair again and dragged her to the front door. He opened the door and threw her outside. She fell down on the concrete hard. Sean walked back inside as Niyah lay there in pain. He came back out. He threw her purse, her phone and her laptop outside. "I have the pictures in my email. Don't try anything dumb. Happy birthday."

He slammed the door. One of the neighbors came outside and ran over to Niyah.

"Ma'am! Ma'am, are you okay? Should I call the police?" the lady asked and helped Niyah to her feet.

Niyah shook her head no.

"No, no I'm fine," she said.

Niyah took a few steps and then fell to the ground. The neighbor helped her inside her house.

Niyah's friends were gathered in Brooke's apartment decorating for Niyah's birthday. Her friends had a cake and food prepared for her. They stacked her gifts on the table. They were drinking, getting worried about Niyah's whereabouts.

Alyssa looked at the time.

"It's ten. Where is she?" she said.

Brooke took out her phone and called her. She hung up the phone.

"Her phone keeps going to voicemail."

Alyssa turned to the guys.

"How come no one knows where he lives?"

Dante shrugged his shoulders.

"He moved, and no one really talks to him anymore," he said.

There was a knock at the door. Brooke ran to answer it. Niyah walked in, scratched up and crying. Everybody ran to her. Brooke carried her in.

"Nini! Oh my God! What happened?"

"Me and Sean had a fight and he grabbed a knife—"

At the sound of that, Gary rushed towards the front door.

"What's his address? I'm going to kill him!" Gary said.

Everyone grabbed him trying to hold him back. Niyah grabbed his arm.

"Gary, please! Don't go over there! They were trying to call the cops, and I can't have you going to jail over me!"

Gary pushed the guys off of him.

"Look at your face, Niyah! Look at your face!"

"Gary, please! Don't go over there!" Niyah cried, still holding on to Gary's arm.

Gary looked at Niyah and sighed. He punched the wall and walked over to the couch.

"I don't mean to make things worse, but, Niyah, look at your Facebook," Alyssa said and gave Niyah her phone.

Niyah took a look at the screen and her eyes widened.

"Oh my God. He leaked those naked pictures of me onto my Facebook account."

Niyah tried to sign into her Facebook, but her password had been changed. Brooke's phone starting ringing frantically as people saw the photos on Niyah's Facebook. Her friends were going crazy. It was chaos in Brooke's house. Niyah fell to the floor bewildered. No one knew what to do.

The commotion at Brooke's house had died down as everyone headed back to their rooms. Niyah rested in Brooke's bed staring out the window. Brooke walked into the room.

"Everyone is gone now. We thought you were asleep," Brooke said.

"I can't even look at anyone right now. I'm so embarrassed."

Brooke went and sat on the bed next to Niyah.

"Are you okay?" Brooke asked.

Niyah shook her head no.

"I just want to forget this day ever happened. I'm scared to turn my phone back on. Even Rochelle saw the pictures," she said.

"Well, we got them off and changed all your passwords. At least people were calling your pictures sexy," Brooke said.

Niyah sat up and smiled. Tears formed in her eyes as Brooke hugged her.

"I'm sorry. I just wanted to make you smile," Brook said. "It's going to be okay, Niyah. I'm back in your life now."

"After all I've put you through, you still my ride or die. I don't understand," Niyah said.

"Because I love you, and I already forgave you. Besides, I never liked Kevin that much. He was great but he was just a little too clingy." They both laughed. "But I never felt anything like that for him. And I was jealous," Brooke said.

Niyah looked at her confused.

"Of what?" Niyah asked.

Brooke looked away.

"Nothing."

Niyah grabbed her chin and turned her face back towards her.

"Tell me."

"Of you liking Sean so much," Brooke said.

"Why would that make you jealous? I've had boyfriends before."

"Yeah but this was different. You were gone. Mentally and physically, he had you gone. And I've never cared about any close friend as much as I care about you. You were in a toxic relationship, and I couldn't do nothing about it. I'm not gay, I'm just attracted to you."

Niyah looked at her shocked.

"You know you can always tell me how you feel. I feel that way about you too," Niyah said.

"I just…I really love you, Niyah."

Niyah smiled.

"I love you too, Brooke."

Brooke hugged Niyah for a long time.

"Let's just lay down. Get some rest."

Niyah and Brooke lay down in the bed. Brooke wrapped her arms around Niyah.

"I love you, Nini."

Niyah smiled as she looked out the window. Niyah's smiled faded as she grabbed her neck and reminisced on the events of the day. She silently cried as she closed her eyes to try to get some sleep.

22

Losing It

The track was sweltering as one hundred teams crowded the stadium for the outdoor qualifying meet. Niyah, for the first time in her life, was nervous to run. She tried hard to concentrate on her race and not the things going on in her life. She set up her blocks for the 400 meter race and knelt down to pray. "Dear God. Thank you for this day. Please guide my feet around this track. Please let me empty my mind of everything that has happened to me these last couple of weeks. In Jesus name I pray, Amen."

The official blew his whistle. Niyah was in her blocks ready to run. The official did his "Ready, Set" routine and shot his gun. Niyah pushed off her blocks and started her race. She was in the lead at first. Her friends and family cheered for her. Suddenly, two competitors were on her heels at the 300 meter mark. Niyah got nervous and tried to pick up speed, but her legs felt heavy. Her arms became tired as they were fifty meters from the finish line. The two competitors passed her. Niyah finished third in the race and walked off the track upset.

Coach Jones ran to her.

"Niyah what happened?" Jones said.

Niyah shook her head frustrated and tired.

"I don't know, Coach. I just wasn't mentally ready."

She began to hyperventilate. Coach Jones grabbed her shoulders as Niyah caught her breath.

"Calm down. There's still a chance you made it to nationals."

Niyah walked over to her bag with Coach Jones and put on her sweats.

The announcer came over the speakers, "And there you have it folks! Your top eight girls that will advance to nationals in the 400 meter dash has been announced and is on the board."

Niyah and Coach Jones looked at the board. They saw "Niyah Coleman-eighth place." It was a bittersweet moment. Coach Jones hugged Niyah.

"You made it! And we have plenty of time to practice!" he said. "Cheer up, okay. You did great. Let's go."

Niyah and Coach Jones walked off.

Niyah walked into her dorm and set her bag on the floor. "Laurie, I'm back from study hall. Want to get some food before practice?"

Niyah heard what sounded like someone puking in the bathroom. She went inside to see Laurie vomiting in the toilet.

"Laurie! Laurie, are you okay?" she asked.

Laurie wiped her mouth with some toilet paper.

"Yeah, I'm fine. I'm just pregnant," Laurie said.

Niyah was stunned. Laurie burst into tears. Niyah hugged her tightly.

"How do you know?"

"I took a test. Three tests actually. They all were positive, and now I'm throwing up all over the place. And my boobs are finally getting bigger."

Laurie tried to laugh at her joke but started crying even harder. Niyah handed Laurie more toilet paper as she wiped throw up from her face.

"Is it Dante's?"

Laurie nodded her head yes.

"He wants me to get an abortion," she said. "He doesn't want Alisha or anyone to find out. I don't know what to do, Niyah. What do I do?"

Niyah rocked Laurie in her arms as she cried.

"It's okay. Laurie. We'll figure it out. It's okay."

Gary and Dante were in the locker room getting dressed for their afternoon workout talking about Laurie's situation.

"Damn, Dante! You don't know how to pull out man?" Gary joked.

"Man, I did! I fucked up!"

"Does Alisha know?"

"Hell no! Not yet."

Gary laughed and shook his head. He said, "And we would have sprints on the track today with them. What if she doesn't get an abortion?"

Dante looked up at Gary with his mouth wide open.

"Then I have a big problem," Dante said.

They both walked out of the locker room and into the hallway. They were getting ready to walk outside to the track when Gary spotted Sean walking down the hallway.

"Hold up real quick," Gary said.

He walked over to Sean.

"Sean! Let me holla at you," he said.

Sean stopped and turned around.

"What's up?"

Gary finally reached him and stepped up to him.

"I'm going to make this quick. I just want to tell you this. If you put your hands on my cousin again or expose her pics, I will kill you."

Sean looked Gary up and down with an annoyed face.

"I didn't do anything to that girl! And I don't appreciate you rolling up on me like this," Sean said.

"Don't put your hands on my cousin no more. I'm not going to tell your weak ass again!"

"Man, fuck you and that ugly bitch!"

Gary punched Sean in the face, and the boys tumbled.

Gary screamed, "Don't put your hands on her no more!"

Sean threw Gary into the wall and punched him in the face. Gary threw Sean to the ground and started punching him in the head. The two guys threw blow for blow. Dante and some of their teammates ran over and tried to stop the fight. Gary and Sean continued to fist fight up and down the hallway.

The girls were on the field running with leg weights. Laurie stopped and ran to a trash can to throw up. Coach Jones watched her.

"Laurie, what's the problem?" he asked.

Laurie took a drink of water.

She said, "I don't feel good today, Coach."

Alisha yelled, "Maybe you should stop drinking, alkie."

Laurie wiped her mouth.

"Not today, Alisha," she said.

Coach Jones walked up to Laurie.

"Alisha, stop. Laurie you can finish. Get some more water and let's go. You might just be dehydrated. It's hot out here," Coach Jones said.

"I'm not dehydrated, Coach."

"Then what is it?"

Alisha screamed, "It's liquor!"

Her friends laughed. Coach Jones became aggravated.

"Alisha, enough!"

Laurie walked up to Alisha slowly.

"How about you ask your boyfriend why I'm throwing up?" she said.

Everyone got quiet. Alisha's face dropped. Laurie smiled smugly. Alisha stood there for a second thinking. Her hands started shaking. Alisha suddenly rushed towards the school. The track team and Coach Jones ran after her.

Coach Jones shouted, "Alisha, where are you going? Alisha!"

As Alisha was running, Gary and Sean's fight spilled out the doors and outside. They brawled, punching each other like professionals. The team finally broke them apart. Sean rushed off toward the parking lot.

"Fuck you, Gary!"

It took everyone to hold Gary back. Niyah ran up to Gary.

"Gary, what the hell is going on?!" she asked.

Alisha spotted Dante. She pulled him from holding Gary back and slapped Dante in his face. Everyone else stopped. Dante grabbed his cheek and was about to rush toward Alisha. His teammates held him back.

"What in the hell is your problem, girl?" he shouted.

"She's pregnant, isn't she?!" Alisha yelled and pointed towards Laurie who was standing with the rest of the girls' track team watching.

Dante didn't speak.

"It's yours, isn't it?"

Dante said nothing as Alisha started crying.

"After all I've done for you! You go and get another girl pregnant!" she said.

"Man, I don't know if it's mine," Dante said.

"But it could be, right?"

Dante looked at Laurie then back at Alisha.

"…yeah," he said.

She spit in his face and slapped him. Dante raised his hand as if he was going to hit her. Coach Jones ran over and grabbed him.

"That's it! I've had enough! What the hell is wrong with you guys?" Jones shouted.

No one responded.

Alisha ran off. Dante snatched his arm away from Coach Jones and shot a look at Laurie who was staring at him.

"Fuckin' bitch!" he screamed at Laurie.

"Fuck you, Dante!" Laurie shouted back.

Dante looked at Coach Jones then Laurie and walked off. Coach Jones pointed to Laurie.

"You are no longer on this team!"

Laurie screamed, "Coach! What the hell?"

"You cannot run on this team while pregnant! I will not have this shit!" he said.

Laurie ran off crying. Coach turned to the football team.

"I'll let Coach Robinson deal with you meatheads in a minute," Coach Jones yelled and turned back to his track team. "Did I tell y'all to stop running?! GO!"

The girls hustled back to the track. Niyah stood there staring at Gary. Coach Jones pointed back towards the track.

"Niyah, go," he said.

Brooke jogged up and grabbed Niyah.

"Come on, Nini," she said.

Niyah gave Gary one last look. He nodded his head toward the track telling her to go back. Niyah ran off with Brooke. The football team went back inside the locker room. Coach Jones tossed his hat to the ground.

"Shit!" he said standing there in disbelief.

The team finished up practice and packed up to go home for the night. Niyah went to sit alone in the bleachers. After all the girls left, Coach Jones walked up to Niyah.

"Why are you sitting up here alone?" he asked.

Niyah shrugged her shoulders.

"I feel bad. I knew everything. Everything that was going on with Laurie and Dante. I feel bad that I'm the reason Gary got into that fight with Sean. It's just a lot going on."

Coach Jones shook his head.

"I don't understand how you can have everything going for yourself and ruin your life over a boy," he said.

Niyah turned to Coach Jones.

"Love can make you do some crazy things, Coach."

"You guys are young. You don't know what love is yet."

They both become silent. Coach Jones sat down next to Niyah. He looked out at the sun setting. He finally broke the silence saying, "You've been doing very good, Nini. In class and on the field. Coach Tatem and I have been talking. Even though you didn't do as well as we wanted you to in qualifying, we're going to let you run at championships. I'm going to need you for those points."

Niyah's eyes lit up. She hugged Coach Jones.

"Don't let me down, Nini."

"I won't. I promise," she said.

"Okay. I have to go deal with this Laurie situation. Are you going to stay out here?" he asked.

"Yeah I'm going to go get my good spikes and come practice block starts.

I feel like my start could be better."

"You just have to push off harder, get lower. You know this. You want me to stay out here with you to help?"

Niyah shook her head no.

"No, I just kind of want to be alone," she said.

"I understand. Okay, put the blocks up when you're done."

Coach Jones got up and began to walk away.

"Coach..."

Coach Jones turned around. Niyah smiled at him.

"Thank you. For everything."

Coach Jones smiled and walked away. Niyah sat in the bleachers for a while and then got up and headed toward the locker room.

Niyah was at her locker getting her running spikes when she heard someone crying. She closed her locker and walked around the locker room.

"Laurie?" Niyah said before she turned a corner and found Alisha on the floor in tears.

Niyah started to walk away but decided to walk over to Alisha. She sat down next to her. Alisha tried to wipe her face.

Niyah smiled and told her, "Hey, you can cry in front of me. I understand how you feel."

"I'm fine, Niyah, thank you. I don't need your sympathy."

Niyah smacked her lips.

"Fine, Alisha, I tried! I am your teammate. Not your enemy."

"Teammates? Fuck teammates! My teammate got pregnant by my man, and all my 'teammates' knew about it."

"Maybe if you weren't such a bitch, someone would have told you!" Niyah yelled.

She got up and began to walk away.

"Wait, Niyah. I'm sorry," Alisha said.

Niyah sighed and sat back down.

"I'm sorry. I'm just so mad!" Alisha said and wiped the tears from her face with her shirt. "Promise if I tell you something you won't tell anyone?"

"If I didn't tell anyone about Laurie and Dante, why would I tell your secrets?" Niyah said.

Alisha shot an angry look at Niyah. Niyah smiled and rubbed Alisha's shoulders.

"My bad! My bad! Too soon! I'm sorry. Yes, I promise not to tell."

Alisha took a deep breath and started talking.

"I got pregnant by Dante when I was in tenth grade. My dad made me get an abortion and pushed me in track even harder. That was my focus. He trained me himself. All he wanted was to see me at state. The day you beat me was the worst. He took me off my summer track team and trained me night and day. He made me hate it! He put me on a diet saying if I was smaller I would have won. He embarrassed me. He treated me like a dog training for a race. I hated him, and I hated you."

"Damn, Alisha. I had no idea. I'm sorry you had to go through that."

"It's not your fault. None of this is. I just can't believe all of this was going on in my face."

"Trust me, I know how you feel. My girl in high school did it to me."

"Really? What did you do?"

Niyah laughed.

"Went to a basketball game and fought both of them."

Alisha wiped her tears and laughed.

"No wonder they call you crazy, Nini!"

They both giggled.

Niyah turned to her.

"Want to know something crazy?"

Alisha turned to her and asked, "What's that?"

"I had an abortion too. I was young and dumb. I was with my boyfriend, Caleb, since we were about twelve years old. Thought I was in love. But I wasn't. It hurt every day. It was a selfish thing to do, and I regret it. It hurts me just to think about it. But God knows I wasn't ready. I just didn't want to have to do something like that you know. Ever. So when I say I know how you feel, I know how you feel. It's going to be okay. I promise."

"Wow. I didn't know that. That's crazy that we all really go through some of the same things. Thank you for talking to me, Niyah," she said.

Niyah turned to her and smiled.

"No problem."

The two girls attempted to hug then stopped.

Niyah laughed and said, "Okay, I guess we're not there yet."

They both laughed and gave each other a high five. Niyah got up and extended her hand to Alisha.

"Now come hold my blocks for me before one of them boys ask just so they can look at my butt," Niyah said.

Alisha smiled and got up. "You ain't got no butt, Nini."

They both laughed and walked out of the locker room together.

Niyah was walking into her dorm room from practice. She didn't see Laurie in the room.

"Laurie?"

She went into the bathroom. Laurie was lying on the floor with a liquor bottle next to her. There was blood running down her pants and blood seeping from her head. Niyah ran to her.

"Laurie! Oh my God! Laurie!" she yelled.

She lifted Laurie's head. Her eyes were closed, and she was barely breathing.

"Laurie! Laurie, baby, wake up!"

She set her head down and ran to grab her phone. She called 911 and ran back into the bathroom. "Hello! Yes I need an ambulance immediately! Someone help me! Please! Oh my God, Laurie, wake up!"

Niyah stayed on the phone with the operator holding Laurie in her arms.

Laurie lay in a hospital bed sleeping. Her head was wrapped, and she was hooked to IV's through her arm. Niyah sat in a chair next to her on the phone with Brooke.

"Yeah I'm here with her now," she said. "Just tell coach, and whenever you guys can get here, please do. She scared the shit out of me."

Laurie woke up slowly.

Niyah told Brooke, "I think she's waking up. Just get here please. Call me when you pull up. Bye." She hung up the phone and stood up next to Laurie. "Hey, beautiful."

Laurie slowly smiled and looked around the room.

"Hey, you. Where am I?" she asked.

"You're at the hospital, my love."

Laurie looked at the machines and tubes in her arms. She looked at Niyah scared. "What happened?"

Niyah hesitated and moved in closer to Laurie. She grabbed her hand.

"I came in the room and found you on the bathroom floor. Do you remember anything?"

Laurie shook her head. "I just remember coming home and drinking until I passed out. I hope I didn't hurt the baby. I was just so upset, Niyah. I was so upset!"

"I know, honey."

Laurie grabbed her stomach.

"Is my baby okay?" she asked.

Niyah stared at her for a moment and began to cry a little. She held her hand tighter.

"You were drinking and you ummm…" Niyah cleared her throat struggling to bring herself to tell Laurie what happened. She finally said, "You got a little drunk and you fell. You hit your head…and your stomach. You had a miscarriage, Laurie. I'm so sorry, baby girl."

Laurie began to cry and scream.

"No, Niyah! Not my baby! I wanted my baby! Don't tell me that! Please!"

Niyah grabbed her trying to calm Laurie.

"It's okay, Laurie. It's okay."

Niyah held her as they both cried.

The next morning, Niyah was helping Laurie get dressed as Brooke, Alyssa, and Coach Jones walked in. Brooke and Alyssa ran and hugged Laurie.

Laurie hugged them slowly.

"I'm okay, you guys. I'm okay," she said.

Brooke grabbed her arm.

"Don't scare me like that!" Brooke said.

Niyah looked at Brooke.

"Scare you?" said Niyah. "I'm the one who almost had a heart attack!"

Coach Jones looked at the girls.

"Ladies, could you give me and Laurie a second?" he asked.

The girls all walked out leaving Laurie and Coach Jones alone. Coach Jones pulled a chair up next to Laurie.

"How do you feel?" he said.

Laurie cracked a smile.

"I'm fine. A little sick, but I'm fine. I can be up and moving again in no time."

Coach Jones sighed.

"Listen, Laurie, I am so sorry this happened to you. And I'm sorry for yelling at you in front of everyone like that. I really am. No woman should have to go through this. But you are worth more than Dante. I was just extremely disappointed in the news."

Laurie lowered her head then looked back up at her coach.

"I know. I'm sorry I disappointed you. I just want to focus on running now," she said.

"Laurie, I can't let you run. Not the rest of this season. I have to remove you from the team. Now, I can red shirt you this year, and I will talk to Coach Tatem about next year. You just need to get some rest," he said.

Laurie teared up.

"How did I know you were going to say that?"

Her tears slid down her cheeks.

"Hey, hey! It's not over for you. Just this season. Don't let this get you down. You have to rest and you know that. Take this as a lesson. Okay?"

Laurie shook her head yes as she wiped the tears away. Coach Jones walked up to her and gave her a hug.

23

Bathtub Blues

Niyah was walking down the hallway to her dorm. She pulled out her keys as she reached her door. She noticed that there was a note on the door that read, 'We need to talk- Sean.' She snatched the note off the door and looked around scared. She swiftly opened the door and walked in. She crumpled the note and threw it to the ground. She closed the door behind her and locked it. Niyah began to undress. There was a knock at the door. She jumped up, scared that it was Sean. She didn't answer as the knocking continued.

She heard a girl's voice on the other side of the door ask, "Laurie, are you in there?"

Niyah let out a sigh of relief and went to open the door.

Alyssa was standing on the side of the door. She smiled when she saw Niyah.

"Hey, honey!" said Alyssa.

They hugged. She walked in.

"Is Laurie here? She's not answering her phone."

Niyah walked over to her bed.

"She just got out of the hospital a week ago, dang, let her breathe," Niyah said.

Alyssa frowned and plopped on Laurie's bed. Niyah laughed and sat next to her on the bed.

"I'm kidding. But, seriously I don't know where she is."

"Damn. She was supposed to go with me to North Hill. Get her away for a minute."

"North Hill College. Ain't that two hours away?"

"Yeah I was going to spend the night with my boyfriend and come back in the morning. I didn't want to drive by myself. They're having a little party. I wanted to cheer Laurie up. No drinking for her though," Alyssa said.

"She don't need to be around that at all right now anyways."

Alyssa frowned and said, "I know. I just didn't want to drive by myself." Alyssa thought about it and turned to Niyah. "Wait, you want to come?"

Niyah got off the bed and shook her head no.

"No, not today! I'm tired!" Niyah said.

Alyssa hopped up and began to plead with Niyah.

"Please! I'll bring you back! I don't want to drive by myself at night. Please! Please! Please! Please!"

Niyah gave in and laughed.

"Okay! Okay! But I'm not drinking! Let me get dressed."

Niyah and Alyssa were in the car laughing and singing speeding down the highway toward North Hill College.

Niyah's phone began to ring. She looked to Alyssa.

"It's Laurie."

Alyssa turned down the music.

Niyah answered the phone saying, "Hey, honey."

Laurie was in the dorm room sitting on the bed.

"Hey, Niyah, where are you?"

"Alyssa's dragging me to North Hill with her. You okay? We were looking for you."

"Yeah I'm okay. I'll just talk to you when you get back. Just making sure you were okay," she said.

"Okay. Love ya, Laurie."

"Love you too."

Laurie hung up the phone and looked to Sean who was sitting on Niyah's bed staring at her.

Alyssa and Niyah arrived to Alyssa's boyfriend's house. They got out of the car and ran to the door. Alyssa knocked on the door loudly. A tall, green eyed white guy answered the door. His tan on his arms made him look like a churro. He was holding a bottle of liquor.

"Hey, baby! Finally!" he said.

Alyssa kissed the guy. Behind him in the house were a group of people were partying. They were all drinking, smoking and playing beer pong. Kids were scattered around the house, drunk.

Alyssa pointed to Niyah.

"This is my friend, Niyah," she said. "Niyah, this is my boyfriend, Nick."

Nick hugged Niyah.

"The track star!" he said. "You wanna race me?"

They all laughed. He was extremely drunk, slurring his words and barely able to hold himself up on the wall. Nick handed Alyssa the bottle of liquor.

"Okay, our rules here are that you have to take a shot to get in the party," he said.

Alyssa laughed and took a shot from the bottle. She tried to hand the bottle to Niyah. Niyah pushed the bottle back toward Alyssa.

"No thank you. I told you I'm not drinking tonight." She turned to Nick and said, "I just came to make sure your girl got here and back safely."

"Come on! It's a party," Nick exclaimed.

Alyssa put the bottle in Niyah's face.

"Come on, Niyah! Just a little peer pressure!" she said.

"Yeah, you can't get in unless you take a shot! Let's go," Nick shouted.

Niyah looked at them, rolled her eyes and smiled. She grabbed the bottle from Alyssa and screamed, "YOLO!" She took a shot of liquor. She gagged as she handed the bottle to Nick. "That was so nasty."

Nick moved to the side and let Alyssa and Niyah inside the house.

"You may enter," he said.

They walked in, ready to party.

Hours later, Niyah was lying on the couch drunk. Alyssa and a couple of girls from the party came and sat by Niyah. Alyssa handed Niyah a cup and made her drink.

Niyah pushed Alyssa's hand and said, "No more!"

"Drink it! It's good!"

Niyah took a small sip. The girls laughed. Alyssa made Niyah drink some more.

"Come on! Don't give up on me now," Alyssa said.

Niyah chugged some more liquor from the cup and Alyssa pushed the cup to her mouth. Niyah finally dropped the cup and bent over coughing.

The girls laughed as they danced and smoked. A guy came over and stood in front of Niyah.

"You're a pretty little thang. What's your name?" he asked.

Niyah looked up at him.

"Who me?" she said.

The guy smiled showing his perfect teeth.

"Yes, ma'am," he said.

Niyah stuttered, "It's ummm...Ni...ni..."

Alyssa laughed and said, "It's Niyah."

The guy grinned and extended his hand to Niyah.

"Hi, Niyah. I'm Jeff. You looking real good."

Niyah tried to stand up and shake Jeff's hand, but she fell back on the couch. The girls laughed. Alyssa lifted her up.

"She's a little drunk right now," Alyssa said. "And now we have to dance."

Alyssa and all the girls grabbed Niyah. They got in the middle of the room and started dancing. Jeff sat on the couch eyeing Niyah lustfully. Jeff's friend, Joey, came and sat on the couch handing Jeff a beer.

"I know that look," Joey said.

Jeff pointed to Niyah.

"The black chick is kind of hot," he said.

All of a sudden, Niyah looked as if she was going to vomit. She ran to the bathroom. Alyssa and the girls ran after her.

Jeff smiled. "I think I might want that tonight."

Joey looked at him disgusted.

"Dude, she's drunk," he said.

"Yeah, so?" Jeff said then smiled and took a gulp of his beer.

The girls were in the bathroom holding Niyah's hair back as she vomited.

One of the girls, Tracy, held Niyah's hair out of her face.

"Oh my gosh! This looks like the exorcist," she said.

They laughed as Niyah finished throwing up. Alyssa flushed the toilet and grabbed some toilet paper. She wiped Niyah's mouth.

"You all done throwing up, crazy girl?" she asked.

Niyah nodded her head yes and moaned. She climbed into the bathtub and laid down. Another girl, Megan, stared at Niyah.

"Should we just leave her in the tub like this?" she asked.

Niyah lay in the tub with her eyes closed, drunk out of her mind. Alyssa laughed and replied, "She is knocked the hell out! I don't even think she knows where she is." She walked up to Niyah and rubbed her face. "Niyah, baby. We're going to leave you in the tub because you're drunk. If you have to throw up the toilet is right here. I'll come and check on you okay?"

Niyah said nothing as she lay in the tub.

Alyssa shook her trying to wake her up. "Niyah! Niyah, did you hear me?"

Niyah nodded her head yes and slumped down into the tub.

The girls laughed as Megan said, "She has made the tub a bed." The girls left the bathroom and closed the door behind them.

The girls returned to the party and began drinking and dancing again. Jeff noticed Niyah was not with them. He snuck off from the party to go find her.

He looked in the bedrooms until he reached the bathroom. He opened the door and found Niyah hunched over the tub. He closed the door and locked it. He went over to her and grabbed by her stomach. "Woah! What are you doing?" Jeff placed Niyah back in the tub.

Niyah tried to talk. "Alyssa...Alyssa..."

Jeff looked around and smiled. He placed his beer on the floor and climbed in the tub on top of Niyah. He took off her shirt and her shorts. He grabbed her breasts and rubbed her stomach.

"You are so pretty for a black girl," he said.

He lifted her up to un-snap her bra. She slightly hit her head on the tub as Jeff placed her back down. She slowly woke and rubbed her head. As she looked around disoriented, Jeff pulled a condom from his pocket.

Niyah finally realized that Jeff was on top of her. She tried to push him off. He pinned her hands down. Arms heavy from alcohol, she squirmed as she tried to get her hands free. She tried to scream. "Help, Aly... Help me." Her screams were slurred and the music in the other room was too loud for anyone to hear. Jeff unzipped his pants and straddled Niyah. Mustering her focus, fighting the booze she yelled, "Stop get off of me! Get off!" She did her best to loosen his grip, but he was too strong. "Get off of me! Help me!"

He covered her mouth.

"Shut the hell up!" he said.

She bit him. He punched her across her face. Niyah spit out blood and thrashed her body, throwing her limbs into the sides of the tub and against his legs which held her in place. Jeff grabbed both her hands with his left hand. He took his right hand and pulled down her underwear.

Niyah continued to kick and scream trying to get Jeff off her. The alcohol made her movements slow, and she struggled to speak.

"Please, don't do this," she said. "Get off!"

Jeff choked her.

"Just relax, Shaniqua," he said. "I'm going to take care of you."

He unzipped his pants. He grabbed his penis from his underwear and put on the condom. He thrust inside Niyah hard. It burned her as he went inside. Niyah jumped and screamed. Jeff laughed.

Niyah began to cry and scream, "Please get off of me! Get off…"

Jeff thrust against Niyah as she cried, sweat dripping down his face onto her body. He choked her, silencing her yells. As Jeff continued to have sex with her, Niyah's vision tunneled into blackness. Her lungs burned, his hand still closed around her throat. Her mind sunk into unconsciousness while her body jostled around the tub with Jeff.

The party was starting to die down. Drunk kids lay everywhere, and the music had been turned down. Alyssa was sitting on Nick's lap on the couch sipping a mixed drink out of her cup. "Let me go check on Niyah. Be right back." Alyssa took one last sip and then put her cup down. She stumbled to the bathroom. She tried to open the door, but it was locked. She knocked hard.

"Niyah… Niyah open the door," Alyssa said.

No answer. She put her ear to the door. She heard a male's voice. Alyssa began beating on the door.

"Open this door!" she yelled.

No answer.

Alyssa ran to get Nick and the girls. She began to panic.

"Nick! Come with me! I think someone is in the bathroom with Niyah, but the door is locked!"

Nick, Alyssa, Megan and Tracy ran to the bathroom.

Inside the bathroom, Jeff had pulled up his pants and was getting dressed. Niyah was passed out in the tub. Jeff threw the condom in the toilet and flushed it. He wiped the blood from Niyah's lip with some toilet paper and flushed that down the toilet as well.

"At least I didn't punch you that hard," he said.

He then pulled Niyah's underwear and shorts up. He lifted Niyah attempting to put her bra back on. Niyah lay there, lifeless. Jeff struggled to get her bra snapped.

"Come on, Shaniqua, help me out here," he said.

Jeff heard knocking on the outside of the door. He dropped the bra. He grabbed Niyah's shirt and put that on her. He threw the bra across the room.

Nick was outside beating on the bathroom door.

"Open this door!" he yelled.

He began to kick it attempting to break down the door, but it wouldn't open. Nick kept kicking. Suddenly, the door flew open. Alyssa and the girls ran to Niyah as Nick charged towards Jeff.

"What the hell were you doing, man?" Nick asked.

The girls tried to get Niyah out of the tub as Alyssa attacked Jeff.

"What the hell did you do to her, you asshole?!" she yelled.

Jeff yelled at the group.

"Nothing!" he said. "I was just helping her out! She's drunk! Get off of me!"

Nick punched Jeff. Jeff fell to the floor. Alyssa noticed Niyah's bra on the floor. She could see bruises forming on Niyah's face and that her shorts were unzipped.

"Oh my God! Oh my God!" she yelled, beginning to cry.

Nick noticed the bruises too and turned to Jeff. Nick punched Jeff in the nose. Jeff fell to the floor in agony. Nick moved the girls out of the way and picked Niyah up in his arms. Niyah lay there, not moving a muscle. Nick turned to Alyssa.

"Come on, let's go! We have to go!" Nick said, and the girls rushed Niyah out of the party into the car.

Alyssa was crying, holding Niyah.

"I'm so sorry, Niyah," she said. "I'm so sorry! Oh my God. Nick, get us to the hospital! Please!" Nick put his foot to the gas and sped down the street toward the hospital.

Niyah was rushed to the hospital as nurses and doctors worked to get her stable. She lay there as the nurses asked the group of kid's questions and gave her a rape kit. She was lying on the hospital bed with her eyes closed, imagining she was on the track about to run. She imagined herself smiling and getting down into her blocks, looking into the sunset. She could hear her name being called.

"Niyah. Niyah."

Niyah woke from her dream when she heard the nurse calling her name. Her eyes adjusted to the light and were wide open as she looked around the well-lit hospital room. She sat up slowly and realized she was still in the hospital bed instead of on the track. Alyssa was sitting at the table next to her bed.

A nurse was at the edge of her bed looking up at her.

"Niyah, you have a visitor from the rape council," the nurse said. "Is it okay if she comes in?"

Niyah nodded her head yes. The nurse motioned for Mandy, a young red headed woman, to come in.

"Hi, Niyah. It's nice to meet you," Mandy said.

Niyah stayed silent and stared at the hospital band on her arm. Mandy continued to talk.

"I'm with the rape council of North Hill and the hospital calls us when things like this happen," she said. "I just want you to know that we from the rape counsel have all been where you have, and I know this is difficult for you to overcome."

Niyah continued to stay silent.

Mandy continued. "I know they took your clothes for more tests, so I bought you some pants and a shirt to wear home. I also bought you a little teddy bear and some pamphlets on how to talk to your loved ones about what happened."

Mandy tried to hand Niyah all the materials. Niyah didn't move. Alyssa got up and grabbed the materials from Mandy.

"I'll take it," she said, setting everything on the table next to her. Mandy turned back to Niyah.

"If you need to talk, Niyah, please don't hesitate to call."

Niyah looked up at her and said, "Thank you."

"And we want you to know, alcohol is not a green light. This was rape. It's not your fault." Mandy walked out of the room and closed the door.

A police officer walked in.

"Okay, Ms. Coleman. We have all your clothes and your kit. We are definitely going to continue to look into this. We do not let stuff like this go. We have questioned all your friends, we just have to wait for all the tests to come back. We will be in touch, okay?"

Niyah nodded her head yes.

Alyssa chimed in.

"So you just can't go and arrest him?" she said.

The officer turned to Alyssa. "At this point, no. He has been questioned, but it's her word against his until we get the test results back." The officer looked back to Niyah. "I'm sorry about this. I will be calling you soon." The officer walked out of the room.

Alyssa got up and sat next to Niyah on the hospital bed.

"I am so sorry I left you in there. This is all my fault. I am so sorry," said Alyssa as she began to sob.

Niyah looked down at the floor.

"It's not your fault, Alyssa. I should have never been drinking," Niyah said.

Alyssa grabbed Niyah's arm.

"No. I made you come along," she said. "I made you drink. Don't do that to yourself. Don't blame yourself. It's not your fault! I shouldn't have made you drink at all after you said you didn't want to!"

"No one can make me do anything, Alyssa. I just need you to take me to Brooke's house," she said.

"Of course. Let me ask the nurse can you leave."

"No, I want to go. Now," asserted Niyah.

Alyssa looked at Niyah sadly. She nodded her head yes.

"Okay. I'll go get all your paperwork," she daintily replied.

She got out of the bed and walked out of the room.

Niyah got up and grabbed the clothes Mandy brought her. She walked into the bathroom and sat on the floor. She threw the clothes and punched the wall. She kept punching until her knuckles bled. She plopped down to the floor and puked in the toilet. She fell to the floor and cried.

The afternoon was approaching as Alyssa pulled into Brooke's apartment complex. She parked the car and turned off the engine. She looked at Niyah and sighed.

"Niyah, I really am sorry," she said.

"I know."

"Do you want me to go in with you?"

Niyah shook her head no. She grabbed the pamphlets and put them in her purse. She grabbed the teddy bear and opened the door to the car. Her knuckles were wrapped, and she still wore the hospital band on her wrist. Alyssa hugged Niyah, but Niyah did not hug her back. Alyssa let her go and Niyah got out of the car. She closed the door and walked up to Brooke's door as Alyssa stared at her then drove off. Niyah took a deep breath and knocked on the door.

Brook answered. She saw that it was Niyah and hugged her.

"Hey, you! I didn't know you were coming! Where have you been? I been trying to call you." Brooke stopped hugging Niyah and looked at her face. She grabbed Niyah's wrapped hands and saw the hospital band. She frowned at Niyah and rubbed her arm.

"Nini, what the hell happened to you?" she asked.

Niyah stood there in silence before shedding tears.

"I was raped last night, Brooke."

Brooke stood there shocked and grabbed Niyah.

"Oh my God! Niyah, are you okay?"

Niyah fell to the ground in tears. Brooke sat next to her in the doorway as they both quietly wept.

Later that night, Niyah lay in Brooke's bed, speechless. Brooke brought her a plate covered with baked chicken, rice and mixed vegetables. She also bought

Niyah a bag of skittles. Niyah cracked a smile and sat up in the bed. She grinned as she took the plate and skittles from Brooke. Brooke sat down next to her on the bed.

"Now you know I can't cook, but you need to eat," she said. "And I bought you your favorite thing in the world! These skittles."

Niyah smiled and stared at the food.

"I'm just not hungry," she said.

"Yeah, well you need to eat. Is it just my food?" Brooke asked.

Niyah laughed a little and grimaced at the food. "You know I love you, Brooke, right?" she claimed while smiling.

Brooke laughed.

"Yeah, you know I can't cook. I'll order you some pizza," she said and took out her phone to order pizza as Niyah lay there in silence.

"All right, got you some pepperoni pizza on the way," Brooke said and rubbed Niyah's hair. "I'm so sorry this happened, Niyah. I blame Alyssa's stupid ass. Why would she leave you in the tub like that?" Brooke choked on the words.

Niyah sighed and told her, "It's not her fault, B. It's mine."

Brooke jumped up out of the bed and bawled, "Niyah, look at me! Don't do that! This is not your fault!"

Niyah stared at Brooke but said nothing. Brooke sat back down next to her and embraced Niyah.

"I'm sorry," Brooke said. "I'm getting emotional because she should have never left you there like that."

Niyah hugged Brooke back.

"I know, Brooke. I know."

Brooke handed Niyah her cell phone.

"Laurie called looking for you. I told her you were over here, but that's all I said. I didn't tell her anything else."

"She keeps looking for me, and I don't know why," Niyah said. "I'll call her later. She doesn't want anything."

Laurie was in her dorm room when there was a loud bang on the door. She opened it. Sean was standing there with a vexed looked on his face.

"Did you find out where she was?" he asked.

Laurie stepped forward trying to make sure Sean did not get in the room.

"Yes, but I'm not telling you where she is, so stop asking me," Laurie stressed.

"I just want to talk to her," he said.

Sean pushed Laurie into the room and into a wall. He snatched her by her neck. "Now where is she?"

Barely breathing, Laurie looked up at him terrified and stammered, "She's…she's at Brooke's!"

Sean tightened his grip around Laurie's neck.

"And where is that?" he said, finally letting go of Laurie's neck.

"Bay Student Apartments. Apartment 115," she uttered while trying to regain her breath.

Sean put his face so close to Laurie's she could feel his hot breath on her eyelids. He looked at her and threatened, "You better not be lying either, or there will be a problem."

He exited the room fast, slamming the door behind him. Laurie ran for her phone and started dialing.

"Gary! Where are you?"

Back in Brooke's bedroom, Niyah and Brooke were still sitting on the bed talking. Brooke asked Niyah, "Are you going to tell your family?"

"I'm scared of what my brothers will do when they find out," Niyah confessed. She pulled out the pamphlets Mandy gave her from her purse. "I don't want to talk about it. I'm just going to let the police do their job."

"Well are you ever going to take that off before Gary sees?" Brooke pointed to the hospital band on her wrists.

Niyah looked at the hospital band and stayed quiet. Brooke sighed and rubbed Niyah's shoulders.

"You want me to run you a bath? I'll sit in there, so you won't be in there alone. I know you're still a little freaked out," she said.

"You go ahead. I'll take a shower after you. Me and the tub thing right now is not a good idea," she said. "I just want to sit here for a second."

"Okay. You just sit here and wait on the pizza. You're going to eat, Nini. Please eat." Brooke kissed Niyah on the forehead. She grabbed some clothes, her phone, and towel and went into the bathroom.

Niyah put the plate of food Brooke had made her on the side table and started looking through the pamphlets. She came across one that read "How to tell your significant other you've been sexually assaulted." She heard the shower running and looked at the bathroom door. She started to imagine herself in the tub with Jeff on top of her. She visualized him pulling her pants down and kissing on her. Her eyes twitched as she became infuriated. There was a loud knock at the front door. Niyah snapped out of her daydream. She looked at the bathroom door. She could hear Brooke in the shower singing through the falling water drops. Another loud knock came from the door. She got out of the bed still holding the pamphlet and phone. She headed towards the front door whispering to herself, "That pizza was fast."

She heard another loud knock. Niyah paused for a slight second. She walked into the front room and opened the front door. Sean was standing there. Niyah jumped at the sight of him. Her legs trembled underneath her. She nervously asked, "Sean, what the hell are you doing here? How did you find me?"

Sean smirked and replied, "I should have known you were at Brooke's house. We all know you like bitches."

"Sean, please just leave me alone."

Sean grabbed Niyah's face. She moved her head away from his hand.

"Your lip looks a little swollen, Nini. What happened?"

He tried to touch her lip.

Niyah slapped his hand down.

"Nothing," she lied.

"Nothin, huh? Come outside. Let's talk. Now," he commanded.

"I don't want to talk to your ass," she snapped. Niyah tried to close the door.

Sean yanked her arm causing her to fall forward. She dropped the pamphlet and her phone. She tried to pick up the pamphlet, but Sean snatched it before she could grab it.

He read the pamphlet and glared at her.

"What the hell is this for?"

Niyah said nothing. Sean noticed the hospital band on her arm.

"Were you... were you raped?" he asked.

Niyah looked at him in tears. He burst out laughing.

"This is great! This is fantastic! Oh shit! You go around telling everyone I beat you up, and then you go and get your ass raped. How does that make you look?" Sean started laughing even harder. He went on asking, "So you let some guy take what's mine?"

"I didn't let him Sean! He raped me!" Niyah hollered.

"You probably led him on, knowing you," Sean teased.

"You're such an asshole." Niyah whimpered as she yelled, "I hate you!"

Sean wasn't done taunting Niyah. He leaned against the door and grinned. "So tell me how did this happen?"

"I was drunk at a party and my girls... the girls left me in the tub. He came in and did it."

Sean looked into the sky at the twinkling stars and pondered. He rubbed his beard and repeated, "So you were drunk at a party? And you let some dude rape you? And you were complaining because I didn't let your dumb ass go to parties. That's what you get!"

"What the hell is wrong with you? It's not like I went and was like 'hey I'm drunk, come rape me.'" Niyah at this point was embarrassed and hurt. Her stomach turned in knots.

"Might as well have! You hang with dumb bitches and do dumb things, then dumb things happen to you!" Sean roared with laughter.

"You are so evil I swear! I hate you!"

"Does your mom know?"

"No she does not!" Niyah claimed.

Sean grabbed Niyah and pulled her outside. He picked up Niyah's phone from the ground and found her mom's number. He dialed it and put the phone to his ear.

"What the hell are you doing?" Niyah tried to grab the phone from Sean.

Sean pushed Niyah down to the concrete. Niyah banged her knee on the pavement, ripping a hole in her jeans. Her knee started to bleed as she held it in pain.

Tammi answered the phone. "Hey, Niyah. What's the matter?"

Sean started talking to Tammi. "Hello? Is this Mrs. Coleman?"

Tammi paused before replying, "Yes! Who is this?"

Niyah got up and grabbed Sean's arm. "Sean, what the hell are you doing? Stop it! Please don't do this," she pleaded.

Sean pushed Niyah into a car. Her back hit the rear view mirror. She fell back to the ground in pain.

Sean continued to talk on the phone. "I'm calling to let you know that your daughter was raped, and she needs to take her ass home now!"

Tammi screeched, "What?! What are you talking about? Where is she? Let me talk to her! Hello? Hello?"

Sean hung up the phone.

Niyah got up slowly rubbing her back. She was in tears.

"Are you crazy?" she said. "Why would you do that?"

Niyah tried to get the phone from him.

He held her back with one arm laughing at her.

"That's what you get!" he said. "You let someone take what's mine!"

Sean pushed her to the ground once again.

Niyah got up and pushed him back screaming, "That's my mom! Why would you do that?" Her tears were flooding down her face. She went for the phone again.

Sean laughed at her attempts and pushed her again. Niyah gave up.

"Fuck it! Keep the phone. I never want to see you again!" Niyah exclaimed as she walked off.

"No! We're going to talk about this!" Sean threw the phone at her. It hit Niyah in the back of the head. He ran after her and grabbed her by her neck choking her. He threw her into another parked car. Then he ran over and started choking her again.

"I loved you! Why would you do this to me?" He threw her to the ground on her back. He put his knee on her throat and rested his weight on it.

She tried to scream, so he covered her mouth with his hands. She slapped him hard across his face trying to get his knee off her throat. He removed his knee and snatched her up by her hair.

Niyah screamed, "Stop it, Sean! Stop! Get off of me!"

Sean hurled her to the curb. He kicked her in her stomach three times. Niyah rolled on the ground holding her stomach. Sean picked her up and tossed her on the hood of a car. She kicked him in the face. He tumbled to the ground. Niyah gasped for air. Sean licked the blood from his lip. He grabbed Niyah and threw her across the parking lot to the concrete. He slapped her in the face and punched her in the ribs. Niyah screamed. Suddenly, a female neighbor from across the street came outside.

"What the hell are you doing to her?" the woman yelled.

Niyah lay on the ground, not moving.

Sean turned to the neighbor, screaming at the top of his lungs, "Mind your own goddamn business! Y'all don't know the hell she's put me through!"

Niyah, at a snail's pace, picked herself up. She picked a rock and threw it at his face. It hit him in the nose. He ran after her and grabbed her by her shoulders and slapped her hard, busting her lip. She fell to the ground in agony. The neighbor's boyfriend and four of his friends were now outside. The neighbor's boyfriend stepped into the parking lot.

"Hey! What the hell are you doing?" one of the men said. "That's a girl, man! She small as hell! What the fuck is wrong with you!?"

Sean ranted, "Fuck you! You don't know me! You don't know what she does to me. How she makes me feel! This is her fault! And this ain't got nothin' to do with you. So what you wanna' do?"

The neighbor's boyfriend and his friends were surrounding Sean. They argued back and forth with Sean. Words were tossed from the friends and Sean. Before he knew it, Sean punched the neighbor's boyfriend. He punched Sean back. The guys all rushed towards Sean. He fell to the ground in a fetal position, trying his best to cover his face. The guys punched and kicked him until he started spitting out teeth and blood. Niyah screamed to the top of her lungs.

"No! No! Stop before you kill him. Please!" She pleaded with the guys, but they continued to beat Sean. She ran over and tried to stop the fight. The girl neighbor ran over and grabbed her.

"Let them beat his ass!" she said. "He deserves it!"

Niyah cried out, trying to stop the guys from killing Sean.

Brooke was out of the shower blow drying her hair. She grabbed her phone and saw ten missed calls from Laurie. She stopped blow drying and heard Niyah's screams. She ran into the bedroom and saw Niyah was not there.

"Niyah?" she called out.

Brooke heard another scream from Niyah outside. Brooke ran out of the bathroom and out the front door.

Brooke ran outside and saw Niyah being held back by her neighbor. Niyah was screaming at the top of her lungs. Her screams ripped through the apartment complex. Brooke ran and grabbed Niyah. Police sirens were heard close by as the other neighbors piled into the parking lot to see what the commotion was about. The guys ran off. The neighbor's boyfriend kicked Sean one more time in the face.

"Bitch ass, hitting a female!" he said, then looked at Niyah before he ran off. They hopped the fence and disappeared into the night as the police pulled up. Sean was lying in a pool of blood. Niyah broke free from Brooke and the neighbor. She limped to Sean as the police car pulled up. The policeman called for an ambulance and hopped out of the car. Sean's blood covered Niyah's jeans as she tried to help comfort him.

She held on to his head, crying. She then looked down at her clothes and felt her face. She swallowed the blood inside her lip. She bent down and whispered in Sean's ear, "This is what you get." She dropped his head on the pavement.

Sean staggered to his feet, pushed Niyah off as the police grabbed him and sat him down on the curb. His jaw was hanging, and blood dripped to the ground. Gary and Laurie pulled up in the car. They hopped out and ran to Niyah. Sean spit out more blood and teeth as the police carried him towards a cruiser. Gary rushed toward Sean and tried to attack him. The officer held Gary back as Sean fell to the ground. The crowd watched as the unraveling situation came to an end.

Niyah was getting her face looked at by paramedics and talking to the cops. Sean was in the ambulance getting worked on. Neighbors were still outside watching as the police questioned Niyah.

"According to your other neighbors, Sean, that guy over there, was hitting you, and some guys ran out and fought him. Can you identify these men?"

Niyah shook her head no. The police officer wrote in his notepad. He continued, "Would you like to press charges on Mr. Sean Johnson?"

Niyah looked at Sean. He continued to spit out blood. He caught Niyah's eyes. They stared at each other. Niyah nodded her head yes. Gary noticed the hospital band on Niyah's arm and grabbed it. He rubbed her wrists as she looked away into the night, ashamed. Gary turned his attention to the paramedic.

"Is she going to be okay?" he asked.

"Well, she sprained some back muscles and twisted her ankle a little bit. Might be hard for her to walk for a couple of days. A busted lip, a black eye and some minor bruising and scratching," the guy said. "Sean on the other hand has a broken jaw and will need immediate surgery. He will be eating from a straw for at least a month or so. I'd say she's pretty lucky."

Niyah's friends all looked at him when he said the word lucky.

The policeman cleared his throat and said, "She will need to come downtown to finish the report if she wants to press charges. She's free to go for now."

The policeman handed Gary a copy of the report. Gary thanked him.

Brooke grabbed Niyah.

"Let's go, Nini," she said. Brook and Gary helped Niyah up and into the house.

In the apartment, everyone sat down in the living room.

"I gotta use the bathroom," Niyah said, managing to stand.

She limped toward the bathroom and closed the door.

Gary got up and punched the wall. Brooke stood up and scolded Gary. "Hey! Look! I know you're mad. We all are! But don't tear up my house!" she said. "Calm down, Gary." Brooke walked up to him and grabbed his shoulders. "Come on. Sit down."

Gary's legs were shaking.

"I swear to God, I'm going to kill him!" he said. "I should have done so a long time ago. Should have put an end to this shit. Fuck!"

Brooke asked, "How did he know she was here? How in the hell does he even know where I live?"

Laurie looked down, disappointed in herself.

"He came to the dorm threatening me to tell him where she was," she admitted.

Brooke retaliated, "Damn, Laurie! Is that why you called looking for her? What the hell!?"

"I'm sorry! He threatened me! He pushed my ass against the wall and choked me. Scared the hell out of me. I tried to call you!"

Gary looked at Brooke and asked, "But why did she already have a hospital band on her arm?"

Brooke sighed struggling to find the words to tell Gary about the night before.

"She was raped at the party Alyssa took her to."

Laurie and Gary mouths dropped as they reacted to the news.

Laurie cried out, "Oh my God!"

Gary buried his head in his hands.

Niyah was in the bathroom staring at herself in the mirror. She lifted her shirt and saw some bruises on her back. The past two days' events played back in her head like an old movie. She thought about the rape, the fight with Sean, the fight with Alisha, and her entire life for the past year. She pulled down her pants and saw blood running down her legs. She closed her eyes and cried. Niyah looked in the cabinet and found some of Brooke's pills. She poured a handful of them in her hand. She put them all in her mouth. She turned on the water facet and drank hand-fulls of water. She swallowed the pills. She then took a razor and made two deep cuts in each of her wrists. She dropped the razor on the floor as blood splattered everywhere. The blood poured from her wrists into the sink. Niyah looked in the mirror, grabbed the counter and fell to the floor.

Gary, Laurie and Brooke were still sitting on the couch in silence.

Brooke got up and headed towards the bathroom.

"I'm going to check on my baby," she said.

She walked in the other room and knocked on the door.

"Niyah, are you okay?" she called.

There was no answer.

"Nini, can you just say something so I know you're okay?"

Still no answer.

Brooke started to panic. She began beating on the door. She tried to open it, but it was locked. Brooke yelled, "Niyah, please open the door! Come on open the door!"

Gary and Laurie ran into the room and looked at Brooke.

"What's wrong?" he asked.

"I don't know, she's not answering! The door is locked, and she's not answering!"

Gary looked around the room. He ordered Brooke, "go get me a hanger or something!"

Brooke went to her closet and grabbed a wire hanger. She handed it to Gary. He twisted the hanger and stuck it in the lock. He wiggled the hanger around until the door unlocked. They rushed in and saw Niyah on the floor. Spit foamed from her mouth. Her wrists were bleeding and her eyes were half way open. They tried to wake her up.

Brooke ran and started to shake her screaming, "Niyah baby, please wake up!"

Gary turned to Laurie.

"Go call an ambulance," he said.

Brooke looked up at Gary crying out loud.

"Gary, what do I do? Do I make her throw up? What do we do?"

Gary grabbed Niyah and held her.

"Niyah, what did you do, baby girl?" he asked.

The empty bottle of pills lay on the floor. Brooke cried as Laurie called the ambulance.

The doctors worked to keep Niyah alive. They pumped her stomach and tried to get her breathing. Laurie, Gary and Brooke watched from outside the hospital room until a nurse made them go to the waiting room. Brooke and Laurie begin crying as Gary tried to console them.

24

Will to Live

Hours later, Niyah was lying in the hospital bed sleeping. The doctors saved her life. Her breathing was stable, but her blood pressure was high. Tammi walked into the room, went over to Niyah and started rubbing her head. Niyah woke up slowly. She saw her mother and smiled.

"Mommy, when did you get here?" she asked.

"I got in the car as soon as I got that phone call," Tammi said. "We all drove up here." Tammi looked as if she had been crying for hours. Her eyes were baggy, and her eyeliner was smeared. She kissed her daughter on the forehead. "How are you, my baby," she asked.

Niyah whimpered, "I'm fine, Mama."

"No you're not fine, Niyah. You tried to kill yourself, baby. That scares me! I've been crying my eyes out. What happened?"

Niyah began to cry. "I just lost it! After getting beat up by my boyfriend and then raped, I didn't know what to do! Why is God punishing me? What did I do?"

Tammi held her daughter and began to cry.

"Baby! I'm so sorry I wasn't there to protect you. Why didn't you say anything about him hitting you? You have too many people that love you that would have helped you!"

Niyah wailed in her mother's arm.

"I don't know!" she sobbed. "He made me feel so alone and low. I started to believe him and believe he was all I had."

"Look at me, Niyah. Nothing in this world makes me more proud than my children. You are my pride and joy. I am always here! I love you more than life itself. I would do anything for you!"

"I love you too, Mom. I'm so sorry!"

Tammi grabbed Niyah as they cried together.

Niyah sat in bed surrounded by her family. There was a knock at the door. Coach Jones stood at the door with flowers.

Niyah noticed him and smiled.

"Coach!"

Coach Jones walked in and placed the flowers on the table next to the bed.

"How are you feeling?" Coach Jones asked.

She sarcastically replied, "I'm in the greatest mood ever." She smiled at her coach and continued, "I'm just ready to get out of here! I'm missing too much practice!"

Coach Jones looked around the room and then placed his eyes back at Niyah.

"Well, there are some things that we need to discuss first," he said.

Tammi turned to everyone and said, "Hey, guys, let's go downstairs and get some food while they talk."

Everyone got up and left Coach Jones and Niyah alone. Coach Jones sat in a chair next to Niyah's bed.

"How are you really feeling?" he asked.

Niyah answered, "I'll live."

"Niyah, why didn't you tell me Sean was hitting you?"

Niyah shrugged. "I'm fine now, Coach, I'm just ready to run."

Coach Jones sighed, "I don't think that's going to happen, Niyah."

Niyah reassured, "Coach, look. If this is about my injuries, the doctor said I'll be fine. As long as I use a mixture of heat and ice, wrap myself, take my meds and…"

Coach Jones interrupted her. "It's not that, Niyah. You just tried to commit suicide! You were sexually assaulted. I don't think in two weeks you will be mentally ready. Track is a mental sport. Eighty percent mental, twenty percent physical," he said. "Your parents and I have already talked, and we think it's best if they take you home and transfer your credits to a junior college. If you do well there in a year maybe you can come back."

Niyah sat up and said, "What? No! Why do I have to leave and come back? I'm okay now!"

"You're not okay, Niyah. We all care about you and love you. We all want you to do well."

Niyah begged, "Coach, people that go to junior colleges don't come back! Please don't do this," Niyah cried.

Coach Jones put his hand on Niyah's shoulder.

"Niyah, no one in this world wants you to run more than I do," he said.

"Then why are you sending me home?" Niyah whined.

"Because your life is more important than track."

Niyah snapped and yelled, "This is my life! If you send me home, I will die! That guy raped me in a bathtub and less than 24 hours later, the guy I thought loved me beat the hell out of me! Of course I'm going to have a breakdown, but I can run! That's the only thing I know how to do! That's the only thing that keeps me sane! Please don't take that away from me!"

"I'm sorry, Niyah. I want you to run, but I need you to live. You're going to go home, get you some help, and come back stronger."

Niyah wept harder and put her face in her pillow.

"I'm so sorry, Niyah."

Coach Jones sat there trying to console Niyah as she cried.

25
It's Over

Niyah was in her dorm room packing up her stuff.

Laurie walked out of the bathroom and hugged Niyah from behind.

"I'm going to miss you," she said.

Niyah turned around and hugged her saying, "I'm going to miss you too."

Laurie began to sob.

"They took away my scholarship for now," Laurie said. "I actually have to go to class."

Niyah laughed and replied, "At least you get to stay. What did the doctor say?"

"He just didn't clear me for this meet. I'll be a walk on next year and try to earn my scholarship back. When are your parents coming?"

"Tonight. They asked if I wanted to go to the track meet. I said no."

"Coach is letting me go as the water girl. We leave tomorrow. You can still change your mind."

Niyah continued to pack her things.

"It would just make everything worse," she said. "I want to run so bad. I've been at the track every day."

Laurie put her hand on Niyah's back.

"I know. Have you talked to Sean?"

Niyah grimaced and said, "Hell to the no. I pressed charges and put a restraining order on him. I told them everything. I mean, I've hit him too, but he really has tried to kill me. Even when I didn't want to fight him no more, he still wanted to fight me."

"Well I'm glad you put a restraining order on his crazy ass. Listen, Nini, I'm sorry I told him where you were. I'm so so…"

Niyah stopped her and said, "Laurie, don't. You were scared. I understand."

"These men in this school are crazy. We got what we asked for, some men. Dante called and checked on me, but that's over."

"Don't talk to him, Laurie. Please, just leave that behind you," Niyah advised.

Laurie smiled and agreed.

"Trust me, girl, I know. Never again. He still fine as hell though." They both laughed. Laurie started to help Niyah pack. Her face frowned as she said, "I just don't know why you didn't tell us what was going on, Niyah."

Niyah stopped packing and shrugged her shoulders. She confided in Laurie.

"I really don't know. I was embarrassed. Prideful. Lonely. I wasn't necessarily scared of him. I was just… real nervous about what he could do to me. It's like I was stuck. I didn't know what to do. I was really just ashamed."

"You had no reason to be. I told you about Dante. Now that was embarrassing."

Niyah laughed. Laurie grabbed Niyah's arms. She lectured, "Just know we would do anything for you. Including kill some crazy bastard that put his hands on you. We would have gotten you out of there. Don't ever do that again. Like for real. You almost died. You were depressed. Cutting yourself and pills and shit. No, ma'am. You can come to us."

Niyah smiled.

"I know, Laurie. I feel that way too about your drinking. You can come to me, seriously. Just call me, write me a letter, whatever you need to do!" She walked over to Laurie and put her hand on her stomach. "I'm so sorry about the miscarriage."

"Me too," Laurie said. "I can't believe that happened. I'm going to cut down on the drinking. Just like track is for you, the alcohol was the only way I could cope. I'll find another way."

They embraced each other in a long hug. There was a knock at the door. Laurie went to open it. Alisha was standing there. Laurie looked at her surprised.

"Oh. Hi, Alisha," Laurie said.

Alisha forced a smile.

"Hi, Laurie. How are feeling?"

"I'm fine. How are you, Alisha?"

"I'm good," Alisha replied. They stood there without speaking for a couple of seconds. Laurie spoke up first and apologized.

"Look, Alisha. I never apologized for anything I did. I'm sorry if I hurt you. I didn't know about you at first and when I did, I was already caught up and…"

Alisha interrupted her, "Hey. It's okay. We good. He cheated, not you. We straight."

Laurie smiled at her. Alisha smiled back.

"Is Niyah here?" Alisha asked.

Niyah came running up.

"Yeah, I'm here," she said. "I stayed away. I thought y'all were going to kill each other."

They all laughed. Alisha hugged Niyah.

"How are you?" she asked.

Niyah shrugged.

"I'll get better," she said.

Alisha asked, "You want to go to the track with me for a run?"

"Yeah let me get my ankle wrap and my shoes." Niyah ran, grabbed her tennis shoes, and they headed out the door.

Coach Jones was sifting through the new spikes he ordered. Coach Tatem walked into Coach Jones's office.

"How is everything?" Tatem asked.

"Good, just finishing up some things before we head out tomorrow."
Coach Tatem took a seat at the desk.

"You think we'll be okay," Tatem questioned.

Coach Jones lifted his head from the boxes and said, "Yeah, I think we have a great chance."

Coach Tatem nodded his head in agreement.

"Even without Ms. Coleman?"

Coach Jones stared at him. "Tim, she's just not mentally ready. I don't want to put her through that pressure. She's been through enough. Besides, you were the one most concerned about her and damn near pushed her out the door yourself."

"You know I went to see her in the hospital," Tatem said, smiling. "She begged me to run."

Coach Jones retorted, "And what did you tell her?"

"I told her it was up to you and she says, 'Well that's a hell no!'"

Coach Jones laughed as Coach Tatem got up from the chair.

"Look, I'm not just saying this because I want to win. I agree she needs help. But what if track helps her? What's wrong with letting her run and prove herself?"

"What if she has a mental breakdown?" Coach Jones asked.

"And What if she runs her ass off?" Tatem noted. "We'll never know. She's already qualified. It's just going to be an open lane."

Coach Jones sighed.

Coach Tatem finished up by saying, "Just think about it. I'll see you tomorrow." He got up and walked out the office.

Coach Jones contemplated the conversation for a minute and sat behind his desk. He grabbed the phone and made a call.

"May I speak to Tammi Coleman, please?"

Alisha and Niyah were jogging on the track. They finished two laps and sat down on the ground. It was one hundred degrees, and the humidity had both girls huffing and puffing. They grabbed their water bottles and chugged down the ice cold water. Alisha tapped Niyah's ankle lightly.

"That ankle healed up!" she said.

Niyah rubbed her ankle. "Yeah! My back still a little sore, but I'll be okay."

Alisha took another drink of water and murmured, "I wish you were running tomorrow."

Niyah looked down the track.

"Yeah me too," she said. "I love it so much."

Alisha inquired, "How did you start running? We all have our reasons. You know my dad made me. What got you running?"

Niyah stayed silent for a minute before she responded.

"When I was a little girl, my parents used to fight a lot. I would hate to hear them yelling and screaming. I know everyone fights. My parents were just everything to me and usually happy, so I wouldn't want to hear it. I would sneak out the kitchen window and just run! I would run so fast, I would forget about all my problems! Just sprint and pray. That's when I felt closest to God. When it was just me and him. I guess I thought if I talked to him at night, he would focus on me. Then I would go home and everything would be fine and I felt like my problems were gone. Running became a release for me. Every time something bad happened, I would go to the track and run. I would leave all my anger on the track. But when I got here I couldn't..." Niyah shed tears and sobbed and admitted, "I couldn't run away from Sean beating me, and I couldn't run away from getting raped in a tub, and I couldn't run away from getting sent home. I couldn't run away from those problems! So what do you do when your problems run faster than you?"

Alisha put her arm around Niyah's shoulders. "You can't run from your problems, Niyah. You have to face them. You just need to get yourself together and show the world who you are. If God was done with you, you would be dead. You have more things to accomplish. You will overcome this."

Niyah wiped her face and smiled.

"Never in a million years would I have thought I would be sitting here crying and confiding in you."

They both laughed. Niyah's phone rang. She answered the phone, confused.

"Coach?"

26

The Finish Line

The girls pulled up to the Outdoor National Track Meet. It was extremely crowded as family, friends and fans piled into the stadium. Coach Jones turned and spoke to his girls before getting off the bus.

"This is it," he said. "All year long, this is what we've been practicing for. I am so proud of everyone for making it this far. We got this! Just get out there and do what you're supposed to do. You know you are champions. So go out there and show them. This has been a rough year, but let's leave all of that on the track."

"Where it belongs," Niyah said making her way onto the bus.

The girls looked up surprised to see Niyah standing in uniform with her family.

Brooke stood up in her seat saying, "Is this real? Are you running?"

Niyah looked at Coach Jones. He smiled and turned to the team.

"It's real," he said.

The girls all came running to hug Niyah. Renae even hugged Niyah and pulled her close.

"Listen, I'm sorry. For everything. I'm glad you're okay," she said.

Niyah smiled and said, "It's all good. I'm not worrying about any of that. I just want to win today! Let's get it!"

The girls all cheered and hopped off the bus.

The track meet was under way. Races and field events were going on every minute. Coach Jones and Niyah were standing on the field. Niyah was getting ready for her 400 meter dash.

"Are you ready, Niyah?" Coach Jones asked.

Niyah shook her head saying, "Yes, sir."

"You understand why I didn't let you run the four by 100 today right?"

Niyah acknowledged that she understood.

"I know. I understand. They got second. That's good enough," she said, jittery as she paced back and forth, stretching.

"You sure you ready?" Coach Jones laughed, watching her.

Niyah looked at him and said, "I'm ready."

Coach Jones grabbed her shoulders.

"Hey you have to relax. Breathe," he said.

Niyah closed her eyes and inhaled deeply.

"Okay. You know how to do this," he said. "Get out the first fifty meters. You're in lane eight, so I need them to waste their energy having to catch you. I need you to shoot out those blocks, Niyah. Like a bat out of hell. Push out! Do not let up a lot! Stride to the 200 mark but don't ease up too much. They will be on your ass! At that 200 I need to bring it home. All the way. Don't stop until you cross the line. You know you have a tendency to slow down when you're almost at the finish line. Run past that! Lean in. You got this."

Niyah nodded her head saying, "I got this."

Coach Jones patted her on the back and said, "I know. Okay, go ahead. They're calling for you."

Niyah walked over to the official who was gathering all the girls for the 400 meter dash. Niyah's friends and family started applauding her.

As Niyah walked to the track she thought to herself, "you can't let them down, Nini. You have to get out there and win this. Don't doubt yourself. You've done this a million times. You got this."

Niyah stepped on the track in lane eight. She set up her blocks and knelt down to pray. "Dear God, Thank you for this day. Thank you for letting me get another chance to run. Thank you for my second chance at life. Please Lord, guide my feet around this track and empty my mind of all the negative thoughts. Please let me focus on this race. Run fast as I can. In Jesus name, Amen." She finished praying as the shooting official blew his whistle.

The shooting official yelled, "Ladies, stand behind your blocks!"

All the girls stood behind their blocks.

The announcer came over the speakers, "Quiet at the start please." The crowd grew quiet.

The starting official held his gun as he shouted, "Runners, to your mark."

Niyah jumped in the air three times bringing her knees to her chest. She shook both of her legs before bending down, placing her hands on the track. As she lowered her head, she started having flashbacks of her rape and fights with Sean. She shook her head and tried to focus. She climbed back into the blocks and placed her knees on the track. She set her hands apart and took a deep breath.

"Set…"

Niyah rose her butt and knees towards the sky. She looked down at the track. She imagined herself as a little girl running at night in peace. She closed her eyes, waiting for the gun. Her breathing got heavier. Her legs moved slightly. She heard the gun and ran for her life. She heard another gunshot which signaled a false start. All the competitors stopped running and returned to their blocks.

Niyah stood there shaking nervously as the officials walked over to each other to have a conversation. Everyone was anxious to find out who false started. Niyah looked up at her coach and family.

They smiled at her and yelled, "You're fine! You got this!"

Niyah smiled and turned back to the officials. One of the officials headed towards her. She became nervous. Her vision blurred as she lost her breath. Her palms got sweaty, and her heart beat increased. The official walked past her into lane six and removed the competitor's starting blocks. The runner in lane six started crying, and was removed from the track. Niyah let out a loud sigh of relief.

The announcer came back over the intercom saying, "Lane six has been disqualified."

Niyah settled herself. The shooting official got back on his podium. "Runners to your mark… Set…" The shooter shot his gun once again. The girls pushed out of their blocks and sprinted around the first curve. Niyah's family and friends rooted for Niyah as the competitors raced for the title.

Niyah was in second place as they came to the first straight away. Memories began to flash again in Niyah's mind and she slowed down. Competitors passed her as Niyah began breathing heavily. They hit the second curve. Niyah caught up, but it was too late. She had let her competitor get too far ahead. Her legs started to give out, and the heat made it hard for her to breathe. She finished the race in fourth place. Niyah walked off the track disappointed, grabbing her back. Coach Jones ran up to her as she walked off.

"Are you okay?" he asked.

"You were right! I'm not mentally ready. I couldn't get this past year out of my head. Take me off the four by four. I can't…"

"Niyah, listen to me. You wouldn't be here if I didn't believe you could do this. You are not one to give up. We still have a chance to win this. You hear me?"

Niyah muttered, "Yes, sir," as she held back tears.

"You did great, okay. You're fine."

The scoreboard showed that Bay University and Alabama were tied in points.

Later that evening, the girls were ready for the last race of the day, the four by 400 meter relay. Coach stood in the middle of his relay team.

"This is it," he said. "This is the one. The last race. How y'all feel?"

All the girls replied with, "Good."

"Okay, I want Renae on first leg, Alisha second, Brooke third and Niyah fourth."

Niyah's muscles tensed up when she heard that she was anchor leg for the relay. Niyah worriedly replied, "Coach, I thought I was running third. Just to be safe."

Coach Jones repeated himself, "You're fourth leg. I want you anchor."

"But coach…" Niyah whined.

Coach Jones motioned for Niyah to step aside with him.

"Everyone here has been fighting for you, Niyah," he said. "But it's all for nothing if you don't fight for yourself. Now I can't make you run, no more than I could make a horse drink water. We are tied with Alabama, so they're going to be on our asses. If we win this, we will win this meet."

"But, Coach I don't wanna' let you guys down."

"Then run. Run like we all know you can. You can do this." Coach Jones touched Niyah's shoulder. "Now let's do this. Finish it. This is what you're here for. Prove yourself."

Niyah looked at her surroundings as Jones walked away. Seeing the score board and her opponents getting ready for their race, everything seemed to be moving in slow motion. She closed her eyes and calmed herself down.

Alisha pulled out the baton saying, "All right, let's pray." They put their hands on it according to their legs. The girls looked back at Niyah. The moment was tense. Tears welled up in Niyah's eyes. She jogged over to the prayer circle and took her rightful place.

Alisha looked at Niyah and said, "Niyah, will you do the honors?"

Niyah smiled and prayed for the team.

"Dear God, thank you for this day. Thank you for allowing us to be here. Especially me. This is what we've been working for all year long. Please let us get the baton around safely and as fast as we can. We love you and thank you. In Jesus name we pray, Amen."

The Alabama girls stared at them as the official stepped up to the competitors and said, "Alright, first and second leg come with me. Third and fourth leg on the fence." Renae and Alisha walked to their spots. Brooke and Niyah walked to the fence.

Brooke walked up to Niyah. "Hey, you got this. You've done this a million times."

"I just don't want to let y'all down," Niyah said.

"You could never let us down," said Brooke, kissing Niyah on the cheek. "Run your ass off."

The starting official blew his whistle. "Runners, on your mark." The girls got in their blocks. "Set…" The girls rose in their blocks. The shooter shot the gun. The girls were off. Everyone was cheering. Renae was doing great on first leg. She paced herself enough to stay in the front with the lead competitors. She ran around the track and back to Alisha. Renae handed the stick off to Alisha third. Alisha took off behind Alabama and Louisiana.

The top three girls were running neck and neck. Brooke got on the track next to the other runners waiting for the baton. She looked back at Niyah and winked. She turned back around and yelled for Alisha to bring it home. Alabama had a small lead. They darted down the straight towards their teammates. Alisha handed the stick off to Brooke. Brooke took off.

Niyah closed her eyes and whispered to herself. "I can do this. I can do this."

She started hyperventilating, trying not to psych herself out of the race. Coach Jones called to her from the bleachers, "Niyah!" Niyah looked into the stands. Her family and coach were smiling at her. Coach Jones gave her a thumbs-up. "You got this!" he yelled.

Niyah turned back to the race and stretched. Alabama still had a gap on the girls. Brooke and Louisiana were running side by side. Niyah yelled to Brooke. "Let's go, Brooke!" Brooke was darting towards Niyah. As Brooke inched closer to her, Niyah got into position, awaiting the baton. Niyah waved Brooke in. Brooke was inches away from Niyah as Niyah sped off behind Alabama. She turned and grabbed the baton from Brooke and took off. It was time to shine. She passed Louisiana and headed straight for the Alabama runner. Niyah thought to herself as she ran, "Come on, Niyah, get her!" The girls hit the 200 meter mark. Niyah was right on the Alabama competitor's tail. Niyah started edging closer. The crowd got to their feet cheering. They were finally at the 300 meter mark with 100 meters left in the race. Niyah was now inches away from the first place runner. They got to the 350 meter mark. Niyah sprinted as fast as she could. She caught up to her. Niyah was right on her heels. She edged up closer. They were now side by side, sweat flying everywhere as the girls zoomed down the track. The finish line was in their sight. They both strained for it.

The race was over. The board did not show the winner immediately. Everyone stared at the board. Niyah stood there anxiously.

The board finally showed the results. The crowd cheered. Niyah dropped to her knees. It read "Alabama 1st place 3:40.07. Bay University 2nd place 3:40.08." Niyah lost by a split second. Niyah's track team, family and Coach Jones ran up to her and hugged her as she cried.

Brooke hugged her first.

"Niyah, you did so amazing!" Brooke shouted.

Laurie kissed her on the cheek and yelled, "Without you we would have gotten like third! Why are you crying?"

Niyah desperately said, "I wanted to win for you guys! I just wanted to win."

Brooke grabbed her hand saying, "You did win! You hit a personal record! We did amazing!"

Coach Jones turned to all of his athletes. "I am so proud of all of you! Second place is way better than tenth like last year!" He walked over to Niyah and hugged her. "You did amazing."

Niyah wiped her face and hugged her coach.

"Thanks for everything, Coach," she said. "I'll try my best to come back after junior college."

Coach Jones let her go and stared at her. "Junior college?" he said. "I could never let you go home after that."

Niyah smiled and laughed through her tears. She was so excited to hear she would be staying. Tammi, David, Junior, Tristan, Gary and Rochelle came and hugged Niyah.

Tristan said, "We are so proud of you!"

David kissed his daughter.

"Just like her daddy," he said.

Tammi laughed and said, "No, like her mama. Stop telling her that. Go on and get your medal, girl."

Gary kissed Niyah on the forehead.

"I love you, cousin," he said. "You still slow!"

She smiled at him and gave everyone another hug. She walked to the podium and took her place with her team on the second place block. The official placed a nice silver medal around her neck. Everyone cheered.

The stadium began to clear out. Everyone walked towards their cars and the buses. Niyah stood on the field, staring at the scoreboard. Brooke came up and put her arm on Niyah's shoulders.

"This was a rough ass year," she said.

Niyah snickered and agreed, "Oh my God. Tell me about it."

Brooke laughed and said, "You did great. I'm so proud of you. Things are going to get better."

Niyah smiled as she reached up to touch her medal.

"I know. God wouldn't put me through all of this if it wasn't supposed to get better."

Brooke smiled and said, "Come on. Let's go celebrate."

Niyah smiled as Brooke ran to the bus. Niyah began walking to the bus then stopped one last time. She turned around and took one last look at the scoreboard. It still showed Bay University at second place. She looked down at her medals and back at the scoreboard. She looked to the sky and smiled.

"I can take second place," she said.

Brooke, Laurie and Alisha yelled for Niyah to come on.

"We have celebrating to do!" Brook shouted as the girls smiled out the windows. Niyah wiped her tears, ran off and hopped on the bus. The team made their way back to Bay University.

About the Author

Denisha Raychelle Hardeman, better known as Dede, was born in Houston, TX. Denisha was born to Angela Hardeman (Pharmacy Administrator) and Dennis Hardeman (Postal Service) on Feb. 18, 1991. Denisha is the third child of Angela and Dennis. She has two older brothers, Kenneth and Tristan and one younger sister, De'Angelique. Denisha grew up performing at a very young age in church. She performed in church plays, speeches, and praise dancing. Denisha also took on another hobby, writing. She won many creative writing contests in school and her poem "Halloween Night" won a poetry contest and was published in a poetry book when she was 8 years old. Denisha continued to perform and write throughout her school years. She won many acting and writing awards along the way. While attending Southern Methodist University on a track scholarship, Denisha was cast as a background actress in the Oscar winning film, "Django Unchained." While on set, Denisha caught the attention of Samuel L. Jackson who encouraged her to follow her dreams and move to Los Angeles. In Aug. 2012, she moved to Los Angles to attend the New York Film Academy. Denisha starred and worked on many commercials, indie films, and television shows including "Glee" and "CSI." Denisha also appeared in the record breaking film, "Straight Outta Compton." Along with the help of her mentor, Paula Jai Parker (The Proud Family, Hustle and Flow, Friday), Denisha got into screenplay writing, producing and casting. She has written 9 screenplays and one book. Denisha recently finished her first book as a published author, "8

Lanes." "8 Lanes" is loosely based on Denisha's early years in college as a track star dealing with domestic violence, sexual assault, suicidal tendencies, addiction and depression. This sparked the creation of Denisha's new charity, "The Un-Hushed Foundation." The Un-Hushed Foundation was created to help those that are going through the darkness into the light. Un-Hushed brings forth the truth that hides behind the smile. Denisha plans on taking the novel "8 Lanes" and reaching the world with its message. To help those in need find ways to cope with their past and follow their dreams.

About the Publishers

Jones and Wright Publishing was established to cater to first time authors and nurturing established authors to navigate through the publishing process. Working with a broad spectrum of authors, we strongly believe in working diligently in helping our authors to create excellent works. Providing hands-on workshops to enhance an authors' ability to produce quality books and distribute them worldwide.

Contact Jones and Wright Publishing at

www.jwpublishers.com